A SNARE OF VENGEANCE

A SHADE OF VAMPIRE 58

BELLA FORREST

Nightlight

NEW GENERATION LIST

- **Avril (vampire):** adopted daughter of Lucas and biological daughter of Marion.
- **Blaze (fire dragon):** son of fire dragons Heath and Athena.
- **Caia (part fae/human):** daughter of Grace and Lawrence.
- **Fiona (vampire):** daughter of Benedict (son of Rose and Caleb) and Yelena.
- **Harper (sentry/vampire):** daughter of Hazel and Tejus.
- **Scarlett (vampire):** daughter of Jeramiah (son of Lucas Novak) and Pippa (daughter of Cameron Hendry).

FAMILY TREE

If you'd like to check out the Novaks' family tree, visit:
www.forrestbooks.com/tree

HARPER

This wasn't the first mess we'd gotten ourselves into on Neraka, but it was by far the biggest. Needless to say, there was always room for "improvement," and, in our defense, this mess was more or less deliberate.

We'd gathered enough knowledge, resources, and allies to confidently take over the fortress on top of Ragnar Peak. We hadn't expected Cason and his cohorts to successfully follow Avril's team back from Athelathan, but we had planned with similar worst-case scenarios in mind. We should've anticipated that big-ass horn that Cason had used to summon more fighters from across the land. Not that we could've guessed the daemons possessed a horn whose swamp witch charms allowed it to ring loud enough for distant cities to hear, but still. Given our circumstances and the scope of our mission, defending a fortress from ferocious armies fit within our GASP job description.

Cason's charred remains were still smoking on the south side of the stony mountain, approximately a hundred yards from the gates —the closest he would ever get to us. His soldiers lined the southern horizon, their drums of war echoing in the distance.

The sky darkened to an intense tourmaline shade, covered in a blanket of stars as the first moon rose over Neraka. The purplish asteroid belt glistened in a lazy arch above us, but what really caught everyone's eye was the Adlet flare, burning bright red at an altitude of approximately five hundred feet. The downside was that anyone could spot it, but given that we already had hostiles headed our way and Cason had blown that wretched magical horn of his, it didn't really matter what other fiends would head toward it. What mattered was that the Adlets had seen it, too. Our new allies, the giant Nerakian werewolves, were hopefully on their way to Ragnar Peak.

For the first time, I could breathe, despite the oncoming war, because I knew we were not alone anymore. It was the kind of hope that kept me going, filling me with enough strength to tackle an entire army of daemons. As it happened, one was already on its way.

Avril had released Nevis's weird little snowflake, too. Not only was it a direct link to the Dhaxanian prince, but the icy, never-melting pendant had also worked as a daemon detector of sorts, burning cold whenever Avril got too close to the enemy. Unfortunately for us, it hadn't stopped Cason from tailing her group, albeit from a considerable distance.

I'd sent the Ekar bird back to the Manticores in the northwest, too. With a bit of luck, our allies would be here by dawn. We needed all the fighters we could possibly get for what came next. We could've just escaped from Ragnar Peak, but we had to make some dangerous gambles in order to truly progress. We'd already dealt a significant blow to Infernis, and we'd also disabled Draconis, the daemons' prison city. We needed to cripple Shaytan's forces even more, in order to cause enough chaos and disruption on Neraka for us to smoothly sneak back into Azure Heights and snatch the swamp witch.

Lumi was our only chance at bringing down the shield that isolated Neraka from the rest of the In-Between and GASP. Our families and our friends, our partners and allies were most likely worried sick and desperately trying to get here, but the shield didn't let anyone in or out. It had to come down, and we needed Lumi for that. Besides, stripping the enemy of their only swamp witch was Warfare 101 in these parts of the world.

We assumed specific positions on the fortress walls, covering all sides. We switched things up and took turns overlooking the south, the north, the east, and the west. Caspian and I were consistently at the front, facing the incoming soldiers from the south, along with Fiona and Zane.

We'd fended off rogue attacks from daemon hunter packs after we settled in the fortress—they'd tried to come at us stealthily, but our red lenses had come in handy. Now we were on the lookout, aware that more packs would come before the daemon army. There was a hefty price on our heads and, after what we'd done to Draconis, I doubted they still wanted us alive.

The adrenaline from our earlier fights had dissipated, but we were still quite sharp and alert. I used my True Sight to constantly monitor the southern horizon. The daemons were still too far away for me to spot any useful details, but they were bound to reach us by morning. One thing I could tell for sure was that their numbers exceeded a thousand grunts, and, according to Zane, they were hardcore mercenaries and not the average soldiers we'd dealt with before.

"They're killers for hire, then?" I concluded, my gaze fixed on the trembling black mass making its way across the flatlands.

Zane nodded, scratching his stubbled chin. "And expensive,

too. The southern cities are particularly pricey, and deservedly so. They are *very* good at what they do."

"What should we expect, then?" I asked, slowly leaning toward Caspian.

With everything that was going on, just feeling him there, next to me, was enough fuel to keep me burning for the rest of the night.

"Increased strength," Zane said. "Their speed is more or less the same, depending on how much armor they're wearing. They're bigger than the regular grunts. That muscle mass is directly tied to the increased strength I just mentioned. You'll want to keep your distance and try not to engage them in direct combat. The more we can kill from afar, the higher our chance of survival."

Faint screeches pierced through the night. Death Claws, still many miles away.

"Also, that." Zane scoffed. "They love bringing their pets. Death Claws and pit wolves are the norm. They will usually send them out as their first line of attack. A brute, ferocious force."

"Sounds like we're in for quite the... um, treat," Fiona replied sarcastically, then nodded at the fortress's tallest tower, on the southeastern corner. "But we have plenty of that, too. Ours also spits fire."

Blaze and Caia had settled at the top of the tower. The structure was thick and sturdy enough to withstand his dragon shifts and landings, especially since it didn't have a roof. For the time being, Blaze stayed in his humanoid form, leaning against the edge and gazing out into the distance, like the rest of us. He didn't take pleasure in killing any creature, and it always took a toll on him. It was written all over his face. However, he never hesitated when it came to protecting his people. Whatever or whoever came at us, Blaze was ready to burn them down.

"Oh, and let's not forget the Druids." I chuckled, pointing at

Ryker and Laughlan, who'd taken the second fortress tower on the right, southwestern corner. "I mean, we started out nicely with our default formula, but those two up there are absolute gems."

Though still weak from millennia of having their souls snacked on, Ryker and Laughlan were holding up surprisingly well. Their thirst for vengeance was monumental, to say the least. Most noticeably, after thousands of years spent inside the meranium prisons of Draconis, both Druids were thrilled to be out in the open. The prospect of spending the night on top of a tower, beneath the starry sky, seemed very appealing to them. Neither could take his eyes off the first moon.

On the northern wall, across the inner courtyard, stood Patrik and Scarlett, covering the back. Hundurr had managed to rescue one of Cason's pit wolves earlier, and he'd been keeping the creature company. We'd named the pit wolf Rover, at least until we got a chance to figure out where he'd come from, what Adlet pack he'd belonged to prior to his capture. Both were circling the fortress, enjoying their newfound freedom. Neither of us could understand what they were communicating to one another, but we could all see how thrilled they were to be out of those charmed collars. They'd lost their Adlet forms and had been reduced to these giant, hairless, black-skinned versions of themselves, but their red eyes yielded a semblance of hope that further encouraged me, too. These were resilient creatures, and we had a lot to learn from them when it came to overcoming Neraka's adversities.

"How are you on blood and water supplies?" Arrah asked, joining us. Pheng-Pheng was with her. They moved along the fortress walls to replenish our food and whatever else we needed.

"I caught a couple of moon-bisons down on the northern ridge," Pheng-Pheng said, offering us a leather bladder filled with fresh blood. I took it, then gave her a thankful nod and a smile. The young Manticore was an excellent hunter and a much-needed ally. Our journey through Draconis would've been a lot worse without her, for sure.

"Thanks, Pheng," I replied, then poured myself a tin cup, passing the rest to Fiona. "How are you girls holding up?" I asked.

Pheng-Pheng and Arrah looked at each other, then back at us, and shrugged.

"Still breathing, so that's good, right?" Arrah chuckled.

"There's fresh meat below if you're interested, daemon prince," Pheng-Pheng said to Zane, nodding at the courtyard behind us.

"I'll help myself later," Zane replied, then gave her a playful wink. "You didn't sting the animal, though, did you?"

"Of course not. My venom is potent enough to kill you even if ingested through another creature's flesh," Pheng-Pheng said.

"Which is why I was asking." Zane smirked.

"Is that blood?" Avril called out from the east wall.

Avril, Heron, Rush, and Amina had settled on that side, and, judging by the eager looks on their faces, they were getting hungry. I couldn't blame Rush and Amina in particular, since they, too, had been locked up in Draconis for eons, their souls weakened but their appetites recovering. We always made sure to feed the Druid delegation more, to expedite their healing process. It would take months, even years for them to get back to what they once were, but they were still strong and capable enough to assist us in the upcoming fights.

Pheng-Pheng nodded, then she and Arrah took the two remaining leather bladders over to Avril's group, who welcomed the fresh blood with radiant smiles. Rush and Amina's fangs were already out, glistening with delight as Avril filled their tin cups. I could only imagine what it must've been like for them. This was their second night out in millennia.

Vesta, Rayna, and Idris covered the west wall. Our warrior fae was taking advantage of the momentary peace to catch up with her parents. She'd yet to recover any of her childhood memories, but her attachment to Idris and Rayna was natural. Their unbreakable bond transcended all other conditions.

Jax and Hansa stayed in the courtyard with Velnias, but occasionally came up and toured the watchpoints, ready to intervene if we needed them. Dion, Alles, and the other Imen covered the ground-floor hatches and made sure we had a steady supply of arrows ready. The surrounding area of the fortress had already been rigged with explosives, and Arrah had helped prepare more over the past couple of hours, to use for our arrows. We needed all the firepower we could get, and, thankfully, Neraka's soils and mines were rich in minerals and volatile substances that we could mix into literal bombs.

"Incoming!" Vesta shouted, pointing to the west ridge of our mountain.

This wasn't the first nor the last group of rogue daemon hunters to attempt an attack. Cason's horn had been heard by many, including some who had already been out in the wild. They all died whenever they tried to approach the fortress, yet more came after them, even more persistent. Some perished when they tripped on explosive wires. Others made it all the way to the walls, just in time for Hundurr and Rover to tear them to shreds.

Caspian and I shot to our feet.

"Stay here, Fi. We'll go check it out first," I said, then rushed over to the western watchpoint.

With my red lens on, I scoured the mountain below. I could see them—five daemon hunters. They didn't even have armor on, just rapiers and shields. I let out a short whistle. Vesta stretched her bow, ready to launch a poisonous arrow, courtesy of Pheng-Pheng's deadly scorpion tail.

Two black shadows rushed through the thick greenery. "Firing one," Vesta murmured, while Caspian and I pulled our own bows out, Manticore poison glimmering black on the metallic tips. She released her arrow.

We heard it swish through the darkness before it got lodged in a daemon's throat. The creature choked, giving away their position to the pit wolves. It didn't take much for Rover and Hundurr to spot the air ripples and recognize the fiends. They'd been around daemons for long enough to get used to following them even in their invisible form.

Caspian and I shot two more arrows, clipping two hunters, just before Rover and Hundurr jumped the other two. Three minutes of yelps and whimpers later, all five daemons were dead. Four were ferociously spread across twenty square feet of stony mountain, but I was in no position or mood to criticize the pit wolves' killing methods. What mattered was that they were dead.

"I'm still not comfortable with staying here until the mercenaries arrive," Vesta muttered, looking out to the south.

"We can't risk them tracking us back to Meredrin or Azure Heights," I replied. "Had Cason not blown his stupid horn, we might've had a chance. Now all the daemons of Neraka know we're here. Fortunately for us, however, not all of them will make it here on time. We'll lay as much waste as we can to the mercenaries, and our allies will hopefully join us and help us flee, preferably undetected."

"You do realize it's easier said than done, right?" Vesta smirked.

I nodded. "Yeah, but we're all together now, stronger than yesterday," I said. "We went over all possible avenues back at the farm, and this is our best option. We need to hold out here and deliver as much damage to those mercenaries as possible, then escape to Meredrin. Jax says we're at war and we need to think like we're at war, not like we're on the run."

"Strategic approach, I get it," Idris replied, nodding slowly. "It is reasonable. Let's hope it's also doable."

I smiled. "With you, Rayna, and Vesta on our side? Absolutely doable."

Another horn sounded, its echoes rippling across the night sky. Our smiles faded. My blood froze, almost instantly, as I looked to the west.

"A little sooner than I'd hoped," I murmured, identifying another daemon army stretching toward us, two hundred miles away.

"How many, do you think?" Caspian asked.

"They're too far for me to see, but I estimate eight, maybe nine hundred more, based on how they're spread," I replied, my voice trembling.

"This is merely the first wave," Zane interjected from the southern wall. "It's how they carry out a siege. They send out the first wave from multiple angles. In this case, these are your first responders," he added, pointing to the south, then the west. "Mercenaries from the southern territories and seasoned grunts from the western city of Davoth."

I let out an audible sigh.

"They'll be here by morning, huh?" Vesta asked, squinting as she looked to the west.

"Dawn, most likely," I replied. "From both sides. They seem to be moving steadily," I added, then glanced at Zane. "You said this will be the first wave. Then what?"

"Well, provided we survive the first wave, the second attack will come in one, maybe two days. What we're seeing now are the only troops they had available close to Ragnar Peak. Rest assured that more—many more—are being geared up as we speak. We won't survive a second wave. Not in this formula. Not even with allies. We lack numbers. Believe me, the second wave will aim to obliterate, and they will be bringing in more swamp witch magic."

"We won't be here that long, anyway," Jax interjected from

below, his brow furrowed. "We need to hold out against this first wave until our allies get here."

"Like I said, easier said than done." Vesta smirked.

"And like I said, let them bring it. We're stronger together," I replied.

Vesta nodded, then pointed a thumb at the incoming hostiles from the west. "Besides, you know what 'seasoned grunts' stands for in daemon-speak, right?"

I shook my head slowly. Zane chuckled.

"Old farts who've seen one too many battles," Velnias said, then pointed a finger at Vesta. "Don't laugh just yet, little fae. Old or not, they can still tear you to shreds if you let them get close!"

Either way, we had more work cut out for us. That meant more arrows and more explosives. While the ground team went on a second search of the fortress, we started gathering our ammunition and distributing it evenly on all four wall positions. The night was still young, but our enemies had just doubled their numbers, and we needed to be ready.

We've made it this far, dammit. This is not where it ends.

2

FIONA

By the time the second moon came up, Vesta, Arrah, and Pheng-Pheng had gathered more supplies from the fortress —there were several hidden storage rooms that we hadn't tapped into before. They prepared small linen satchels filled with an explosive mixture that detonated upon impact. The leftovers they'd brought over from Athelathan had been carefully rigged on a five-hundred-yard radius down the mountain, concealed and fitted with wires.

Once triggered, they reacted much like the landmines that humans used back on Earth. Some were loaded with shrapnel; others were filled with toxic, acid-like substances that burned through pretty much anything.

"They are really good at this whole explosives thing," I murmured, watching Arrah as she skillfully tied a leather string around one of the satchels, keeping her mouth covered with a cloth so as not to inhale the vapors of the volatile mixture.

"They've had decades, if not centuries, to perfect the technique," Zane replied, his eyes on the gates below. Caspian and Harper were farther to the west, close to the Druids' tower, worriedly looking at the incoming daemon armies.

My stomach was tied up in painful knots, but Zane's presence kind of took the edge off. I kept watching the girls. They were done with the satchel explosives and had moved on to fitting smaller doses on arrowheads, while Pheng-Pheng dipped another batch of arrows in her venom—she'd collected a hefty amount in a stone bowl for this. They were quiet, calm, and focused, and I couldn't help but admire them for their strength and resilience.

"That's what thousands of years of hostile occupation will do to you," Zane added, noticing my fascination. "They toughen you up. These girls have seen some horrible things in their short lives, and yet look at them go, unflinching. Feisty little things. Like you."

I briefly glanced at him, instantly warming up at the sight of his smile. My heart fluttered, but I had a hard time enjoying the sensation. My nerves were stretched too thin. The war drums grew louder in the distance. The daemons sure loved making their presence known.

"I'm nothing compared to them. This is literally the first combat experience for half of us on my team," I replied with a shrug. "We're trained and all, but we haven't lived through what they've experienced," I said, pointing at the Nerakian girls.

Zane gripped my chin between his thumb and index finger, lifting my head so he could get a better look at me. His touch alone was enough to light tiny little fires that spread through my skin, and I once again found myself stunned at how stealthily he'd gotten under my skin.

"You should give yourself more credit, little vampire," he replied, his voice low, raspy and sweet at the same time. "You've already accomplished something incredible during your short time on Neraka."

I scoffed and tried to look away, feeling my cheeks burn, but he held me in place, his red gaze dropping lead weights into my stomach. "You give me too *much* credit." I chuckled nervously.

"You're all unbelievably capable, Fiona," he insisted. "You've managed to get the Adlets on your side. You found Manticores and Dhaxanians, hidden in the most extreme corners of Neraka, and you've brought them into the fold, too. You've given people hope, darling. I've never seen anything like this. Not in this lifetime, I assure you. Up until I stumbled upon you in that underground prison, I didn't even think I'd see such a successful rebellion. You crippled Infernis. You got *me* out of Draconis, then tore it down on your way out." He chuckled. "I'm giving you the credit you deserve."

In hindsight, and looking at what we'd managed to achieve up to our arrival at Ragnar Peak, Zane did have a point. We'd come to a planet whose people were jaded and exhausted, weakened by predators like the Exiled Maras and the daemons. We'd managed to escape a city riddled with lies and illusions, and we'd survived not one, but two hostile cities. I didn't have the tragic life experiences of Arrah and Vesta, for example, but I was a survivor, and I was definitely a fighter. I never should've forgotten that, not even for a minute.

"They're strong, though," I murmured, gazing at the girls. "So freaking strong."

"They are. All Nerakians are, in fact. But my people and the Exiled Maras have spent thousands of years tearing their societies apart, separating and isolating them. But you, Fiona, you and your people have brought three of this kingdom's most powerful creatures back together. The Dhaxanians of Athelathan, the Adlets of Lagerith... the freaking Manticores of Akrep! I'm in awe of you.

Only a short while ago, I was contemplating running away from Infernis and settling somewhere by the southern seas, away from my entire family. Yet, here I am, helping you."

I cupped his cheek with one hand—small and soft against his rugged, sharp jawline. "I know it can't be easy for you," I breathed. "Killing your own people, I mean. I'm sorry you have to do this."

Zane inched closer, his gaze darkening as it dropped to my lips, which I parted on instinct.

"You still don't understand, do you, little vampire?" he replied, and I shook my head slowly. "I will burn this entire planet down, if that's what it'll take for me to be with you."

"Please don't. There are innocent people here," I muttered, stifling a grin.

He narrowed his eyes at me, though visibly amused. "I was going for a figure of speech there, but you're right. Let me be more literal," he said, then regained his serious expression, his crimson gaze drilling into my soul. "Fiona, I will not let anyone hurt you or put you in a cage ever again. I did it once out of curiosity, and I still feel like a miserable schmuck for it. I'll take my entire kingdom down to keep you safe. I mean it."

My heart sank, ever so quietly, as I listened to him say those words. Deep down, I started wondering where this would lead. Was this a relationship? I was definitely falling for him. I'd stopped denying that already. But where were we going with it? Would one of us follow the other into their home world? Would we spend half the time in my world, and half here, on Neraka? Or, when and if we succeeded in ridding Neraka of its daemon and Mara problem, would we just go our separate ways?

Judging by the painful pang in my stomach, the latter didn't feel like a good option. I breathed out, then closed the distance between us and kissed him. Zane didn't hesitate, responding immediately. He parted his lips and took control. He tasted like honey and spices, making me quiver as he wrapped his arms around me and pulled me closer.

He groaned softly against my lips, then brought our kiss to an end. It took a lot of energy on my part not to let out a whimper of discontentment, until I noticed the amusement flickering in his eyes. His gaze was darting between me and Harper and Caspian, who were just twenty feet behind me.

"I think we're distracting them," Zane whispered. "Though I would love nothing more than to keep tasting you."

I giggled, my face flushed. I smoothly distanced myself from him, then looked over my shoulder. Like two little kids caught staring, both Harper and Caspian instantly shifted their focus back to the southern horizon, pretending we weren't even there.

Zane chuckled softly, then leaned back against the wall. It took us a minute or so to get our breathing under control, occasionally stealing glances at one another. Zane then fixed his sights on Caspian. "You know, he's one hell of a fighter," he muttered. "One of the best I've ever seen."

"Yeah, he is. What's even more impressive is how well he gets along with Harper in combat," I said. "I've never come across such synergy before. They're so fluid, so natural in covering one another, almost completing each other's movements. It's always such a pleasure to watch them."

"Oh, I agree. Harper is equally phenomenal, I'll admit," Zane said. "It's like they read each other's minds when they fight. Thing is, it doesn't just come from one of them. It comes from both. Harper is obviously exquisitely trained. And Caspian has a similarly impressive military and law enforcement background, which I think you know about."

"Yes, House Kifo has an ancient tradition in this discipline, if I remember correctly. Policing and warfare," I replied.

Zane nodded, then grinned, his expression lighting up as he

remembered something. He looked at Caspian, raising his voice. "Oh, crap, you're still under that blood oath, huh?"

Caspian sighed, then pointed at the symbol behind his ear. Zane then laughed lightly, briefly glancing at the girls fiddling with explosives below.

"Which means our friends don't know about your involvement in the resistance," Zane said. "You can't talk about it, but you can clearly do it, otherwise you would've burned up by now."

"Obviously," Caspian replied with a smirk.

"What are you talking about?" Harper asked, slightly confused.

"You see all these explosives, the whole technique behind them?" Zane asked, pointing at the pile of linen satchels behind Arrah. "These are all little snippets of knowledge that the likes of Vesta and Arrah have inherited from elder Imen, all gone from this world already. But where do you think the elders got them from, huh?"

As if struck by the same lightning of realization, both Harper and I stared at Caspian, our eyes wide with surprise. "You?" I croaked.

Caspian couldn't confirm, but he looked at Harper and blinked, prompting her to then look at me and nod. "Yep," she confirmed.

"Lord Kifo here leaked the hell out of his own military archives." Zane chuckled. "Shortly after the Lords pushed the rebel Imen farther to the west, Caspian gave them explosive recipes galore, instructions on how to extract certain volatile substances, where to draw them from, how to handle them so they wouldn't blow themselves up, everything! Arrah wouldn't have all these nifty little tricks today had it not been for Caspian a couple of centuries ago."

All of a sudden, Caspian seemed even more amazing—not just to Harper, but to all of us. Murmurs of gratitude and admiration emerged from below, and all my team gave Caspian a series of appreciative and thankful nods, while Harper wrapped her arms around his neck and dropped a soft kiss on his cheek.

He smiled shyly, like a little boy who wasn't used to getting credit for the incredible things he'd done. Needless to say, it was about time. He'd spent too long suffering in silence, struggling to do the right thing, while his people further eroded the once-beautiful way of life of the Nerakians. He deserved a pat on the back and a round of applause.

Had it not been for his willingness to risk his own safety, his own life and integrity by passing explosives recipes on to the rebel Imen, we would've been royally screwed here, on top of Ragnar Peak, with armies of daemons headed our way.

Thanks to him, we had a good fighting chance and a better shot at rescuing the swamp witch and getting our freedom back.

3

HANSA

Jax and I went on our hourly round of the fortress walls, the third moon rising overhead. Its beams came down in a warm off-white, casting a milky glow over the stone structure. We'd just checked on Scarlett and Patrik. The north side was quiet, and while the west wall had seen some action over the past couple of hours, it was nothing two pit wolves and three of our best fighters couldn't handle.

"We've certainly come a long way since we first got here," I said, walking with Jax by my side and occasionally glancing over the wall into the dark wilderness below. "I remember our first encounter with daemon hunters. We were so confused."

"With good reason, though," Jax replied, the corner of his mouth twitching. "Remember, we had no idea what we were dealing with, and they were using their invisibility spells. We've had a lot more practice since then. They're not the boogeyman anymore. They're palpable enemies, with strengths and weaknesses. As long as they bleed, they can also die, as we've repeatedly proven on an almost daily basis."

I scoffed, one hand resting on my broadsword's bejeweled handle. "One thing is certain, as far as I'm concerned: I hate the Exiled Maras now more than ever. That second chance they got was a complete waste of time and lives. Look at how they've squandered it. They've festered and spread. It was bad enough the daemons were pillaging and murdering left and right."

Jax stopped walking and leaned against the wall. He caught my hand and pulled me close, wrapping his arms around my waist and holding me tight. For a few moments, it was as though the entire world disappeared, and it was just me and him, casually standing on a fortress's wall in the middle of nowhere on a planet far away in the In-Between.

He tucked a black curl behind my ear, then trailed his fingers along my jawline. His touch was deliberately soft, sending ripples of electricity through my skin. "Hansa, we're about to go to war in about five hours. Forgive me if I don't feel like talking about the scourge of my species," he muttered, his bitterness about the Exiled Maras impossible to ignore. His gaze softened once it settled on my face, his thumb gently brushing over my lower lip. "Whatever happens here, I want to enjoy every minute left with you. Screw Azure Heights, screw the daemons and everyone else who aspires to be a wedge between us. I've wasted three months avoiding you instead of loving you like you deserve. I'm not letting anyone else distract me."

I couldn't help but smile, leaning into him. His muscles were hard against my flesh, even through the layers of leather between us. The effect that Jax had on me was undeniably strong and incredibly addictive. He held my heart inside his, and, judging by the look in his eyes, I had him all to myself, body and soul. Sure, there were armies of daemons getting closer to our location, but who gave a damn? At that moment, it was just me and Jax beneath three full moons.

"You know I love you, right?" I asked, raising my head, touching the tip of his nose with mine.

"Meh, you say it once in a while," he replied, smirking like a mischievous little kid. He made me laugh when he was like this—the complete opposite of Jaxxon Dorchadas, the Lord of Maras on Calliope, ruler of his kind and warrior extraordinaire. He was hot like a volcano beneath that dark and icy surface, but I loved every bit of him just the same. "If it's worth anything, I might as well remind you that I love *you*, Hansa."

"Oh, good," I said, my tone flat. "So I'm stuck with you."

"Forever," he whispered, then gripped the back of my neck and pulled me into a kiss. He was firm and commanding, intense and possessive. It took everything I had not to unleash my succubus nature on him, although I was tempted. We needed some sliver of clarity left, though, even in that little moment, just in case it all went south fast.

Jax's tongue circled mine, his lips soft and his breath hot, lighting my senses on fire. He paused to look at me, panting slightly. I could see myself glowing in his eyes, my skin reacting to the intense emotions that he triggered in me. He sighed, then tightened his embrace and rested his lips against my forehead.

"Let's assume we'll make it out of here alive," he murmured.

"So let's be optimistic?"

He chuckled softly. "Let's be determined and focus on an agreeable outcome," he replied.

"Good grief, you were made to lead, Lord Dorchadas. You sure have a way with words, though you're quite conservative when sharing them with the rest of us."

"Hansa, let's think about it. Now. Before dawn, before all hell breaks loose," he said, his voice low and scratchy, making my spine tingle.

I looked up at him, losing myself in those dark jade pools he had for eyes, and nodded slowly.

"Let's assume we'll find Lumi. She'll bring the shield down. We'll go back to Calliope," he continued. "What then? What do we do?"

"You'll go on to lead your people, while working with GASP. I will continue to speak on behalf of the succubi, while working with GASP. Isn't that what we've been doing?" I replied, resting my palms on his chest.

"That's correct. I'll go back to White City. But... Hansa, will you come with me?" he asked, his voice trembling, his breathing heavy. I could feel him getting nervous. Most importantly, I could feel my heart swelling, to the point where it had trouble fitting inside my ribcage.

"Jax," I breathed. "I'll go anywhere with you. I'm no longer bound to a tribe, to a patch of land, to anything. I'm free. Free to love you, to be with you. I don't care where I am, as long as I'm with you."

He sighed deeply, then kissed me again, this time so tenderly I felt tears forming in my eyes. There was so much love infused into a simple peck on the lips, I could almost cry. I put my arms around his neck and lifted my head. He looked perfect under the moonlight, like a living, beautifully sculpted statue filled with a dazzling whirlwind of emotions that I longed to feed on, every day for the rest of my life.

"There's one thing I'm a little worried about," he said. "Though I don't think we need to address it just yet. Not in these circumstances, anyway. But I still want to voice it, for you to think about once we go back home."

"What is it?"

"You're a succubus. I'm a Mara. Your blood is toxic to me. I know, stating the obvious. But I can never do Pyrope with you; I can never taste your blood in an act of love without getting myself poisoned. I worry that, should you want to have children, I may not be able to help with that, Hansa. I don't think our species are compatible on that level."

I thought about it for a second. I'd thought about it before, back on Calliope, during the few moments I had to myself to fantasize about what it would be like to be in a relationship with him. *Go figure, huh?*

"Would you like for us to have children of our own?" I asked gently.

I felt him shudder in my arms. He nodded. "Not now, but at some point, yes. But if I can't, that's okay, too. Having you is enough. Not being with you is unacceptable. I'd rather have you than an heir."

It hit me then. In Mara tradition, Lordship was transmitted exclusively via the bloodline, or by the existing Lord's nomination, with the support of his subjects. If he didn't have an heir of his own, Jax only had his brother, Heron, to leave the Lordship to. However, that had rarely happened in White City—Lordship belonged to the offspring, not the siblings. On top of that, I wasn't even sure Heron would've wanted the role, given his independent nature.

But Jax didn't really care about all this. He wanted to be with me, and that meant the world to me. I'd seen enough in this lifetime. I'd lost enough and then some. Yet the universe had still managed to find a way to surprise me because, as I stood there, looking at Jax, I felt as though my life was only just beginning. I gave him a soft smile, caressing his face.

"You know, I had seven daughters," I replied, my own voice shaky and tears gathering in my eyes. "I buried six of them. Izora is all I have left, and she's still very young. She could do with a father figure in her life, if you want to give that a try?" I asked, carefully analyzing his expression.

I registered astonishment... pondering... then a surge of love and warmth as he leaned forward and kissed me, deeply, once again filling me with everything that animated him.

"It would be an honor," he whispered.

"And, later down the line, we could adopt," I suggested. "Calliope was left with many orphans after Azazel's war. I'm sure there are Mara younglings who need a loving family. Should you start considering an heir to your Lordship, I'm sure your subjects would be more than happy to support your adopted son or daughter. The Maras of Calliope would know that the heir was raised by Jaxxon Dorchadas, the greatest of them all, after all."

He stared at me for a while, genuinely impressed, his lips lazily stretching into an appreciative smirk. "By the Daughters, succubus, you've already thought of everything, haven't you?"

I burst into laughter, feeling my cheeks literally light up.

"I did. You know me: I think of all the details, big and small."

"I wouldn't expect anything less from the Red Tribe Chief," he replied, running his fingers through my hair. "You paint a pretty picture, though. I'd like it. All of it. Everything you've just described. Yes, Hansa. We could do all of that and more, together."

"We most certainly could," I breathed against his lips.

"You know," he said, changing the subject, visibly amused. "Stories about you spread all the way to White City, long before you made your way there with Serena and Draven."

"Oh, really?" I chuckled. "What do the stories say?"

He glanced around me, as if trying to remember the exact words.

"That you are fierce and cunning. Deadly, and seductive to the point where absolutely no creature could resist you. That you could crush a Destroyer's head between your thighs—"

I yelped and covered my mouth to stifle a wave of hysterical laughter. Such stories were always insanely fun to hear, especially after all my adventures on the battlefield.

"Well, I'd heard stories about you, too," I replied, pressing my index finger against his lips. "That you were like a shadow, bending the minds of your enemies, planting nightmares in their heads, mercilessly cutting them down. That you led your people with an iron fist. That you'd sold your soul to the Daughters a long time ago, in return for your ability to syphon energy from your wards and perform mass manipulation, corrupting the wills of hundreds at once. Let's just say you were depicted as quite the fearsome, soulless character."

He scoffed, slightly amused. "Well, they got most of it right. Though I didn't sell my soul for my wards. I rescued a swamp witch. And I do have a soul, though I refrain from showing it to just anyone."

"You don't mind showing it to me?" I asked, raising my heels so I could reach his lips and kiss him.

"Showing it to you? Hansa, I'm wholeheartedly sharing it with you," Jax said, then lowered his head and captured my mouth in another kiss. This time, he was hungry, greedy for more, eager to make me understand how hot he burned for me. It was easy for me to understand, because everything he felt mirrored my own emotions.

We were two sides of the same coin, only we were fortunate enough to face each other. He grunted softly against my lips, then stilled and froze. I peeled my eyes open, but before I could ask what was wrong, I heard it.

The shrill, brain-scratching, bloodcurdling screeches of Death Claws.

"Oh, crap," I croaked and quickly turned around.

Two hundred yards to the south, a black cloud hovered toward us. The sound of Blaze turning and stretching his dragon wings on top of the left tower pulled me deeper into the impending reality.

"That's a swarm," Jax muttered, then grabbed my hand. We ran along the wall toward the front, where Harper, Caspian, Fiona, and Zane were already preparing for the attack. "They made it before the mercenaries."

"It's what they usually do," Zane replied, visibly annoyed. "I was hoping I'd get to take a nap, at least."

My heart thudded, my blood rushing as all my senses went into overdrive. I mounted an arrow on my bow, stretching my arm back and aiming at the swarm. They were moving fast, squealing and squawking incessantly.

Growls erupted from below.

"Dammit, pit wolves, too?" Zane groaned, childishly exasperated.

A gust of warm wind hit us as Blaze took off and flapped his wings. He was going ahead, eager to burn those creatures down. I took my aim at one of them and released my arrow.

Swish... Right in the chest it went. It screamed, then plummeted to the ground.

The first round of beasts had reached us, but we were more than ready. If anything, we could do with a little warmup.

"Buckle up, kids!" I hissed. "It's time for target practice."

4

SCARLETT

There were at least a hundred Death Claws coming in, screeching and spreading across the night sky like a black cloud. We had less than a minute to get ready.

Blaze took off in dragon form, eager to greet the creatures.

Velnias coordinated with the Imen on the ground floor—their task was to disable as many charmed collars as they possibly could, and shoot to kill when saving pit wolves was not an option. Hundurr and Rover went out to rescue as many of their kind as possible, and I could hear them shuffling and growling through the woods below.

Everyone else was up on the walls and in the towers, ready to strike. The Death Claws were just yards away now, shrieking with the excitement of tearing into us.

I lit a fire on a stone slab and used it to light my first arrow after I mounted it on my bow. The tips were loaded with a mixture of flammable and explosive powders, soon to ignite. I stretched the bow and released it.

It swished through the air, swiftly joined by dozens more shot by the rest of my team. Patrik launched blue fireballs with his bare, glowing hands. The first round of projectiles, both arrows and fireballs from Druids and fae, went right into the center of the swarm.

Boom! One after another, the loaded arrowheads exploded. Amber fires bloomed in the middle of the black mass of Death Claws. The creatures hissed and wailed. Five of them collapsed. The others became even more aggressive. However, they didn't get to retaliate straightaway. Blaze snapped open his jaws and released a devastating stream of fire.

It engulfed a large number of Death Claws, while the several dozen left scrambled to get out of his range. They scattered overhead, which meant we had to deal with them on an individual basis. Growls erupted from below, but I couldn't afford to worry about Hundurr at that moment. I could only hope that he and Rover were getting more pit wolves on our side.

I released a second flaming arrow, then a third, a fourth, and then kept shooting, using my unnatural speed in the reloading process. One by one, Death Claws screamed, then fell in the middle of our courtyard, where Dion and Alles rushed to kill the ones still moving, jamming spears into their muscular chests.

One of the pit wolves must have tripped on a wire—a string of explosions fifty yards down from the fortress on the west side rocked us to the core. Fiery orange blossoms burst out from the woods. Several pit wolves whimpered, while others snarled. I could hear fangs clamping down on metallic, charmed collars.

In the meantime, Patrik and I kept firing at the Death Claws. Two of them got dangerously close, flying in low, but I managed to turn and release one arrow, just as Patrik shot out a fireball. Both creatures crash-landed into the northeastern corner of the wall. They ended up in the courtyard under a pile of rubble.

Movement below caught my eye. Freed pit wolves came in, guided by Rover. I counted ten. It wasn't enough for what armies were coming for us, but it was definitely better than what we'd counted two hours before.

"Cover the eastern part," Patrik said, then muttered another spell and released a flurry of smaller fireballs. They hummed and shot through the night, smacking several Death Claws at once. They then spread like wildfire, swallowing the creatures whole. I watched them drop into the courtyard, where the newly freed pit wolves proceeded to rip their throats out.

"Oh, a pit wolf scorned is not a creature you want to be around," I muttered, pleased to see my theory about pit wolves quickly becoming a fact. The Adlets never forgot who they were, despite losing their forms. The charmed collars served to restrict and control but did nothing to the creatures' long-term memory.

The fight was dirty, but we still had a massive advantage. Said massive advantage kept flapping his dragon wings, chasing isolated groups of Death Claws around. He maintained a head-on approach, spitting fire then ripping through the beasts with his humongous fangs.

The sea of growls in the woods outside the fortress began to subside. Hundurr and Rover had more pit wolves to help them, leaving the Imen to focus less on shooting charmed collars off and more on killing the incoming crashed Death Claws. There were about six or seven left, and they seemed particularly adept at dodging Blaze's attacks.

I loaded another arrow, ready to fire at the Death Claw leading a trio over on the east side. Blaze came in from behind, so I decided to move my aim toward one of the three flying loosely on the south side. I shot my arrow and missed a Death Claw by inches

—but that wasn't the worst part. The beast suddenly changed its trajectory and went after Blaze.

"Watch out, Blaze!" I cried out, as the Death Claw caught Blaze by surprise. He was so focused on the three hostiles in front of him, he didn't see the fourth coming in.

The fiend clawed at his eye. Caia screamed from her position in the tower. Blaze growled and jerked his head, then slapped the Death Claw away with his wing. I caught a glimpse of him shifting back to his normal form as Caia summoned winds to help him land in the tower, where she immediately started applying first-aid measures.

The rogue Death Claw was badly hit and struggling to stay in the air. I loaded another arrow and shot it right in its bony throat. It screeched, then spotted me and feverishly flapped its wings, gaining a concerning amount of speed.

"Oh, crap, it's going to crash," I breathed.

It was headed right for us, and I couldn't let it damage the fortress wall. Patrik was busy shooting fireballs at another Death Claw. There was no time to move away from the impact point.

I had to do something, and fast.

The Death Claw came toward us like an overgrown bullet. I cursed under my breath and jumped out to break its course. Its large body rammed into mine and knocked the air out of my lungs, but I managed to keep it away from Patrik and the northern wall.

I heard Patrik cry out my name. "Scarlett, no!"

The Death Claw squirmed as I coiled my arms around its neck and constricted it tighter than a boa snake. I put in all my strength. The world moved around us. It fell off its axis as I struggled with the Death Claw. Up was down, left was right, and—we both slammed into the hard stone pavement of the courtyard.

I gasped and wrestled the Death Claw, despite the burning pain in my right shoulder and upper back. It hissed and growled, desperate to get a bite out of me. With lightning speed, I managed to draw my sword, and rammed it into the creature's throat. Crimson blood gushed out and poured all over me like a warm glaze.

"Ew!" I groaned. The Death Claw choked on its own gurgling blood, heavy on top of me.

My entire body hurt, but I'd taken the beast down. I couldn't breathe anymore. I had to get it off me. I pushed, barely managing to lift it a few inches off the ground.

"Good grief, you're heavy," I muttered through gritted teeth.

I heard a familiar growl, then felt the Death Claw getting dragged off me. Two pit wolves got busy shredding its throat, and I managed to get back on my feet. Hundurr rushed toward me, nuzzling my face with his giant, bloody head.

I held my breath for a second, quickly checking him for injuries.

"Not your blood. Okay. Proceed, you fantastic mutt!" I chuckled, then gently patted the side of his neck. Hundurr huffed and ran back outside. Judging by the rustling and crackling sounds beyond the walls, there were still hostile pit wolves out there.

Another shriek pierced the sky above. I looked up just in time to see a flaming arrow get lodged in the last living Death Claw's forehead. I moved back a couple of feet, as the creature came down hard, breaking most of its bones in the impact. It wheezed and groaned, its wings and legs twitching.

I ended its misery with one sword hit, then climbed back onto the northern wall. I'd been so busy trying to stay alive and assessing our combat situation that I didn't even notice Patrik's expression until I got back to him.

Patrik's face was drained of color. He was shaking like a leaf, his lower lip trembling and his eyes wide, as if he'd seen something so horrible that it couldn't be described with words. He was speech-less, staring at me.

"Are you okay?" I asked, wiping some of the Death Claw blood from my chest and neck.

He didn't say anything for a few moments, making me worry. I moved closer, trying to figure out what was wrong with him. It dawned on me then that I was still covered in blood, and chances were he thought it was mine.

"The blood isn't mine, don't worry," I said, smiling.

Patrik then took me in a tight embrace, wrapping his arms around me and burying his face in my neck. He shuddered, breathing heavily. I still had trouble figuring out why he'd gotten himself so worked up—until the adrenaline cleared off a bit and it hit me. Kyana.

"I thought I'd lost you," he whispered.

Something wet and warm found my neck. Tears.

"Oh, Patrik," I mumbled, suddenly feeling horrible for not having thought of it sooner. "I'm sorry. I didn't mean to—"

"I thought it had you."

I held him tight, trying to find the right words. He knew very well that he couldn't be angry at me. I'd made an executive deci-sion that I didn't regret. We were at war. Our lives were bound to be at risk. There was no denying that, and Patrik knew it. But it didn't stop him from coming undone whenever he saw me in such a tight spot, especially when a Death Claw rammed into me midair. Just over three months ago, he'd buried the love of his life after a war.

He had every reason to fear that history was going to repeat itself, given our circumstances. He was distraught, but he was also underestimating me. I wasn't Kyana. I was a GASP fighter.

I caressed his face and kissed him, then gave him a soft smile. "I'm okay. I'm okay, Patrik. A Death Claw won't be the end of me, babe."

"I know," he replied with a nod, "but I can't help it. I got the worst flashbacks. I should be the one apologizing, not you," he added, regaining his composure. His steely eyes were red, but his gaze and expression were firm.

"How about neither of us apologizes, and we move on, huh?"

He chuckled softly, then put some space between us. We looked around. We'd all made it. The Death Claws, however, had not. Some were collapsed in our courtyard, and the pit wolves were already dragging them out through the back gate. The rest were scattered throughout the woods, several still burning.

Blaze was going to be okay, but he needed a few hours of rest for the healing paste to work its mojo on him. This wasn't his first dragon-related injury, and something told me it wasn't going to be his last, either.

"Nice tackle on that Death Claw," Harper said, from the south wall.

"Tackle and grapple, baby!" I shot back, prompting her to laugh out loud.

Hansa wiped some Death Claw blood off her shoulder, then looked out into the distance. Our enemies were still coming. The persistent beat of their drums was getting louder.

"All right, let's clean up and get ready for the next wave. This was just a preview of what's coming, and we all know it," she muttered.

Patrik caught my hand and squeezed it. He didn't need to say anything. I knew what he was thinking—the intensity of his gaze and his erratic heartbeat told me more than his words ever could.

"I know," I told him gently. "And it's okay. I'd be worried about me, too, if I were you. I took a big risk earlier, and I'm aware of it. But I couldn't have you get hurt, and I couldn't let the Death Claw compromise the wall's structure, either. Not with what's coming at us in a few hours."

He nodded slowly. "I agree. Just don't tell me to toughen up." He smirked.

"You're tougher than all of us put together," I replied. "You reversed your Destroyer form with sheer willpower, remember?"

Patrik sighed, then wiped some of the blood still smearing my face. "You're a mess."

"Yeah? Well, you should see the other guy." I chuckled, pointing at the Death Claw in the courtyard.

5

HARPER

A few hours later, Blaze was back at full strength. Both Ryker and Laughlan had helped speed up the recovery process with a couple of spells. The Imen scoured the fortress for more arrows, but, upon a final count, we discovered we only had about three hundred left.

"This won't be enough for what's coming," Hansa said, frowning.

The sky was beginning to light up, the moons descending into the horizon as dawn gleamed in the east. I, along with the other vampires and Maras in our group, was already covered up, ready for daybreak. Our nerves were stretched. Our stomachs churning.

Daemon mercenaries spread out from the south, and soldiers occupied the western fascia of flatlands. Their boots thundered on the ground. Their war drums were loud, incessantly beating with the sole intent to intimidate us, to put fear in us... to make us lose hope.

They were just a few miles away now, and I could see them clearly with my True Sight. Their armor was thick, their swords broad, and their shields sturdy enough to resist consistent hits. They could still be killed, though. They weren't unbeatable.

"Death Claws," I announced, pointing to the south.

Another swarm of winged beasts was coming in, albeit smaller than the previous one. It wasn't meant to deliver a significant blow. Their sole purpose was to distract us from what the daemons were about to unleash on us. Looking down, I counted eight horrifying contraptions—large wooden crossbows, big enough to launch arrows that were the length of two Zanes. The arrowheads looked heavy and sharp enough to maybe even pierce Blaze's dragon skin.

"They've brought some serious toys," I added, then looked up at Blaze, who stood in the tower with Caia. "You'd better be careful, Blaze. Those things were made specifically with you in mind."

"My skin's pretty thick," Blaze grumbled.

"Don't risk it, though," Hansa replied. "Keep your distance. Change your position as often as you can. Don't let them lock their sights on you."

Blaze replied with a nod, then slipped out of his pants and burst into full dragon form. He stretched his wings and shuddered briefly before he took flight.

"Be careful!" Caia shouted after him, staying behind in the tower.

"Everyone ready?" Hansa raised her voice.

I briefly glanced around me—we were definitely ready, our team members in their assigned positions, armed and geared up. The Imen held the ground floor with Velnias. The thirty pit wolves we'd rescued, including Hundurr and Rover, left the courtyard and spread around the fortress, hiding below the thick foliage. They were ready for the next wave of hostile, collared pit wolves. I could see and hear them at the base of the mountain.

"We're ready," I said, then felt Caspian's soft nudge. We exchanged glances and instantly knew that, no matter what happened next, we had each other's backs.

Pheng-Pheng had joined our group, while Arrah stayed with the Imen below. One-third of our rigged mines had been blown by previous attacks, and we had a limited supply of arrows. However, the fortress's position, along with our Druids, fae, and dragon, was going to help us survive for quite a while. On top of that, we had pit wolves ready to defend us. We were not going down without a fight.

We're not going down, period.

Blaze roared as he reached the Death Claws and released a curtain of fire.

"I take it he's still pissed about the eye poke." Zane smirked.

"Well, the boy's grudge does come in handy," Jax replied.

We all stared, watching as Blaze didn't even give the Death Claws a chance to scatter. He viciously bombarded them with a constant, thick stream of fire, flying in a wide circle around them. He'd learned something from his previous experience for sure— this time, he didn't let them break formation.

One after another, the Death Claws were burned alive and darted into the ground and the woods covering Ragnar Peak like meteors. They crashed in a hail of flaming flesh, and Blaze continued to mercilessly attack them.

I surveyed the daemon armies and came to an unsettling conclusion.

"Guys, they're spreading out," I said. Hansa followed my gaze, then cursed under her breath. "They'll come at us from all sides."

The thick mass of armored daemons began to stretch evenly as they reached the mountain base. They split into squadrons of twenty to thirty grunts, then moved around to cover the eastern and northern slopes, too. Their generals barked orders and whipped the pit wolves. The beasts lunged forward and began their climb, growling, desperate to get to us.

Several Death Claws landed in the middle of the southern army. The daemons cleared the impact area and continued their advance, banging their swords on their shields. It sent shivers down my spine. My blood boiled as a direct response to the fear sneaking into my heart. There was the possibility of failure here. There was a chance that we would not make it off of Ragnar Peak.

I shook my head slowly and decided to focus on the mercenaries' giant crossbows. I couldn't let fear sabotage my resolve. Not while Caspian stood by my side. I looked down and spotted Hundurr and Rover by the gate, then whistled. Both pit wolves looked up at me. If Scarlett was right, then the creatures understood every word we said.

"We need to disable those giant crossbows," I said.

Farther ahead, Blaze was finished with the last of the Death Claws and began his descent toward the mountain base. The mercenaries were loading the giant crossbows—commonly known as ballistae—with equally large arrows. Hundurr growled and rushed down the mountain, followed by Rover. I had a feeling they understood exactly what we needed them to do.

"No sign of our allies yet," I muttered, my gaze shifting between the southern and western armies. "And about seventeen hundred daemons are about to climb this peak. Zane was right. These guys are better equipped to fight us than their predecessors were."

"We can still escape through the back hatch when the time comes," Hansa replied. "But we'll have to fight our way down the mountain. Let's focus on disabling all their large-scale weapons first. Once they start climbing the mountain, it'll be death on a first-come, first-served basis."

Pit wolves yelped beneath the dark foliage. Metal collars clanged as they were torn open. Our pit wolf problem was basically solving itself at this point, and it gave me an additional confidence boost. Those creatures were huge and could tackle a daemon general all on their own. Grunts were even easier to break. We needed them to do as much of the groundwork as possible, since we had a limited supply of arrows and only one dragon.

"Yeah, it'll be tough to make a clean exit," Scarlett confirmed after she checked the northern ridge. "The route itself is not easily accessible from the sides, but I wouldn't put it past the daemons to make an extra effort. It's steep, but they could still get to it."

Pheng-Pheng gasped, her amber eyes wide as she turned her head to look at me. She seemed tense and downright stiff, her jaw clenched.

"Harper Hellswan," she said, her voice low and slightly different. "The Ekar has come to me. I can see your enemies surrounding you. Stay strong."

I remembered then that the Manticore queen had this ability to communicate through all her people, including her daughter. That was Neha speaking through Pheng-Pheng. My heart swelled in my chest, growing three sizes. We finally had confirmation of one round of allied forces coming to our aid—and hopefully they would come soon enough.

It was starting to look downright dismal for us, not to mention messy and bloody.

"Queen Neha," I breathed.

Pheng-Pheng smiled, cocking her head to the side. "Worry not, young vampire. We are coming. I do keep my promises, you know."

Before I could get a chance to ask how long till they got to Ragnar Peak, Pheng-Pheng exhaled sharply and blinked several times, regaining her consciousness.

"That was Mother... I could feel her," she murmured, then eagerly looked around. "I think they're close."

"Good," Hansa interjected. "Now, get ready."

We all looked down at the dark mass spreading around the mountain. The drums banged ferociously. Swords clanged against meranium shields. I could hear the screeching of the ballistae being turned and aimed at Blaze. He circled above them, looking for the right entry angle.

When the launch mechanism on a ballista clicked, the dragon's jaws parted wide open, and fire and fury left his throat. The daemons were quick to cover themselves with their shields. A series of metallic screeching sounds caught my attention—the ballistae were equipped with charmed meranium plates that covered them with less than a minute's notice; the dome-shaped casing protected the giant crossbows from fire.

"Oh, crap," I muttered. "It's going to take more than that to disable those things."

Daemons roared below as they began to climb the mountain.

We loaded our arrows and pointed them downward.

This is it.

6

HARPER

For a moment, I was breathless.

My brain was desperately trying to adjust to the scene unfolding before my eyes—hordes of daemons working their way up the peak to get to us. I listened to my own heartbeat, rampant and downright erratic. But beneath the thuds, there was a layer of determination I'd managed to tap into.

This wasn't panic I was experiencing. Not anymore, anyway. It was a sliver of clarity. My brain finally switched gears, and I went into battle mode. My entire body bucked as I took my first deep breath, my bow stretched.

Another swarm of Death Claws emerged from the western ridge. About three dozen.

Hansa was the first to point her bow at them. "Take them down first! Let the dragon deal with the ballistae! Archers, go!"

In one fluid movement, all of us with bows turned to the west and released our arrows. I used my True Sight for target accuracy.

We used explosive arrowheads this time. They blew up everything they hit—chests, wings, heads. Blood sprayed out. Chunks of Death Claws rained all over the western ridge, and we reloaded and fired another round.

Below, our pit wolves ripped off the collars of the enemy hounds, then coaxed them into fighting on our side. One by one, pit wolves regained their freedom and rushed down the mountain, careful to avoid the land mines we'd set.

The daemons roared as they got past the first fifty yards. That was as much hope as we allowed them to have. They tripped the wires and—boom. A chain of explosions ripped through the base of Ragnar Peak. Orange fires bloomed and swallowed the front line of mercenaries. Many were torn to pieces.

Our pit wolves reached them. Jaws snapped shut. Flesh and meranium armor plates were torn. Bodies of daemons and giant hounds tangled. Heads jerked. Swords punctured black, leathery skin. Some of the pit wolves died in battle. But many chewed their way through the daemon ranks.

We had more Death Claws to deal with. We reloaded, then fired a third round. Two of the creatures slammed into the courtyard. The Imen were quick to neutralize them.

Another chain of explosions followed, this time on the north side. Daemons had stumbled upon those mines, too. *Don't worry, fellas. Plenty more where those came from.*

Caspian and I exchanged quick glances as we mounted a fourth round of explosive arrows onto our bows. The Druids and the fae made liberal use of their fire spells. Caia in particular was increasingly destructive. Her fireballs were small, pretty much the size of her head, but concentrated with enough energy to explode and tear into a fully grown Death Claw.

"She's quite feisty today," Fiona muttered, watching her for a few seconds. To my right, Caspian released his arrow. I shot mine too—caught a Claw right in its ugly, drooling face.

"Yeah, she's missing out on a baseball career, at this point," I replied. Fiona chuckled, reloaded, and fired another explosive arrow. It caught a Claw in its side, right above the courtyard. It plunged, screeching, and rammed into the eastern wall, breaking its neck in the process.

The daemons snarled and cursed below. The pit wolves were doing a good job of thinning their ranks, but not enough to keep them all away.

"Switch to burning and poisoned tips!" Hansa called out. "Keep the explosive ones for the grunts. We'll need them!"

We had our arrow ammo stacked in three piles. We reloaded as instructed, alternating between burning and poisoned tips. We had about a dozen Death Claws left to deal with. They circled above, hissing and looking for the right attack angle.

Unfortunately for them, Ryker and Laughlan were two Druids who had a serious bone to pick with anything daemon-related.

"I'm tired of hearing your obnoxious screeching!" Laughlan muttered, then chanted a spell and launched a bright green fireball.

It hit a Death Claw right in the chest and swallowed it whole, then exploded into a flurry of fireworks, scaring the daylights out of the other beasts.

"Nice," Ryker remarked, then tossed a flurry of blue fireballs at the remaining Claws.

Scarlett, Avril, and Heron handled the others with burning arrows, while the rest of our crew shifted focus to the ground. The daemons were making progress, despite the pit wolves, whose fangs couldn't breach the thicker meranium plates of the second line of attack. The mercenaries' broadswords came down hard, and several pit wolves fell. I counted five who didn't get back up.

It broke my heart to see them die, but their help so far had already given us a minor advantage. I caught a glimpse of a ballista spinning on its base. I followed its aim. Blaze was turning back toward the core mass of mercenaries on the south side. I found myself holding my breath.

A third chain of explosions rocked the western slope. The stone wall trembled beneath us. They managed to launch a giant arrow, but it missed Blaze by inches. In the following second, his jaws split open and out came a jet of raging fire. It caught the ballista's handlers unprepared—its shields just halfway up. They burned, and I felt a sliver of relief, counting one ballista disabled, as the flames consumed its wooden structure.

"Avril, Heron, Scarlett! Keep your eyes out for incoming Death Claws," Hansa shouted, constantly looking around and checking every side of the fortress. "There will be more coming. Make sure they don't reach the fortress. They're heavy and damage the walls whenever they land, the clumsy bastards!"

"Druids! Fae! Cover the slopes," Jax added, raising his voice. "It's only a matter of time before the daemons start noticing the wires. Keep them back. Use your fires and detonate the explosives if they pass without setting them off!"

It was impressive to watch Jax and Hansa in action, literally managing the fight. The synergy between them reminded me of Caspian and me. Our minds were perfectly tuned to one another, our reflexes sharp. Their warfare experience, however, was far superior to mine. I only had a handful of battles on Neraka to my credit. Hansa and Jax had won entire wars before they got stuck here. They'd led armies to victory and vanquished their foes.

So, if either Jax or Hansa told us to aim here or shoot there, we did it. No questions asked.

We were so wrapped up in keeping the fifteen hundred or so daemons left at bay, we didn't even notice the Adlets coming in until screams erupted from the northeastern ridge. I turned my True Sight on and immediately saw what was happening, seconds before Ryker announced it:

"Adlets are here!"

There were dozens of them, with rich and beautiful reddish fur coats, giant frames, and lethal jaws. They plowed through the daemon squadrons on that side, their fangs tearing into every limb in their path. They growled as they engaged in a spine-chilling bloodbath. I couldn't help but chuckle when I noticed the freed pit wolves' reaction—sheer delight, as they yelped at the Adlets, then proceeded with their rampage.

"I think it's safe to say the northeast and the east are, for the time being, fully covered," I said.

"About damn time!" Hansa smirked, then pointed her arrow south.

A fourth round of explosions burst through that side. Daemons pushed through, jumping over the fresh corpses of the second line of attack. "This is the third line," I muttered. "Extra armor on them."

"Go for the necks, the sides, the joints. That armor doesn't cover everything," Jax replied.

We stretched our bows once more and released a flurry of poisoned arrows. We'd gone through half of our arsenal at this point. We hit the right spots. The projectiles didn't kill the daemons right away. They grunted from the pain and broke the stems off, but they continued to make their way up. However, in less than a minute, they started collapsing, their veins blackened and their mouths foaming.

"Reload!" Hansa barked. "Burning tips this time."

"Harper, hit the fifth string of mines. Let's go preemptive on these bastards," Jax said.

I nodded and aimed my arrow at the fifth string of explosive devices we'd set up on the southern ridge. The grunts had already passed through the first four and were steadily approaching the fifth. One flaming arrow was enough to cause a chain reaction. The mines exploded in steady, fast succession.

One... two... three... four... all the way to the western ridge. Ragnar Peak shuddered from the deflagration. Dozens of daemons perished. But the third line of attack wasn't dead yet. They were persistent fiends—I had to give credit where it was due.

"Ready!" Hansa shouted, and we stretched our bows again and aimed at the incoming daemons, now less than a hundred yards away from the fortress. "Fire!"

We released a round of poisoned arrows this time, then quickly reloaded and followed up with flaming ones. I used my True Sight and aimed for the biggest of the mercenaries—the generals.

I'd learned something from Hansa's account of the wars against Azazel. *You cut off the head, and the body will flounder.*

So, I pulled on the tail of a poisoned arrow and searched through the third line of attack for the biggest and baddest of their generals. I pressed my lips into a thin line and ignored the little droplet of sweat trickling down my temple.

Deep breath through the nose and—*shoot!*

The arrow whistled through the air, between daemon heads and thick trees, in a perfect line. It caught one of the generals right in his throat, his head turned to the side as he yelled orders at his grunts, eighty yards away from me.

He gripped his punctured throat, blood gurgling from his gaping mouth. Within thirty seconds, he was down, flat on his face and convulsing. Another twenty seconds later, he was dead, and I'd already reloaded another poisoned arrow and pointed at the next big boy on the ground.

Deep breath. *Shoot!*

The Adlets coming in to assist us were not enough to stop the daemons' advance up the mountain. Despite their size and ferocity, they could only do so much against armored mercenaries. The worst part was that the third line of attack was making progress, having spotted what was left of our explosive devices and avoiding them as they made their way toward the fortress.

Patrik, Ryker, and Laughlan did a fine job of taking down incoming Death Claws on the northern wall. Given their thinning numbers, it was a safe bet to conclude that we'd delivered significant damage to the daemons' airborne hostiles. Patrik's blue fires swished across the sky, hitting the Claws before they even got close to the fortress walls.

The last thing he wanted was another instance of a flying beast hurling toward us in its deadly plunge, and Scarlett jumping out again to divert its trajectory, risking her life in the process. So he drew deep breaths, muttered his Druid spells, and shot the Claws with all his blue-fiery might.

On the other sides, our teams were hard at work keeping the incoming daemons at bay. However, it was only a matter of time before the fiends finally broke through our last lines of defense and reached the fortress walls. We needed to cause more damage in their third line, and the remaining mines were a good bet.

I lit up an arrow and stretched my bow, aiming it at one of the mines—specifically, one of the few that was within close range of the incoming daemons. I released the arrow and watched it shoot through the air, flicking past several grunts before it lodged itself into the mine. The fire was quick to spread and react with the chemicals.

The mine exploded, tearing the ground beneath it and several daemons around it apart. I reloaded and prepared to shoot the next mine on the same ridge. That one was closer to the others in its chain. Chances were that it was going to ignite the entire set if I set it alight.

I shot the second burning arrow, then stilled for a split second, hearing a familiar whistle. I saw the steel-tipped arrow headed toward me and ducked. It missed my head by inches, but it cut off a lock of my hair in its flight. I cursed under my breath, then looked behind me to see where the arrow had gone.

It was stuck between two blocks of stone in the western wall, less than a foot away from Vesta's leg. She froze, gawking at it, then looked at me, visibly confused.

As if time slowed down for a few seconds, my mind processed what was about to happen next. That was just one arrow coming from the daemons. More would follow shortly. My breath was cut short, and I quickly took my shield off my back and slipped it onto my right arm, leaving my left arm to pull on the bow.

"They've got archers!" I shouted. "Keep your shields up!"

Not two seconds after I announced that, a flurry of whistles erupted from below. Hundreds of arrows came at us in a slightly arched trajectory. We brought our shields up just in time. Tap! Tap! Tap! The arrows poked and scratched at the stainless steel and meranium discs.

"Reload now! Fire!" Hansa ordered.

We had to move fast, before the daemons reloaded. Suddenly, the stakes were even higher, and I feared they'd yet to reach the metaphorical ceiling. I remembered Harper's barriers as I got up and aimed at the row of daemon archers, who were partially shielded by the third line of attack.

"Harper! Your barrier might come in handy here!" I called out to her, then released and killed one of the archers at the back, approximately fifty yards away from us.

"Ugh, I can try," she replied, then shot an arrow. "Move quick, they're reloading. The third line is covering them!"

"Let's get rid of the third line, then!" Jax said. "Ryker, Laughlan, Caia! Detonate the mines! We'll handle the archers!"

Another round of arrows came swishing in from the daemons. We ducked and put our shields up. Someone cried out in the courtyard. I looked down and saw one of the Imen collapsing, riddled with arrows. One had gone straight through his neck. We couldn't save him, and the thought made my blood simmer.

I reloaded and sprang back up, while the Druids cast blue fires near the mines we'd set up at the forty-yard mark down the mountain. I aimed for another archer and got him right in the eye. Heron released a poisoned arrow, then slipped down to take a short breather. He'd been firing those things like crazy. He'd chosen his brief moment of respite well. A third wave of arrows came in.

Our shields went up. The steel tips never reached us but got two of the Imen below in the legs. Velnias rushed to give them first aid, slapping handfuls of healing paste onto their wounds. The Imen boys cried out from the pain but were soon back in front of their hatches.

When the fourth round of arrows came down on us, Harper summoned all the sentry strength she had and stood up. She grunted as she pushed out a barrier pulse. It radiated outward, and it was, by far, the most potent of all the energy pulses she'd ever released. It broke most of the arrows in half, midair. The others lost their trajectory and just hit the ground.

Harper breathed out, then quickly resumed her archery. "I'll need a little bit more energy to put out another one of those," she said, "and not one of you can spare any, given what we're dealing with."

I aimed a poisoned arrow at one of the daemons in the third line, now thirty yards away. I got him in the neck, just as one of the Druids managed to ignite one of the mines. It caused a devastating chain reaction, aided by the fires already burning from previous attempts. Ragnar Peak was rocked by the explosions, the ground shaking beneath us as we all prepared to reload.

"Use the explosive heads this time," Hansa shouted.

We did as we were instructed, then aimed at the incoming line of hostiles. Many were left behind in tatters, including several dozen archers. Plenty were left standing, reaching into their quivers for another round of arrows.

"Oh, no, you don't," Heron hissed and shot his first.

It hit an archer in the chest and detonated, spreading him over twenty yards. The blowback got others killed or severely injured. I chuckled, then followed up in the same area with another explosive arrow. More bloody gunk was left where archers had stood until a few seconds earlier.

The Adlets continued to work their way through the north and eastern ridges, but we were still woefully outnumbered. Their surviving archers mounted their bows and released another wave of steel-tipped arrows.

"Incoming!" I shouted, then ducked, putting my shield up.

Heron and I bumped shoulders. We could see each other smiling through our masks. We both nodded, then checked on Rush and Amina, who were several feet farther down the wall. They had a millennia-old bone to pick with the daemons, and despite their still-weakened states, both Maras were energized and determined, their state of mind visible in the speed with which they reloaded and the accuracy of their aim. That was a cool couple to marvel at, in my book.

"Avril, do you know what keeps me going right now?" Heron breathed, loading another explosive arrow.

"The thought of having another bedroom all to ourselves for an entire night?" I replied, then got up and released my bow.

The projectile went through two daemons, one after the other. It exploded as soon as it pierced the first one, but, given its speed, it continued well into the second. They both disintegrated, swallowed by the bright orange flames.

I gave Heron a sideways glance and found him grinning beneath his mask as he stretched his bow and fired another shot. Boom!

"Like I said before, you know me so well," he muttered.

I would've laughed, but the urgency of our situation was heightened by the speed with which the daemons were getting significantly closer to the fortress. We were going to run out of arrows soon, and the daemons kept coming. No matter how many of them we blew to pieces or shot down, more came from behind —snarling, growling, and determined to capture us.

I heard Hansa shout. "Reload!"

But something caught my eye—movement below in the woods, just twenty yards from our location. Arrows whistled through the air. We raised our shields and blocked the incoming projectiles, but I kept my gaze focused on a shrub. It rustled and trembled, then moved upward. I gasped, realizing that it had been covering a hidden hatch.

Daemon mercenaries were just feet away from it. Short arrows were shot from inside. Several daemons came down. I couldn't see from that angle, but whoever was coming out through the hatch was an ally.

"Heron, look!" I breathed, pointing at them.

Heron paused in the middle of reloading to follow my gaze. He then nodded to another spot, farther to the left. "There's more than one!" he said.

Indeed, upon second visual inspection, there were tens of those hatches built into the ground, expertly camouflaged by the foliage. There were most likely more of them on the other sides of the mountain.

"Can anyone else see the hatches opening?" I asked, raising my voice for the others in our team to hear.

"Yup, confirming eight on our side!" Harper replied a few seconds later.

"Twelve on the western slope!" Vesta added.

"Six on the north!" Scarlett confirmed.

"Nine on this side!" Heron chimed in. "I think they're friendly."

"No kidding!" Zane shot back, visibly amused. "They just took down six third-liners in one round!"

We released another round of explosive arrows, this time aiming farther down the mountain so as not to hurt our unexpected helpers. A couple of Death Claws screamed above, engulfed in blue flames, before they plummeted into the courtyard, where Dion and Alles killed them off.

"Who are they, though?" Heron muttered, frowning as he reached down to his side for an arrow.

"I don't know, but—"

The clang of a metal hatch opening somewhere in the court-yard behind us made me still for a second. Both Heron and I turned around, then found ourselves equally stunned. There were hatches hidden beneath the stone slabs in the courtyard. Four of them, to be precise, one of which was just a couple of feet away from the fountain.

"What in the..." Heron's voice trailed off, as we finally saw our surprise helpers.

Imen. Dozens of them, pouring into the courtyard. One of them, in particular, stood out—tall and slender, with bushy blond hair, ginger freckles, and piercing green eyes. He looked young, in his late teens, wearing the smile of a permanently mischievous boy.

All of them were armed to the teeth, carrying extra crossbows and quivers loaded with hundreds of short arrows.

"Good morning to ya!" the young Iman greeted us. "You're all probably wondering what we're doin' here!"

"We would, if we had the time to do that!" Hansa shot back, then stretched her bow and released another arrow.

Heron and I did the same, launching a pair of explosive arrow-heads at two daemon archers. The Imen from the hatches nearby followed up with a flurry of short arrows, taking down a dozen more of the third-liners covering the archers behind them.

"Okay, well, long story short, I'm Wyrran. I lead the rebels of Harbir, to be precise," the young Iman replied, then motioned to his teammates to distribute the extra crossbows and arrows, while four of them kept taking out more quivers from the open hatches in the courtyard. "We've heard about you, about Draconis. The southerners told us where to find you, so we thought we'd come by to help."

Holy crap.

Neraka sure supported our rebellion, then! We certainly hadn't expected Imen to come all the way to Ragnar Peak to pitch in, but we absolutely welcomed the added firepower. As the sun rose proudly over the eastern horizon, I found myself smiling beneath my mask.

8

HERON

I didn't even have time to be baffled, constantly reloading and shooting more arrows to kill as many daemon archers as I could before they had a chance to reload.

"So, yeah, we brought some of the good stuff!" Wyrran added. His Imen handed crossbows around, along with fully stocked quivers. Avril grabbed two of each, and we quickly switched to crossbows. I could instantly feel the improvement in speed and accuracy with these simple yet exquisitely crafted beauties.

"That's... That's incredibly thoughtful of you, I guess," Hansa stuttered, trying to find the right words as she released another explosive arrow, before she took hold of a crossbow. "Big one incoming!" she then shouted.

"Crap," I muttered, then yelled at Wyrran. "Take cover!"

Seconds later, a giant arrow made its way up above the fortress, before gravity got the better of it. It pierced through the northern wall just as Scarlett pulled Patrik away. The portion they'd just stood on was damaged in the impact, and chunks of stone crumbled into the courtyard.

"Oh, wow, they brought out the big toys, huh?" Wyrran chuckled nervously, then whistled, earning the attention of his Imen. "Spread out. Take the walls. Groups of five. And give these outsiders some backup. Move! Move! Move!"

Despite his young age, Wyrran displayed military discipline. He was bound to have an interesting story to tell, provided we all survived this siege. The troops he'd stationed through the outside hatches continued firing their crossbows. We added rounds of arrows on top of that, but it took six or seven per daemon to bring them down.

The Adlets had lost tens of their own, their packs thinned as they continued toward the southern and western base of the mountain. The daemons still had the giant ballistae, and we could hear Blaze roaring and raining fire on their asses, but he'd obviously been unable to disable all of those horrible contraptions. He couldn't get too close, either, as each of those giant arrows was meant for him.

Wyrran's Imen took their positions up on the walls and started shooting. The difference was immediately noticeable.

"It's getting hot on this side!" Hansa shouted from the southern wall. "We could use an extra pair of crossbows here, kids!"

Avril and I briefly looked at each other, nodded, then darted over to help. "Coming," I replied and found us a good spot in the corner. The view from up here was downright spine-chilling. The eastern ridge was definitely in slightly better shape, as the Imen from the hatches continued their assault on the incoming mercenaries.

Over on the south side, however, it was getting crowded. The third line was almost down, as were most of the archers on the ridge below, but the fourth and fifth lines of daemon mercenaries were thick and persistent, navigating the plethora of craters and dismembered corpses. Furthermore, there were still four ballistae fully operational. I spotted five large arrows lodged into the mountainside at different altitudes, and we'd just taken one in the northern wall. It was only a matter of time before they released one that could cause more damage.

Wyrran came up on our side with a loaded crossbow and a quiver on his back.

"You people won't be able to get off this mountain through the back gate. You know that, right?" he asked. "The staircase leading to the ground level is compromised, and there are plenty of daemons coming up on that ridge."

"Yeah, we kind of figured that one out already," Jax replied, shooting and reloading his new crossbow with swift movements. He looked as though he'd been born with one of these things in his hands. "We've got more allies coming. Hopefully, they'll keep these daemons busy while we get away through the back, nonetheless."

"No need," Wyrran shot back, then fired his crossbow. A confident smirk crossed his face. "We came through the tunnels. There are four of them leading up to the fortress, plus a network of smaller links between them and the outer hatches. It's how we made it up here undetected. We rigged them with enough explosives to bring down the entirety of Ragnar Peak."

As he said that, he got our full attention, especially Jax's, who was stunned and staring at him. A daemon arrow missed him by inches. Hansa cursed behind him, smacked him over the shoulder, and pulled him back into the crossbow game. They both leaned against the half-wall and fired at the incoming hostiles.

"You can take one of the four tunnels out of here," Wyrran continued. "As soon as you get out of range, a few of my guys will stay back to detonate the whole network and destroy the entire mountain."

"Draconis 2.0," Fiona muttered. "Then we need to get as many of these monsters up on the mountain as possible," she added. "We're not leaving until we know for a fact that the majority of these two armies will be dealt with. We can't afford being followed, given what we have to do next."

Wyrran nodded, then fired another shot, getting a mercenary right in the throat. The kid had impressive marksmanship, for sure. Definitely military. I was officially curious.

"That's fine. We'll hold out here for as long as possible, but as soon as it starts getting too hot, I need you all to go," he replied.

A bloodcurdling roar from below made us all freeze. Blaze plunged toward one of the ballistae, spitting fire along the way, but a second one was turned and aimed at him, while the mercenaries around the giant crossbows scrambled for cover from the melting inferno spreading toward them.

I heard Caia scream from the tower. "Blaze, watch out!"

The dragon managed to disable the ballista he'd been aiming for, but the other one released an arrow. He was too late to completely dodge it. It pierced through his wing, but it didn't take him down. It got lodged halfway through, and it looked horribly painful.

"Oh, crap," Avril muttered. The rest of our team on the south side was forced to resume fire, as more mercenaries from the fourth and fifth lines of offense made their way up.

Blaze wasn't just in pain, though. He was incredibly pissed off —and for good reason. He roared and spat rivers of fire below him, urgently flapping his wings in a desperate attempt to dislodge the arrow. It came loose and landed head down into a squadron of daemons. Two never got back up, while the others scattered and ran for cover.

He obliterated the ballista responsible for his injury before its handlers could reload. Two were left fully operational, but Blaze was injured. He flew back up to the fortress, barely keeping a straight line. The remaining ballistae turned and aimed at him.

"Druids, incoming ballista arrows!" Jax shouted. "Do *not* let either one touch Blaze or the fortress!"

I feared that Druid fire might not be enough in this case. "Harper!" I called out. "Draw some energy from someone and get ready with a barrier, just in case!"

She nodded, and Pheng-Pheng tapped her shoulder. "Take some from me," the young Manticore said. Harper gripped her forearm and syphoned off her, then shifted her focus back to the ballistae—just in time, too, as both released their projectiles.

They came up fast, just as Blaze did a forced landing in the middle of the courtyard. He slammed into the northern wall, making the entire fortress tremble in the impact. Caia was visibly distraught and tried to come down, but Hansa stopped her.

"Focus, Caia!" the succubus shouted. "We need firepower up here!"

Velnias rushed over to Blaze, who shifted back to normal. His left arm was bleeding.

"Incoming!" Jax yelled.

Druid fireballs missed one of the arrows, forcing Harper to release a barrier prematurely. It wasn't strong enough to break the second one's flight. Someone cursed, and I watched the second giant arrow headed right for our wall.

"Get out of the way!" I managed, then quickly wrapped my arms around Avril and pulled her back.

The projectile hit the south wall with considerable strength, piercing the upper edge. The others managed to avoid a direct hit, but stone rubble burst out from the impact and exploded inward.

The blow was severe. Dust billowed, and I could no longer see the rest of my team.

A portion of the wall crumbled, and more dust spread through the air, making it even more difficult to see. I held on for dear life, clutching Avril to my chest as the stone slabs beneath us gave in and sank into the courtyard.

"Crap, crap, crap!" I bellowed, then fell.

9

HARPER

I *didn't draw enough energy from Pheng-Pheng.*

I coughed, struggling to breathe. The dust tickled my throat. My whole body hurt as I lay on the ground in the courtyard. I'd been caught in the partial collapse of the wall. Pain shot through my right leg. I tried to move it, but it was stuck.

"Harper!" Caspian croaked, reaching me.

Not all of us had managed to get out of the way in time. Caspian was injured, too, judging by the blood trickling down his dust-covered face. He freed my leg from the pile of rubble that had pinned it down and pulled me up.

"Are you okay?" I asked, wheezing and breaking into another dry cough.

"I'll be fine," he replied, then briefly checked my injuries. "Nothing serious, from what I can tell."

"Doesn't stop me from feeling like a train ran over me."

I paused, then quickly looked around to assess the state of my

team. Imen had hurried over to get Hansa and Jax back up. Pheng-
Pheng was already standing, panting as she wiped the blood from
her temple.

Heron and Avril were okay, too, though still dazed from the fall.
The ballista arrow had hit the upper lip of the southern wall with
enough strength to dislodge a hefty chunk of it. The entire structure was still standing, but it was only a matter of time before it
would all come crumbling down—if I had to guess, I would've said
three, maybe four more of those big-ass arrows to completely
destroy the entire south side.

Velnias had already taken care of Blaze, whose forearm was
covered with a bandage strip, holding the healing paste in place.
Zane and Fiona were still on the wall with Wyrran and a couple
more Imen, while the others held their own against the incoming
daemons on the other sides.

"We need to get back up," Hansa breathed.

With lightning speed, she and Jax climbed up the southern
wall, next to Fiona, Zane, and the others.

"Guys," Vesta called out. "Big problem on this side!"

I immediately used my True Sight to scan the western part of
Ragnar Peak, all the way to the base, where—I lost my breath.
Catapults. Two of them, and huge. The daemons had taken a while
to bring them forward, judging by the deep tracks they'd left
behind in the hard ground. They had loaded them up with large
boulders and were just about to pull the levers.

"Catapults!" I shouted. "Two at the base!"

I briefly assessed potential trajectories as Zane slipped to the
corner to get a better look.

"High-precision launchers," he said. "They'll go for the towers
first! I've seen them in action before."

I heard the rumble and the release clang. My heart stopped as I
looked up at the towers.

"Caia!" I screamed. "Get down from there! Now!"

The boulders were hurled through the air with bone-chilling precision, proving Zane's point. Vesta and her parents summoned the elements in a bid to stop both incoming chunks of rock, but only managed to take one down. The second flew past them and straight toward Caia's tower.

"Caia!" Blaze growled.

The Druids were halfway down from their tower. Patrik shot out a blue fire spell but missed the projectile by inches.

I kept my True Sight on Caia. The boulder crashed into her tower. I choked up, then cried out, my eyes instantly tearing up. I'd just seen her up there, but she was gone—and so was the tower. It came crumbling down, its stony entrails spilling into the courtyard.

"Caia, no!" Blaze bellowed, utterly distraught as he finally managed to stand.

My heartbeat echoed in my ears. My breath was cut short. I couldn't move. Neither of us could move as we stared at the collapsed tower.

Caspian and I rushed toward it but came to a sudden halt. The pile of rubble trembled and burst outward. Velnias, bless his daemon heart, emerged, holding Caia in his arms. They were both covered in scratches and dirt—but alive.

Blaze and I darted over to them. The dragon took over for Velnias and held Caia tight in his arms. I dropped a kiss on the top of her head, tears streaming down my cheeks. I was shaking like a leaf.

"Cuz, I'm not leaving this place without you, dammit!" I whispered.

Caia gave me a weak smile. "Hey, I'm tiny but resilient."

"No, what you are is lucky," Velnias shot back, shaking his head disapprovingly as he dusted himself off.

"We need some help up here!" Hansa called out, constantly firing and reloading her crossbow. A brief True Sight assessment confirmed my fears: the daemons were gaining significant ground on the south side. The Adlets and the rebel Imen were good at keeping the west and the east flanks back, while Patrik and Scarlett had a good grip on the north. Laughlan and Ryker split up. Ryker took the northeastern corner, while Laughlan moved to provide backup on the west side.

Caspian and I rushed back up the crippled south wall, picking up new crossbows and quivers on the way—courtesy of Wyrran's people. We loaded up and started firing again. My head hurt, and my leg felt a little stiff. My ribs and left shoulder were sore, but I was going to heal soon enough. There was no time to take a breather. The enemy surrounded us, and they were getting dangerously close to the fortress walls.

"Disable the archers," Jax commanded, then looked over his shoulder at Laughlan. "We need those catapults disabled too."

The Druid nodded, then froze. Only then, in the second-long silence, did I capture a familiar, spine-tingling rattle coming in from the northwestern ridge. My heart boomed with newfound energy.

"Manticores!" I breathed.

10

HARPER

The rattling grew louder.

I glanced around and noticed the worried expressions on the daemon mercenaries' faces. They slowed down in their advance. Some even paused as they recognized the sound.

Perfect window for us.

"Reload," Hansa muttered.

We did, then aimed and released a flurry of short arrows. Dozens in consecutive rounds pierced their throats before they continued their advance and used their shields to avoid the incoming projectiles. There was only so much meranium plates could protect them from, especially since their armor didn't fully cover their most critical points.

Pheng-Pheng purred, almost like a kitten, a grin slitting across her face as she reloaded her crossbow and shot it again.

"I can smell the wind of change, comrades," she chuckled.

"Oh, damn," Heron murmured, then stilled.

There were at least eighty, maybe a hundred Manticores working their way up the southern and western slopes. They were fast, vicious, and poisonous in their strikes. Their chests, upper backs, shoulders, and forearms were covered with bronze-colored protective plates that glistened whenever touched by sunlight.

They darted through the fifth line of daemon mercenaries, their scorpion tails rattling and stinging left and right. Our enemies didn't even see them coming. Less than a minute later, the Manticores were breaking through the fourth line.

Some of the daemons were quick enough to react, the remaining archers in particular. I saw them shift their aim onto the Manticores, waiting for a clear shot, but I wasn't going to let them shoot. I reloaded my crossbow and got one of the archers in the throat. His eyes bulged out, blood gurgling out of his gaping mouth, as I prepared another arrow, then released it into another archer.

"Go for the archers," I said. "The Manticores are too fast for them. Now's our chance."

Pheng-Pheng giggled. "Nice to see you're all still standing, Harper Hellswan," she said, her voice low. That was her mom, the queen of Manticores, speaking through her.

"Looking forward to seeing you join us," I replied, trying to drown out the rumbling and growling of the war unfolding around us with the sound of my own voice.

"Oh, I'll be with you shortly," she replied.

We kept shooting, catching glimpses of Adlets tearing through the lower ranks, while the Manticores continued their dash through the fifth and fourth ranks. Their scorpion needles pierced through the daemon skin, delivering considerable amounts of venom. Just to make sure the mercenaries went down, preferably sooner rather than later, we concentrated a number of arrows in their direction.

"We'll handle the archers," Heron said. "You guys take the foot soldiers."

"Perfectly fine by me," I replied, then reloaded and aimed my crossbow at one of the generals.

He was fifteen yards away and twice as big as the others around him. He was a mountainous mass of muscle and heavy bones. The mighty fall harder... I released an arrow. It cut through the air, its feathery tail rippling. He didn't even see it coming until it was too late—specifically, when it pierced his eye. He cried out from the pain, and I heard Caspian scoff.

He aimed and shot a second arrow, piercing the general's jugular. "As much as I would love to see these fiends suffer tremendously for everything they've done and intend to keep doing, we don't have time."

"You make a fair point," I replied, then shot another mercenary in the throat.

The Manticores continued their deadly rampage, while we provided cover and finished off the daemons that were still standing. It was starting to look like we might get off this mountain after all.

Wyrran and two of his Imen pulled open the hatch next to the fountain. He looked up at me. "You'll all need to get ready soon," he said. "Your allies are coming. Your window to escape is almost here."

The clang of a catapult releasing a boulder made my stomach churn.

"Catapults incoming!" I shouted.

Blaze left Caia to handle the southeastern corner of the wall. "Yeah, I'm not done with these assholes yet!" he growled, then burst into full dragon form and took flight.

His wound had closed up. Our fire dragon was back in full force and had a grudge the size of Neraka. I used my True Sight to follow him as he disappeared below the western wall. He glided over the woods and sharp, stony ridges, then shot upward and crashed into the first boulder, knocking it off course.

The impact threw him back, though, and he smashed into the mountainside, breaking trees and daemons as he rolled through the shrubs. I heard the catapult again, then cursed under my breath. Blaze then scrambled to get back up and flew out to intercept the second boulder.

"Come on, Blaze," I muttered, gritting my teeth.

The projectile hurled toward the fortress at high speed, with Blaze hot on its trail. He couldn't use his fire at such close proximity to the fortress—not without hurting the fae covering the western wall.

"Vesta, take your parents and move!" I shouted.

"Yup, I see him!" Vesta replied, then pushed her parents down toward the northwestern corner.

Based on its trajectory, that boulder was seconds away from tearing into the western wall, and, unlike the ballista arrow, that thing was big enough to tear down the entire structure like a boot kicking down a carefully assembled work of dominoes.

Everybody else was busy fending off daemon attacks, now less than ten yards away on all sides. Some didn't even pay attention, particularly below, where the Imen had begun to release a frenzy of arrows at the daemons that got too close to the fortress.

It was up to Blaze to catch it.

He managed to speed up and almost had it, when a white streak shot through the air from the north and took the boulder down. It was instantly frozen and exploded upon impact with the stony ridge, snow spreading out on a twenty-yard radius.

Only then did I notice the dark clouds gathering overhead, as the temperature began to drop.

Blaze came to a sudden halt, visibly confused. The daemons

behind him were terrified when he landed on the western slope and glanced back at them. I heard them curse, before the dragon released his fire and fury on the entire flank. The flames spread on a fifty-yard stretch, as the Manticores pulled back and focused on the lower half of the mountain.

With dozens of daemons charred and scattered on the upper side of Ragnar Peak's western ridge, Blaze took flight and plunged toward the catapults. They were minutes from completing a reload down there, but they never got the chance to launch another pair of boulders. Blaze literally burned them out of existence, then quickly pulled back up.

I didn't understand why he had retreated so quickly until I saw a ballista arrow shoot through the air and miss him by inches in his ascent.

The cold winds grew as I shifted my focus back to the southern slope. The mercenaries had been quick to move the ballistae closer to the western base. The Adlets were losing their battle with the ground forces and began to retreat up the mountain, where it was easier to tear through the climbing grunts, providing valuable backup to the Manticores.

Dozens of our allies had fallen—Adlets, Imen, and even some Manticores—while half of the daemon armies were still standing, their fiercest warriors only now getting involved. The first offensive lines had served to wear us out, just like Zane had predicted.

"We've got more company," Avril said, looking up.

The sun had vanished beyond the swirling dark clouds. Snowflakes began to come down, their natural design a microscopic monument devoted to the geometry of the universe itself. The Dhaxanians were coming.

11

AVRIL

I recognized the snowstorm gathering overhead. I'd seen it before.

The chills trickling down my spine confirmed what was happening. Nevis was here. Heron and I looked at each other as icy, rabid winds smacked into the fortress, carrying hefty pounds of pure white snow.

The daemon generals roared from the bottom of the mountain. The ground troops slowed down, overwhelmed not only by the constant attacks from Manticores and Adlets that they had to keep fending off, but also by the rapidly dropping temperatures.

Blaze flew around the mountain and took advantage of the momentary pause. He headed straight for the ballistae, just as their handlers scrambled to reload them. Battle horns blew in the distance. The rumble of war drums erupted from the southwestern horizon. More armies were coming.

It didn't matter anymore, though. The daemons clearly had not seen the Dhaxanians coming to our aid. Maybe they could've handled the unruly Manticores and Adlets. Maybe they would've eventually overpowered us. Even as we would've escaped from Ragnar Peak, they would've caught our scent and tracked us.

But nothing had prepared them for *this*.

Hope blossomed in my chest once more, the blood rushing to my head. I relished the cold air hugging me from all sides. We reloaded our crossbows and kept shooting at the daemons. They were just yards away from the fortress now. We had to take as many of them down as possible—our allies had come to help us, after all. The least we could do was make it easier for them to destroy our attackers.

Just then, I heard a familiar crackle.

I looked down. "Yup, so the Dhaxanians sure know how to make an entrance," I muttered.

We all stilled momentarily, watching the crystal-clear frost spread out on the ground and all around the mountain base. It came from the northern side, and it stretched across almost two hundred square feet, slipping beneath the boots of daemon mercenaries and grunts.

They struggled to stay upright as the ice expanded and worked its way up the stony mountain. The winds grew even colder and heavier, thick snowfall obscuring the daemons' visibility. I heard them yelping somewhere far below. It seemed reasonable to assume that the frost was starting to swallow them up. I couldn't help but wonder whether that was Nevis's frost or his subjects'. The latter could be broken and melted, at least. Otherwise, the daemons were screwed.

Everything seemed to slow down, gradually. It was as if time itself was winding down with the cold. Frankly, after all the time we'd spent up here, perpetually on edge and, for the past couple of hours, constantly fighting off daemons, collared pit wolves, and screeching Death Claws, I could really use a breather.

I exhaled sharply, and Heron took my hand in his.

"Look over there," he muttered, pointing to the southeastern ridge.

Daemons slipped on ice as the frost finally reached the fortress. Arrows made of pure, hard ice shot through the growing snowstorm, piercing their meranium armor.

"How is that possible?" I breathed. "It's just frozen water."

One by one, the daemons collapsed, blood pooling beneath them, as the ice arrows swiftly melted. Based on the growls and whimpers emerging from the southwestern ridge, the same was happening over there. Soon enough, the entire fourth line of attack had fallen, their large, muscular, and meranium-armored bodies defeated by the simplest of natural elements.

"Well, way to minimize Dhaxanian greatness." Nevis's voice made me turn my head.

Scarlett and Patrik moved back a couple of feet, as Nevis gracefully climbed up the northern wall and smiled at me. Twenty Dhaxanians clad in pale blue silks and silvery armor joined him, lined up on the edge. The prince of Dhaxanians looked as gorgeous as ever, covered in white silk from his neck to his ankles. He was barefooted, frost spreading beneath his pale-skinned soles. His neck and chest piece glistened with silver swirls and a plethora of diamonds. His long white hair was elegantly braided back, cascading beyond his shoulders. His pointed ears were covered in silver and diamond jewels, molded to their peculiar shape. His icy blue gaze found mine, and he kept his hands behind his back and his posture perfectly dignified.

I couldn't help but let the sudden surge of relief wash over me.

"Don't let it go to your head, but, boy, are you a sight for sore eyes." I chuckled.

Nevis smirked, while the killing of daemons continued below. We couldn't see it anymore, as the snowy winds roared and circled the fortress. All we could do was stare at Nevis and his Dhaxanians —all beautiful and calm, almost surreal, with iridescent skin and sky-colored eyes.

"Dhaxanian arrows aren't just... ice," he replied, sounding almost offended. "Dhaxanian arrows carry the force of the fighter, the spirit of winter, and the fury of the defender. Only then can they pierce through anything. Including meranium."

"That sounds a lot like magic," Patrik muttered, frowning slightly.

"Call it whatever you want," Nevis shot back. "What it is doesn't matter. What it does, on the other hand... Well, I assume you can tell already."

"Thank you for coming to help us," I said. "I take it your people are taking care of our problem?"

"The bottom is frozen, though it won't take them long to break free," Nevis replied. "You can hear what's happening around the top."

"How many of you are there?" I asked.

"I could spare fifty of my best fighters," he said, motioning at the Dhaxanians lined up behind him.

"Wait, twenty are up here with you. You mean to tell us only thirty Dhaxanians could plow through almost a thousand daemons?" Hansa gasped, surprised.

Nevis raised an eyebrow as he looked at her. "I'm sorry, you are?"

Ugh. Still with the attitude. I decided to give him a pass, though. He'd solved one hell of a problem for us just now.

"Your Grace, Nevis, Prince of Dhaxanians," I replied, then cleared my throat and motioned for the rest of my GASP crew. "You haven't met my colleagues. These are our group leaders,

Hansa Gorria and Jaxxon Dorchadas, succubus and Lord of the Calliope Maras, respectively."

Both Jax and Hansa promptly offered a respectful nod. Nevis measured each of them from head to toe, curiosity and fascination glimmering in his eyes.

"Good to see there are Maras out there who don't require their heads getting cut off in order for me to tolerate their presence," Nevis said, the corner of his mouth twitching.

"You tolerated *me* just fine," Heron grumbled, crossing his arms and giving me the urge to pinch the bridge of my nose. I loved him so much yet struggled with the occasional and sudden desire to slap him silent.

Nevis glowered at him. "I have not yet made up my mind about you. Appreciate your head while you still have it. I might reconsider."

"And these are Harper Hellswan and Lord Caspian Kifo—" I tried to shift the conversation back to the introductions, but Nevis cut me off.

"I know Lord Kifo," he said, then narrowed his eyes at the Mara. "I'm not surprised to see you here. Even as I signed the treaty with Azure Heights, I could tell your heart wasn't in it. It was only a matter of time, I thought. Nice to be proven right once more."

"I was waiting for the right people to come along and help us liberate Neraka," Caspian replied with a polite nod.

Blaze was still in dragon form, huffing as the cold started to seep through his thick hide. Nevis lazily turned his attention to him and grinned.

"You're a big boy, aren't you?" He chuckled softly, then quickly turned serious. "Can you try to make yourself look less threatening, though? My subjects' teeth are chattering, and it's not because of the cold."

Blaze blinked several times and shifted back to his humanoid form, prompting Nevis to quickly look away and roll his eyes. "Good grief," he added.

"Sorry," Blaze replied with a sheepish smile, as Caia handed him a pair of pants. "Comes with the package."

"Yes, I can see that. Cover it up," Nevis shot back.

I pressed my lips tight, my cheeks burning despite the freezing blizzard pummeling the fortress.

"Your Grace, that is Blaze, our dragon, and Caia, our beloved fire fae," I added, raising my voice to divert his attention from the half-naked hunk of dragon who was still fumbling with his pants buttons. The cold made his hands shake.

"I think we can skip the rest of the introductions for now," Nevis replied, pointing at the rest of our crew. "I can already spot a daemon prince, another daemon, two more Druids, a couple more of your fae and Maras, as well as the Imen—though half of them are, unfortunately, dead."

His tone was so dry, it completely undermined the gravity of the situation he'd been already so quick to gloss over. One brief glance below and I could see our fallen Imen, as snow piled above them. I overcame the pain settling in my stomach and chose to focus on what lay ahead. We didn't have time to grieve, although one could tell from our expressions that we cherished all our allies equally and suffered tremendously when we lost them.

"Moving forward," he added with a cold smile, "you called, Avril. So, I'm here to oblige. How can I be of service?"

I breathed out, steam rolling out of my mouth. I welcomed the icy air filling my lungs and the smell of winter. It covered the layers of blood, death and burnt-everything that spread over Ragnar Peak.

This was it. Time for our great escape.

12

HARPER

At first glance, I both liked and detested the Dhaxanian prince. In some ways, he reminded me of my first encounter with Caspian—he was cold, even glacial, blunt, and seemingly heartless. I could spot that silver spoon in his mouth from a mile away. Then again, he had broken his treaty with the daemons and chosen to help us.

I guess you take the good with the bad, in the end.

In Nevis's case, the good outweighed the bad.

With the siege abruptly frozen to a temporary stop, we had a few minutes to just breathe and focus on our escape. Wyrran's arrival had brought forth a new exit strategy, one that didn't involve anyone seeing us go down the mountain.

War horns kept sounding in the distance. We'd made a lot of noise by battling two armies of daemons—of course they were sending reinforcements. By sundown, this place was going to crawl with twice as many hostiles, maybe even more.

We jumped off the walls and gathered in the middle of the courtyard. Nevis used his frost as a means of getting around; he wiggled his fingers, and ice extended from the northern wall's upper lip onto the ground floor. He slid down to join us. His Dhax-anians stayed behind, surveying the area, while the others in his group continued to strike down the remaining fourth and fifth lines of attack beyond the walls.

Wyrran positioned himself in front of the proposed escape hatch by the fountain, and briefly brought our newly-arrived friends up to speed. "We've got secret tunnels going in and out of this place."

"We're going to sneak out," Avril said to Nevis, "and we need you, our allies, to cover for us. We can't risk daemons tailing us."

"You're lucky the daemons didn't expect to see us," Neha said, emerging from the western wall.

I couldn't help but smile at the sight of her—ever so gorgeous, brown leather hugging her curves, and thousands of tiny red gems braided into her thick, firebrick mane. Kai joined her, and they both slid down the wall and came toward us.

Pheng-Pheng's scorpion tail rattled with excitement. She rushed into her mother's arms and held her tight for a good minute, while Kai watched them both with beaming affection.

Neha chuckled softly. "Otherwise, their first round would've come with a lot more firepower," she continued.

"Thank you," Hansa replied, offering a curt bow. "We would've been lost without you."

"Well, I wouldn't say lost," Colton interjected from the top of the eastern wall. "Maybe sweating a lot more, for sure."

Colton came down and joined us, just as Hundurr and Rover made their way back into the fortress. Rover stayed back, wary of Colton, but Hundurr yelped and rushed to nuzzle his face, thrilled to see the Adlet pack master—his brother and his best friend, before he'd suffered the mutation of the daemons' charmed collar.

"I'm sorry for your losses," Jax said, his voice low and his brow furrowed. "You've all made an enormous sacrifice today."

"Our fallen brothers and sisters have made their peace already," Colton replied, raising his chin. "We'll gladly spill our blood and give our lives for the liberation of Neraka."

"Frankly, most of us were beginning to think we'd never see the day," Neha said, a faint smile stretching her lips. Her amber eyes flickered with grief, but I could also see hope in them. "But you've already surprised me in more than one way. You even found Dhaxanians," she added, then looked at Nevis. "I figured your kind might've gone extinct."

"It will take a lot more than daemons and bloodsuckers to destroy the Dhaxanians," Nevis muttered.

Heron scoffed, visibly insulted by the "bloodsucker" remark, and crossed his arms.

I chuckled. "He was kind of accurate in describing your species, and, by association, ours, too."

"Still. Manners," Heron grumbled.

"I'm hearing a lot of noise." Nevis smirked at Heron. "Was that you talking?"

"Good grief, you're both incorrigible," Avril snapped, instantly silencing them both, while the rest of us tightened our lips, struggling not to laugh.

"We'll keep the daemons off your tails," Colton said, drawing focus back to the matter at hand. "They'll keep trying to reach the fortress, anyway. I doubt they know anything about these tunnels. Otherwise this place would've already been swarming with them."

"Agreed," Wyrran replied with a nod. "This tunnel will take you about two miles to the northeast, virtually undetected. It doesn't connect with any daemon passages, and it runs smoothly, uninterrupted until the end. I can guide you from thereon, while the rest of my Imen stay here and keep the daemons busy."

"The Imen should also leave," Neha said firmly. "Otherwise, you'd all be cannon fodder for the daemons. We can handle them well between us," she added, then grinned. "It's been a long time since the Adlets, the Dhaxanians, and the Manticores have fought together, anyway."

Nevis scoffed, crossing his arms. He wasn't too happy about playing with others, it seemed—yet another trait I'd seen in Caspian during our first days on Neraka. "There's a reason behind that."

"Yes, yes, there's definitely a reason. It's the peace treaty you signed with the daemons, sending the rest of us to our doom," Colton shot back.

"Now, now!" Neha interjected. "We can fight about past deeds later. I've got a list for the both of you, anyway. Let's worry about wiping those horned bastards out, first."

"That being said," Wyrran replied, shaking his head, "the Imen aren't going anywhere. We've rigged the tunnels with explosives, all the way down. Once the outsiders are out of range, you all need to get out of here, because we'll blow this whole mountain to bits."

Nevis, Colton, and Neha frowned, then exchanged glances. Neha scoffed and put her hands on her hips, her golden wrist cuffs jingling.

"You're bringing Ragnar Peak down?" she asked, slightly incredulously.

"Why risk the lives of more of your people in a fight with the daemons, when we can just bury them all in one go?" Wyrran asked, shrugging.

"He makes a fair point," I replied.

"Dhaxanians are generally slower in hot weather. It will take us a while to adjust and lower the temperature properly," Nevis said.

"The Iman is right. I don't want to risk the lives of my men in long-term combat, especially since there are more armies headed our way. It's simply not worth it."

Neha nodded. "GASP will go through the tunnel first, then," she said, then nodded at Pheng-Pheng. "My darling, stay with them. They need you more out there than I do here, as much as I hate to admit it."

"Mother, no!" Pheng-Pheng replied, frowning. "I want to stay here with you and fight!"

Neha smiled and gently held her daughter's face in her hands. "Don't be stubborn, Pheng-Pheng. Your skills are of more value to our new friends. We have plenty of fighters here. Your sisters are out there as we speak. Please, trust my judgment."

Pheng-Pheng exhaled, then nodded slowly. I rested a hand on her shoulder and gave her a soft smile.

"For what it's worth, I'm more than happy that you're sticking around," I muttered.

"Yeah, me too. You're kind of growing on me," she replied, no longer able to contain her smirk.

Nevis clapped his hands once, looking bored. "Okay, ladies, hurry this up and get ready to make your exit," he said. "The temperature will soon be perfect for my people. The battlefield is ours."

Hooves thundered in the distance, getting significantly louder. The sound prompted us all to frown and look at each other. I turned to the southwest and used my True Sight to see beyond the fortress walls and the thick snowstorm outside. My stomach dropped. Instant heat spread through me—and not the good kind.

"Riders," I murmured. "Hundreds of them. Over a thousand, in fact. Daemons on indigo horses," I added, out of breath.

"Of course," Heron groaned with exasperation. "Why the hell not? The Exiled Maras brought indigo horses here and started breeding them, anyway! Why shouldn't the daemons get their claws on a few specimens? Ugh."

"They'll be here in an hour, tops," I replied. "We need to hurry."

The incoming hostiles were heavily armored, most likely with charmed meranium plates, and carrying crossbows and large blades. Behind them, pulled by dozens of indigo stallions per load, were more ballistae and catapults. Zane was once again being proven right. What we'd been dealing with so far was just the beginning—the first wave, to test us, to wear us out.

The real fighters were coming now. And my initial fear of losing this fight was starting to creep back up, curdling my blood and choking me up. We'd fought daemon hunters and grunts, guards and mercenaries. We'd even brought down generals, pit wolves, and Death Claws. However, the daemons coming for us next were visibly bigger and more vicious than their predecessors. They were geared up for creatures like us.

Even with Blaze, we didn't have much of a chance. They'd probably brought swamp witch spells with them, too—as per Zane's predictions, anyway. He'd nailed everything so far, so there was no point in doubting he'd get *this* wrong.

Time was no longer on our side.

13

AVRIL

Despite the cold, my blood rushed hot at the thought of daemon riders. That was a new concept I was not looking forward to experiencing.

We replenished our backpack supplies—healing potions, whatever crystals and herbs and bandages we could cram into them, plus leftover explosive satchels with fuses. We each took a crossbow and a short arrow quiver on our shoulders, then prepared to go down through the tunnel.

The final tally was encouraging, particularly when compared to our initial numbers. Alongside the GASP team, we had Caspian, Zane, Velnias, Arrah, Dion and Alles, Wyrran, and Pheng-Pheng, along with the Druid delegation, Maras and fae included. We also got Hundurr and Rover with us.

"Two pit wolves are better than one." Scarlett smirked, then scratched both beasts' necks as they whimpered and grumbled, their red eyes glimmering with delight.

"The others will stay here with us," Colton said, nodding at the two dozen other rescued pit wolves still standing, as they moved around the courtyard, sniffing the air.

"I'll have the frost loosen up a bit," Nevis said. "We need the remaining grunts at the base to work their way up, along with the incoming riders. They need to think they can still get to you."

"Yes, the more of them we gather on the peak, the better," Neha replied with a nod.

It sounded all good and simple in theory, but I couldn't help but worry about their escape before the tunnels were detonated.

"How will you get off the mountain, then?" I asked, looking at Nevis, Neha, and Colton. "It'll have to be at the very last minute, when the place is swarming with daemons, for the explosive charges to be detonated. How will you all get out alive?"

Nevis's gaze found mine, and he smirked. "You know, you could just say you're worried about me," he replied.

"Get over yourself. She's not worried about you, specifically," Heron shot back, prompting Nevis to scowl at him.

"I am! I care about Nevis," I interjected firmly, drawing the outraged look of my boyfriend and the delighted grin of the Dhax-anian prince. "I care about Neha. I care about Colton. I care about every single one of these creatures sticking their necks out for us," I added, taking a hammer to one's childish insecurity and the other's titanic ego. I could almost hear them both crumble.

In the end, they both got the gist and didn't pursue the topic further.

"I was hoping I'd keep you on the edge of your seat with the grand finale of Ragnar Peak," Nevis scoffed, "but, since you're worried about your *allies*, I might as well ease your heart a little. As soon as you kids get off the mountain and reach a reasonable distance, I'll turn the temperature to a drastic low and freeze our enemies without harming our allies. The rest of us will then escape, leaving the Imen behind to do the honors and... you know, boom."

"Can you do that?" I replied.

"Of course," he said, almost insulted. "I'm simply waiting for that horde of riders to come up. I've already blown my truce with Shaytan to hell. I might as well take as many of his fiends down as possible in the process."

"Fair enough." I sighed. "Okay, we're good to go."

Wyrran pulled the hatch door up. We lined up in front of it, with Wyrran going in first, followed by Jax, Hansa, Harper, and Caspian, then the others. Nevis came closer and gave me another one of his weird, mystical little snowflakes on a delicate silver chain. This one was smaller, roughly the size of my fingernail, and glimmered pale blue.

"What's this?" I asked.

"A gift?" he replied sarcastically. My eyeroll made him scoff. "I can find you anywhere with it. So don't lose it. It might save your life someday."

Heron groaned, then gave Nevis a friendly slap on the back. The Dhaxanian prince froze, flabbergasted. "You're not a bad guy, after all," Heron chuckled. "Just don't use it to stalk my girlfriend. I will break you."

He didn't give Nevis a chance to respond, just slipped down into the tunnel. Nevis blinked several times. I guessed it had to do with physical contact. No one randomly touched the prince of Dhaxanians and lived to tell the tale. Then again, Heron wasn't just anyone, so I chuckled.

"He means well," I replied.

"Right," he muttered, then frowned at me. "Don't get yourself killed."

"You complain about me not giving you enough credit, but I think you're the one who needs to give *me* some," I shot back with a wink, then jumped into the tunnel.

I landed on my feet and put the snowflake pendant around my neck. Half of my group was running ahead through the dark, narrow passage. I went after them, with Heron right in front of me. Behind us, the rest of our team followed, one by one.

We ran fast at a steep angle.

Based on the noises coming from above, Nevis had done what he'd said he would do—he'd tempered the frost, allowing the daemon mercenaries to move. Given how desperate they all were to capture us, along with the boost of confidence provided by over a thousand riders coming in as backup, I didn't have a hard time imagining their resilience. A bunch of Dhaxanians, Manticores, and Adlets could not stand in their way—or so they thought. Their desperation and their fear of Shaytan's wrath in case of failure would eventually be their undoing.

For us, it worked remarkably well. I could hear the boots rumbling on the ground. They were fighting. Harper used her True Sight as she ran and gave us occasional snippets from the ongoing battle.

"The Dhaxanians are taking a bit of a backseat for now. The Manticores and Adlets are tearing through the daemons, though," she said.

"Nevis is probably waiting for the daemon riders," Jax replied. "There's only fifty of his people. Dhaxanian frost or not, they'll still have their work cut out for them."

"Yeah, I hope they don't spend too much time up there," Harper breathed.

"Wyrran, how will your people know we got out of explosion range?" I asked.

"They're working with a relative notion of timing," Wyrran replied. "We've trekked through these tunnels before, in previous years. We know how long it takes to cover two miles from the top to the edge."

I exhaled sharply, pleased to find myself running away from Ragnar Peak. The bigger the distance between us and the fortress, the easier I could breathe. We'd put up a good fight in there, but it was time to move on. We had bigger things to deal with—while our allies helped us deliver yet another devastating blow to Shaytan's armed forces.

A crippled enemy was bound to get sloppy. We needed him to make mistakes and rash decisions.

"You said the word spread fast about what we've been doing," Harper said. "How many rebel Imen are there, Wyrran? That you know of, anyway?"

"Oh, a couple thousand in the south and the west, for sure," Wyrran replied. "The daemon pacifists are coming out now, too. You've emboldened the people of Neraka to stand up and fight. My people are doing everything in their power to keep the daemons and the Exiled Maras distracted. Riots are breaking out in and around daemon cities all over the kingdom. We're doing everything we can to help you defeat them."

"Wow, word travels *really* fast around here." I chuckled. "We can't thank you enough."

"You're damn right!" Wyrran said. "We've got moles all over the place. We use flares and birds to communicate. We even have eyes in Azure Heights."

"Oh, really?" Arrah chimed in.

"Yeah, you'd think that would be difficult, huh? Getting around in a city filled with creatures that could mind-bend you if they caught you." Wyrran chuckled.

"I'm from Azure Heights," she said. "Who do you have there?"

"Are you now? What's your name?"

"Arrah. I worked for—"

"House Rohan. Yes, I've heard about you," Wyrran replied.

"You have?" I asked, suddenly even more curious.

"Arrah is quite famous for her contacts with the rebel tribes living around the Valley of Screams. Her uncles used to smuggle explosives from Azure Heights."

"Until they were caught," Arrah muttered. I could almost feel the grief in her voice. "But I am curious, though. How did your Azure Heights moles keep a low profile? I'm immune to mind-bending, for example, but I've never met another Iman like me. Are they immune, too?"

"What? No," Wyrran said, shaking his head as we kept running. "They just keep a low profile, avoid interacting with the Maras as best as they can. Those bloodsuckers don't go around randomly mind-bending people, anyway. They do it for a reason, and, provided they're not given a reason, they don't engage. Besides, they're not paranoid enough to immediately assume that our guys are moles. We're smarter than that."

The angle of our descent started to drop as we got closer to the ground level. The fighting sounded a little more distant. The daemons were working their way up to the fortress, leaving the mountain base behind.

"What have you been hearing from Azure Heights? Over the past couple of days, at least?" I asked. I was dying to know what the Lords were up to, especially since, as Wyrran had said, word spread fast. Surely, they must've learned about Draconis by now.

"Oh, they are flipping out up there!" Wyrran laughed whole-heartedly, as if he'd just remembered a fantastic joke. "They're scrambling to send more scouts out to look for you. They've heard about Infernis, and there are rumors of the Lords already talking about Shaytan being weak and whatnot. They're so vain and self-assured, it's ridiculous."

"Yeah, we know," Caia muttered. "It's why I'll genuinely enjoy burning them all to a crisp."

"Right?" Wyrran kept laughing. "They think they're the center of the world. The daemons are the cunning brutes that unknowingly serve their purposes in exchange for some souls to feed on. That's what they tell themselves. They'd probably die before they could admit in public that they tremble like worms whenever a daemon walks into the room."

"So their alliance is really shaky, huh?" Jax asked.

"It was always shaky because both sides are greedy and vain. They share the addiction to souls and the access to swamp witch magic, along with the interest in seeing that both are never tapped out," Wyrran explained. "That is pretty much the basis of their alliance. Well, that and the fact that, in their own twisted way, they have kind of a love-hate relationship. Azure Heights is well guarded against daemon attacks with swamp magic, and daemon cities are filled with fire and lava, both of which can terminate a Mara in seconds. They call it mutual appreciation."

"Keeping their enemies close," Hansa replied.

"Pretty much. But this delusion of grandeur started to fizzle out when you guys showed up with a dragon. I mean, up until recently, we just saw them as bloodthirsty conquerors, mindless beasts pretending to be intelligent and fashionable. Absolute frauds but, unfortunately, deadly and destructive frauds. Hope was gone for a long time. Now that we know what the outsiders can do, we understand that our bullies can, in fact, be defeated. It's what kickstarted all the riots."

"So, the daemon attack that we first witnessed in Azure Heights was... fake?" Jax asked.

Wyrran nodded. "They had to put on a show to convince you they were in trouble."

That didn't come as a surprise. I'd thought about it before.

They'd gone to great lengths to fake their daemonic misfortunes. In hindsight, it made sense.

"Have you heard your moles mention the swamp witch?" I asked.

"A few times, yes," Wyrran said. "Though there's nothing concrete. The Lords and the upper-level Maras know where she's kept. Most of us didn't even think she was still alive, but we deduced that much over the past ten years, as the Maras and daemons kept popping up with new swamp witch magic treats. You don't get fresh milk from a dead moon-bison, now, do ya?"

"Fair enough," I muttered. "And the—"

I lost my train of thought as a string of loud bangs erupted from far back. Explosions thundered through the underground. The tunnel shuddered, dust escaping from all its nooks and crannies. We kept running. The ground shook beneath our feet. I counted four large explosions, followed by six muffled ones.

"There we go!" Wyrran exclaimed. "Now, everybody, we need to try and go a little faster. Ragnar Peak is about to come down!"

"We're out of range, aren't we?" Hansa replied.

Wyrran picked up the pace, as did the rest of us, holding up a torch he'd brought with him. Technically speaking, we could've run faster, but Wyrran was leading. We were still extremely fast, and our allies had the benefit of simply sliding off the mountain with Nevis's help—thus making their escape quick and easy. Assuming we'd left the mountain behind and couldn't be crushed when it came down, there was no longer a life-or-death urgency to deal with.

"Yeah, but all that rubble will cave into the tunnels," Wyrran said. "It'll get dusty, fast!"

Just then, I glanced over my shoulder and saw exactly what he meant. With the earth still shaking, a thick cloud of dust and smoke was coming after us, blown through the tunnel in the aftermath of the explosions and the catastrophic collapse of Ragnar Peak.

"Wyrran, I think we need you to keep up with us now," I said, my voice betraying my nervousness.

Fiona slipped past me, leaving Zane behind, and reached Wyrran. "Get on my back," she ordered, both of them running side by side. Wyrran scoffed.

"You're kidding, right?" he replied.

"You either get on my back or I hoist you up. I'm strong enough to carry you without sacrificing my speed," she shot back.

"Do as she says, Wyrran. Trust me," I chimed in, speeding up.

The dust was coming in fast after us. In less than a minute, it would swallow us all, and it would severely slow us down. No one ran well with lungs clotted by dust, smoke, and ash.

"Okay, okay!" Wyrran groaned, then jumped on Fiona's back. "How much faster can you people go, anyw—"

Fiona shot forward, dashing through the tunnel like an arrow. Wyrran's yelp trailed behind him as he held on for dear life. We all followed, darting like gusts of wind and leaving the billowing dust behind.

Within minutes, we could see the literal light at the end of the tunnel, as it curved upward to the surface. That was the two-mile point away from Ragnar Peak. We'd made it.

"Almost there!" Hansa breathed.

Fiona and Wyrran were the first to vanish into the light above. Those of us who were sensitive to daylight instantly pulled our masks, hoods, and goggles back on. Harper, Caspian, Hansa, and Jax got out next. Heron followed, with me, then Zane, right behind him.

I was just about to breathe the air of freedom, when—I came to a sudden halt as soon as my feet touched the surface. Caia bumped into me from behind. My blood froze. My heart stopped.

We had a welcoming committee waiting for us, and it wasn't the nice kind that offered drinks and well-wishes. This was a mixed group of thirty Maras and thirty daemons, led by a uniformed Correction Officer. Their swords were drawn. The daemons growled with anticipation, and the rest of my crew came to a standstill.

"Crap," Heron muttered.

14

HARPER

The Correction Officer cocked his head to the side, leaning on his sword like a cane. He chuckled. "It's so nice of you to finally join us... I would've hated having to come all the way up to that fortress to drag your asses out."

"And who are you supposed to be?" I asked, genuinely annoyed. My initial shock had given way to irritation. These guys had no idea what we'd been dealing with since last night. We didn't have any time or energy left to waste on them.

"I'm the smart one, playing the long game," the Correction Officer grinned. "Tarsis is my name," he added, then shifted his focus to Caspian. "Oh, hey, boss."

Caspian grunted, raising his blade, ready to strike.

"What are you doing here?" Caspian asked, his voice cold and low. It sent shivers down my spine.

"Milord, you taught me to think ahead of the platoon, remember?" Tarsis replied, annoyingly calm and amused. He was pleased with himself and unable to hide it. "I know everything you've been up to since your dragon left Azure Heights. I know about your master plan—which, by the way, is good, I have to admit. I was impressed. I mean, splitting up in two groups, chasing down allies in Lagerith, Athelathan, *and* the Akrep Gorge? Brilliant. Plus, the stunt you pulled in Draconis? Epic. There's a reason you're all such a problem."

That hit us hard. They knew everything? How?

"Did you track us?" Caspian shot back, his eyes darting across Tarsis's entire group, assessing their traits and weapons.

They broke rank and surrounded us in a wide circle, their weapons out.

"Whenever possible, yes," Tarsis replied. "But I kept my distance. I told you. I played the long game. The longest, in fact. I didn't need to follow you all around. That would've been a waste of my energy. I needed to see what you people were up to, first. I made sure I appended my spy to your merry little gang."

He snapped his fingers, and I heard Alles cry out. I turned my head and saw him drop to his knees, holding his head in pain.

"What the hell?" Dion gasped, horrified as he watched his friend writhe and squirm on the ground.

"I've got mind-bent spies infiltrated all over the place," Tarsis replied, chuckling. "Every faction, every village, and every gang of miscreants. I have eyes and ears everywhere, and they're extremely efficient since they don't even know they're doing it. I've embedded suggestions so deep in their subconscious minds, they don't even remember sending their messenger birds out."

"What did you do to him?" Dion shouted, trembling with rage but unable to do anything to help Alles.

We were all stunned at that point. No one could have seen this coming.

"He thinks he's got a crippling headache. It happens whenever

I snap my fingers," Tarsis sneered through his mask. "I've got sleepers and saboteurs in that group of Imen you left with your friends back there, too," he added, nodding at the crumbling mountain behind us. "They'll get a nasty surprise when they get out of the area. I mean, I assume they didn't all die in the explosions. Nice touch, by the way. Luring daemons to the peak, freezing them, then bringing the entire mountain down. Ambitious!"

Dion snapped and lunged at Tarsis, waving his sword around.

"Dion, don't!" Hansa called out and slipped between them, blocking Tarsis's sword hit with her blade. Jax pulled Dion back, though the Iman struggled against his hold.

"Let me go! He's dead!" he shouted, pointing his sword at Tarsis. "You're dead, you hear me? Dead!"

"No, no, little one. You're dead. I've had enough of you for the day," Tarsis shot back, then nodded at his fighters.

They all closed their circle around us. Pheng-Pheng's scorpion tail rattled. Blaze growled behind me. I briefly glanced at Avril. "Make sure they don't mind-bend Blaze or Caia," I murmured. Avril replied with a nod, then nudged Heron. They both shifted closer to the dragon and fae. The last thing we needed was a mind-bent dragon.

The daemons came first, bringing their swords down with great strength. We blocked their hits, dodging and swerving before launching our own attacks. They were the grunts, the muscle. They required brute force and single, fatal blows.

I pushed a barrier out and followed up with my twin blades. Caspian darted forward and went straight for Tarsis's head. Pheng-Pheng took a daemon down with her scorpion sting. The Druids and fae were quick to dispense their fireballs, careful not to stand still for more than two seconds at a time and avoiding direct eye contact with the Maras.

All it would take was one look for everything to go sideways.

Caspian fought Tarsis, hard and relentless in his hits, while I dealt with another daemon. I heard Caspian hiss. I turned my head and saw Tarsis's blade piercing his stomach.

"No!" I cried out, then swiftly dodged a daemon rapier and crossed my swords out against my attacker's neck. I pulled them out in a slash and slit his throat, then rushed over to Caspian's side, just as Tarsis withdrew his sword.

I kept him busy, hitting him over and over in consecutive blows. He didn't have time to do anything other than block my attacks.

We were in a tight spot. The Maras circled in and got dangerously close to mind-bending our people. The vampires and Maras, along with Arrah, were not at risk. But everybody else was, and good grief, that was a lot of magic and firepower that could be turned and used against us.

I dodged a sword hit from Tarsis, then brought my swords up, missing his torso by inches. Cursing under my breath, I slid to the side and cut his left hip. He yelped from the pain and tried to cut me, but I blocked his hit with my right sword, then drove my left blade forward. He was quick to lean backward to avoid getting himself impaled through the chin.

"You're good," he hissed, then brought down his sword.

I caught it with my twin blades crossed. He was strong, pressing hard against my swords.

The fight viciously raged on around us. Fireballs swishing. Daemons growling. A couple of hostile Maras collapsing. Druids muttering defensive spells. Swords clashing. It felt as though everything was happening in slow motion. My stomach churned with worry over Caspian, whom I didn't have time to check up on —not even with a glance.

The pit wolves had fallen prey to mind-bending. I could hear them whimpering somewhere to the side, and Scarlett trying to get them to snap out of it.

"Hundurr, please! Listen to me! It's me! Don't let them do this to you. You're stronger than that!"

Crap.

Hundurr replied with a growl.

A loud roar ripped through the battle. Tarsis hesitated for a split second, looking up in shock. Whatever was happening, it didn't suit him. That was my window of opportunity. I took it and pushed out a barrier.

It bumped him back a few steps. I jolted forward with a three-hundred-and-sixty-degree spin and cut his head off. His blood sprayed out, his body slumping to the ground as his head rolled away from me.

"How's that for a long game?" I muttered, then quickly turned around.

Caspian got up, grunting and holding his side. He'd been well guarded by Fiona and Jax during the fight. He opened one of his belt satchels and scooped out some healing paste, spreading it over his wound through the shirt cut. Another goosebump-inducing roar made me look to my left.

I stilled, watching as our fight for survival took an unexpected turn. The daemons were all down, soaked in puddles of their own blood. There were six Maras left from Tarsis's team, but that wasn't the shocker that had made the Correction Officer falter.

Tobiah and Sienna had joined the fight. Tobiah ripped through the remaining Maras, joining his daemon fellows, Zane and Velnias —who were both amused and thrilled to see him there. Sienna, Vincent's younger sister, wore a hood and a mask, but I could see her face with my True Sight. She quickly moved to break the mind-bending that had been inflicted on both Hundurr and Rover.

Her eyes glimmered gold as she extended her arms and ordered them to sit. The pit wolves froze, then obeyed, whimpering from the distress.

"Stay there, for now!" she commanded them. She briefly scanned our group and lit up when she saw me. "Harper!" she exclaimed, then frowned when she saw that Caspian was wounded. "Lord Kifo!"

She rushed over to us, leaving Scarlett befuddled, with two mind-bent but docile pit wolves.

The last two hostile Maras were taken down, courtesy of Hansa and Patrik. They shook the blood off their swords before sheathing them. The group then gathered around us, and Tobiah joined Sienna in front of Caspian and me.

"What are you two doing here?" I asked, startled and confused.

Sienna sighed, then showed me her blood oath. I noticed that Tobiah had the same marking on his neck, just under his ear. "We can't tell you, but we can fight now," Sienna replied with a weak smile.

Zane chuckled, patting Tobiah's back. "I'm just glad to see you're still alive, you little rascal!"

"Little?" Fiona scoffed, raising an eyebrow. "He's the size of a mountain."

"But fifty years my junior," Zane grinned, then put his arms around Sienna and Tobiah's shoulders. He nodded at Caspian before settling his gaze on me. "These two pledged silence, just like Lord Kifo over there. Those in charge didn't think to get specific and force them to pledge their *loyalty*."

"And given how swamp witch magic operates on the power of the word, semantics got in the way, huh?" Hansa muttered.

"Exactly," Zane replied. "I know about them and their deal with Azure Heights. These two lovebirds were allowed to live on their own, in the Valley of Screams, because Sienna managed to soften up Lady Roho's heart. My father wanted them both jailed, but they settled on the blood oath instead. They were still planning their little theatrics with you outsiders at the time."

I remembered the first time we'd met Sienna and Tobiah, back in the gorges. I'd wondered what they had to do with this whole farce after we learned about the Maras' nefarious alliance with the daemons. I had my answers now, and it broke my heart a little, because I knew how hard it was to not be able to tell the truth. I'd seen it in Caspian's struggle with his blood oath, after all.

"How did you know to find us here, though?" I asked Sienna.

Sienna opened her mouth, then paused, sighed, and pointed at Tarsis's decapitated body on the ground. Zane was quick to deduce what she couldn't say.

"They followed Tarsis," he said, and Sienna nodded briefly. "I'll go ahead and guess that she and Tobiah saw Tarsis roaming around these parts, close to the gorges. They probably found it interesting that a group of daemons and Maras were operating in the middle of the day and decided to follow."

Zane paused, then questioningly looked at Sienna, who replied with another nod to confirm his theory.

"How do you know Tobiah and Sienna?" I asked Zane.

He smirked. "I make it my business to know everyone who has ever crossed my father in any way. A daemon consorting with a Mara is definitely on his no-no list."

"So you two were here by chance?" Caspian murmured, still holding his side. The bleeding had already stopped, but it would take a little while longer for the wound to heal completely.

"We didn't know you'd be here," Tobiah replied with a shrug. "Lucky you, huh?"

"Pretty much," Jax scoffed. "It's a little tricky fighting Maras when they can mind-bend our most powerful agents."

"By the Daughters, our allies! Tarsis's spies!" Hansa gasped.

We instantly looked down at Dion, who was cradling an unconscious Alles in his arms. The young Iman was sobbing, broken-hearted. We couldn't place any blame on Alles but, judging by Dion's fiery red aura, he was in a lot of emotional pain, probably for not having seen this coming.

"Dion, it's not your fault," I said. "You know that, right?"

"I... I know. It's just... I wish I could've prevented this. I didn't know," he replied, sniffing.

Wyrran came forward and sighed. He was just as annoyed. "I wouldn't worry much about the Dhaxanians, the Manticores, or the Adlets dealing with Imen spies. Even if one or more of my men have been mind-bent by Tarsis at some point during our incursions in the area, I doubt they'll have anything on them. The daemons and the Maras are looking for you. They're stretched thin, and they've just lost, what, almost three thousand soldiers back there?" he added, pointing at the cloud of dust covering the ruins of Ragnar Peak.

"Yeah, they'll have to prioritize," Zane agreed. "They'll come for us first. In the meantime, we could send a messenger or a bird to find them and warn them."

Avril lifted her snowflake pendant. "Or I could try summoning Nevis with this."

Heron rolled his eyes, then got his attention drawn by Hundurr and Rover, who were still sitting, mind-bent by Sienna and watching us. He walked over to them and took a close look at each of them.

"Ice prince extraordinaire aside," he muttered, "we need to fix our pit wolves."

"Sorry about that." Sienna sighed. "I had to stop them from attacking you. They were getting restless and aggressive."

"Hundurr did his best to resist the mind-bending, I'll give him credit," Scarlett replied. "But the Mara who compelled them got super persistent with his orders. I mean, I don't know if Tarsis was willing to kill some or all of us, or not, but I wasn't ready to experience a pit wolf bite, for sure."

"How do we fix them, though?" Patrik asked, visibly affected by Hundurr's tormented state.

"Their pupils are not overly dilated," Heron replied. "I can try something. It worked before with animals." He took a deep breath, then channeled his mind-bending ability to Hundurr first. He muttered something in the pit wolf's ear.

The creature whimpered, then growled and shook his head. He shuddered, got up, and calmly padded over to Scarlett and nuzzled her face—his beastly way of apologizing for snarling at her, probably. Satisfied with the results, Heron proceeded to do the same to Rover, who reacted in a similar fashion and nearly rammed into Patrik. Both Scarlett and the Druid hugged the pit wolves, laughing from relief.

"You two are clearly our beast-masters." Heron chuckled.

"And you're the pit wolf whisperer." Scarlett giggled.

I felt my lips stretch into a smile. I took a deep breath, then looked around. There were more horns and drums tearing through the distant horizon to the west, but they couldn't see us. They couldn't even track us at this point. Ragnar Peak was demolished, and we'd taken a now-sealed underground route. There was no trace of us for a two-mile radius.

"They'll probably send Death Claws out to look for us," Zane said, as if reading my mind. "With the damage we just caused them, they'll be conservative with their ground troops. But they will get vicious, fast. What you're hearing are top brass troops coming. Once they catch a scent or once a Death Claw confirms our location, they will come, and we won't stand much of a chance, not even with allies."

"The whole kingdom of daemons is rising against us," Velnias added, frowning as he looked out into the distance. "We still have our advantages for now, but they won't last long. We need to seize this moment."

"Then let's go," Hansa replied. "Meredrin awaits."

Wyrran raised his hand. "It'll take some hours. We don't have horses anymore."

"Oh, damn. The horses," I breathed, instantly wanting to smack myself for not having thought about them. We'd left them in the fortress's stables, and we hadn't even thought about them where our escape from Ragnar Peak was concerned.

"Relax, I set them loose through the back gate while you people were still pushing back on that fourth line of mercenaries." Velnias chuckled.

A wave of relief washed over me. At least they had a chance to escape and roam freely. I would've hated myself if they'd died in the collapse. I sighed, then looked to the northeast, as Caspian gently leaned into me.

"We'll keep a low profile," Wyrran said and took the lead on our group. "Follow me."

I looked at Tobiah and Sienna. "I know you two are bound by silence, but you can come with us, if you want. We could use the extra hands on deck."

"We can't go back to the gorges right now, anyway," Sienna said, wearing a faint half-smile. She looked sad. "The scouts are out, and they're rounding up all the Maras who left or ran from Azure Heights."

"Ah, they're closing ranks, trying to boost their numbers a little." Zane grinned. "The Maras are getting a little anxious. Clearly rumors about my father's failure to capture us have given the Lords some of those crazy, I-might-be-able-to-topple-the-daemon-supremacy thoughts."

"Do you think there's any substance in them?" I asked, and

Zane replied with a short burst of mocking laughter. "I'll take that as a no," I muttered, then looked around.

The Valley of Screams was hundreds of miles away, but I could see its gorges rising to my right, drawn across the eastern horizon. Behind us were flatlands and a fallen mountain. To my left, I could see the green Plains of Lagerith stretching along the line where the sky touched the ground. It reached along the northeast, where we were headed.

We walked in a straight line, the sun heating us up as we put more miles between us and Ragnar Peak. We had a long way to go, but, just like before, we'd come a long way already. For a moment, I felt as though the hardest part was only just beginning.

After all, we could handle all kinds of battle scenarios—we'd proven that, repeatedly. We'd pushed our limits, we'd fought tooth and nail, and we'd stopped at nothing to retain our freedom and integrity.

But now... Now, we had to sneak into Azure Heights and steal a swamp witch, while avoiding capture.

Well, challenge accepted.

15

HANSA

We kept to the shadows and patches of woods along the way, as we headed northeast. By sundown, we could see the so-called lake district stretching a few miles ahead.

The lakes went on for miles, the sky reflected on their calm surfaces. It looked as though Neraka was holding a mirror up to the orange and pink afternoon clouds. Thick woods bordered most of the lakes, with tall pine trees providing shade and refuge to a plethora of wild animals.

The trip had been uneventful so far. We'd left the hot spot behind, anyway. Both daemons and Exiled Maras were most likely busy converging on the collapsed Ragnar Peak, thinking they'd find us there, dead or alive. I had a feeling it didn't matter that much anymore, not after the amount of damage we'd inflicted.

Harper used her True Sight to survey the area on a regular basis, while the pit wolves frequently went ahead and scoured the area, like the wonderful, extra-large guardians that they'd chosen to be during our incursion into Neraka's less-traveled areas.

"Have you been to Meredrin before?" I asked Wyrran.

"A couple of times, yes," he replied. "I haven't been in touch with the town in a while, though. Worst-case scenario, it's been abandoned already. However, I doubt that. It's a good area. The lands are ripe, and the lakes and forests keep it secluded. Unless daemons raided it, there should still be Imen living there."

I looked ahead and noticed the town's silhouette rising over the lake—a solitary island in the middle. "Harper, can you tell us what you see?" I asked.

Harper narrowed her eyes, taking a few moments to reply.

"I see boats by a jetty," she muttered. "Five of them, in good condition. Lights are coming on. Yep, it's inhabited."

"Hostiles?" I replied.

She shook her head. "No, Imen, from what I can tell. I'd need to get closer, though."

"That's a good sign," Wyrran said, smiling. "They can help us with shelter and food for the night."

"We do need to rest," Jax agreed. "If we're infiltrating Azure Heights tomorrow, like we should and like we already discussed, we need a quiet place to put our heads down."

"Meredrin is a pretty tranquil place," Wyrran confirmed.

"And once we get there, we should look into a way to reach out to Nevis and the others," Harper said, frowning. "I'm still not comfortable with the idea of Imen sleepers infiltrating their ranks."

As soon as she said that, I looked back at the end of the line. Dion was quiet and sullen, carrying an unconscious Alles on his back. Velnias stayed behind with him, as did Scarlett and Patrik. They occasionally exchanged words, reassuring Dion that they'd find a way to help Alles.

"Normally, once you remove someone from a Mara's mind-bending influence, all it takes is some time and rest for them to recover," Heron said. "That is, of course, if the subject wasn't mind-bent too many times—the damage can be irreparable. Swamp witches used to be able to cure that. But in Alles's case, I'm not sure how to help him. He had Tarsis's suggestion planted so deep in his head, he didn't even know it. On top of that, I'm pretty sure Tarsis had a backup plan for his 'news delivery', someone else to receive the intel in his absence."

"Have you seen this before?" Avril asked.

"Oh, yeah, plenty of times. But we never questioned the aftereffects. I've never done it myself, but I've seen plenty of incubi back on Calliope with implanted orders. They flipped on their own people when one of my commanding officers gave the signal. It caught them by surprise. It was a bloodbath," Heron replied.

"Maybe you could try something similar to what you did with the pit wolves?" I offered. "What did you say to them, exactly?"

"Oh, I basically mind-bent them again, overriding their original command," Heron explained. "Which, in Hundurr and Rover's case, was a direct order to attack us. Surprisingly, both mutts were unbelievably resilient and didn't immediately give in. With Alles it might be a different story, but I'll try and see if I can get him to forget he ever met Tarsis. My only concern is that he'll have a bad reaction to my suggestion, if Tarsis mind-bent him into forgetting about him first, leaving only the suggestion to send messages or leave a trail or something."

"We don't know yet how Alles communicated with Tarsis. Not in detail, anyway," I said. "We can find out first, then maybe you can try your mojo on him."

Heron gave Dion a friendly half-smile, then nodded. "I'll definitely try."

"Thank you," Dion murmured, his eyes still puffy. He'd cried a lot on the way. I understood the feeling of helplessness that came with finding out you'd been betrayed. In his case, however, it wasn't even Alles's fault. My history with betrayal ran much deeper and was much bloodier. I'd lost daughters and sisters to it.

We reached the edge of one of the lakes and took a few minutes to analyze our surroundings. The lakes were interconnected by thin strips of dry land and thick streams—they all came from the river flowing through the region.

"Over there," Wyrran said, pointing to the far left across the water. I could see the greenery lining the river in the distance, as it cascaded down several rock clusters before spilling into the plain. "It's the River Ebis," he said. "It fills all nine lakes, then continues its flow south," he added, as we followed the stream across the lake district to the right. "Ebis goes through the Valley of Screams, then right past Azure Heights, before it pours into the ocean."

"It's one of three rivers on this side of the continent, right?" I asked, remembering what I'd seen on one of the maps we'd studied for this mission.

Wyrran nodded. "Yes. The others are close, too, but you can't see them from here. You'll need a high altitude for that," he replied, then nodded at the lake in front of us. Its crystalline water was lapping at the grassy shore. "We'll need to cross this, of course."

"Oh, that's easy," Idris said from behind.

He and Rayna came forward, and Vesta joined them. They looked at each other and smiled, then put their hands out.

The air rippled from their fingertips as they wiggled them. The lake's surface trembled. I found myself holding my breath as the waters parted all the way to the bottom, clearing a straight passage for us—all the way to the next strip of land.

"Whoa," Harper gasped, her eyes wide. "This is one hell of a trick."

"It works better when there's three of us." Vesta grinned.

"Can you hold it for long enough?" I asked, a little worried about the lake accidentally swallowing us. This planet had already tested plenty of my hidden fears; I didn't want to deal with the prospect of drowning, too.

Idris nodded. "Don't worry, you'll all be safe. You all go first," he said. "We'll close the line."

We went down to the bottom of the lake and made our way through the natural—yet unnatural—corridor. I could see fish and other aquatic creatures darting through the water on both sides. Their movements were frantic as they moved away from the edge, as if they knew they'd fall out if they came toward us.

A couple of fish did slip out, though, writhing on the ground for a few seconds, before Harper and Fiona picked them up and tossed them back into the water wall. I chuckled softly, then took Jax's hand as we advanced through the first lake.

He held it tight, occasionally squeezing it to make me look at him. We didn't say anything, but we didn't need to. Our eyes had all the words we wanted to say—the sweet stuff we were both saving for later, when we'd be alone again.

Idris, Rayna, and Vesta repeated the water passage move through the next lake, then partially through the third. Halfway through that one, however, Ryker and Laughlan had to intervene. The town of Meredrin floated in the middle of the third lake. The fae couldn't safely keep the waters split *and* raise the ground for us to reach the edge of the city. So, the Druids used their magic to raise mounds all the way to the shores of Meredrin, which we quickly climbed.

As soon as we were all back up above the lake, the fae released the waters. The liquid walls splashed into one another, causing ripples to spread out and lap at the grassy shore.

"Is this a floating island?" I asked. "I assume it is. Otherwise the corridor would've gone up a slope, right?"

Wyrran nodded. "Yes and no," he said. "Technically speaking, yes, it's a floating island. But it's anchored from below."

"Really? With what, exactly?" I replied, curious about the infrastructure.

The town itself was quaint and pretty, with simple, square homes and several bigger buildings, all built from sand-colored bricks. The roofs were thatched and dark gray, and there was an abundance of fruit trees lining the streets. The evening sky took on its signature indigo hue, sprinkled with stars and a rising first moon.

"Giant iron chains, from what I remember," Wyrran said. "I hear it gets a little wobbly during a storm, but they rarely get one that's powerful enough to shake this place up."

There weren't many Imen out. Those who were, however, had frozen, staring at us with a mixture of shock and fear.

"Ugh, I think we've freaked them out," Fiona muttered, checking them out.

"We literally split the lake in half to get here. I'd be shocked, too, if I were one of them," Heron replied dryly.

"We come in peace," I said, raising my voice. "We just need a safe place for the night."

Murmurs erupted from the Imen. Several figures stepped forward and made their way down the wide road connecting the town to the island shore. The closer they got, the paler they looked. My blood ran cold.

Jax cursed under his breath. "Dammit. Maras!"

We instantly drew our swords. The four Maras stopped and put their hands out in a defensive gesture. The one in the middle, looking like he was in his mid-twenties, smiled.

"Relax, we won't hurt you," the young Mara said.

"Said the Exiled Maras in the middle of an Imen town," Jax shot back, his tone firm and unyielding.

"Meredrin took us in!" the Mara replied. "We ran from Azure Heights years ago. I'm Peyton, leader of our small Mara group. We *all* ran from the Lords. I promise you, we have no intention of harming you!"

Somehow, that made sense. Had this been a hostile city, they would've had guards looking out, maybe someone intercepting us. And they certainly wouldn't have come down to chat with us. We would've been ambushed by now.

"I think he's telling the truth," Sienna murmured from the side. "There are many of us who fled Azure Heights. It's public knowledge, actually. That's why they're being rounded up."

"If they're still here, it means the daemons definitely haven't made their way into the area," Jax muttered.

Peyton smiled. "And they probably never will. We left Azure Heights with some stolen swamp witch magic. We couldn't get our hands on a cloaking spell, but we've got plenty of alarms set up across and around the lakes. You set one off, actually, and didn't even know it."

I put my sword away, as did the rest of our crew. "That's why none of you attacked us. And why you don't seem scared of us at all," I breathed. "You saw us coming."

Peyton nodded, then came closer and offered a curt nod. "I know who you are, too," he said. "It's an honor to meet the future saviors of Neraka."

Heron chuckled. "Thanks for the encouragement, I guess."

"But it's true. You're the outsiders! You've accomplished something no one else has!" Peyton replied, obviously thrilled to see us. "You've angered the Lords and the king of daemons. You've destroyed the prison city of Draconis. You have a dragon! We are all in awe of you, believe me."

"What are you and your fellow Maras doing here?" Jax asked, keeping his defenses up, though he'd put his swords away already.

"The Imen took us in. There aren't many of them left, but they're living a good life here," Peyton replied. "We do our best to keep them safe. Especially after dark."

Jax frowned, crossing his arms. I couldn't fault him for his skepticism. We'd been through enough with the Maras of Neraka to not want to fall for the same trick twice.

"Where's the town leader?" I asked, looking to mediate this conversation and make sure we were safe in Meredrin.

"I'll take you to her," Peyton said.

We followed him and his Maras up the road and into the town center. The Imen watched us quietly, but kept their distance, while Peyton occasionally looked around and gave them reassuring nods and smiles. I found it ironic that we were the ones the Imen seemed wary of. Not the freaking Exiled Maras.

A middle-aged Iman female came out of the large building overlooking the town square. She briefly looked at Peyton, then at us, her brow slightly furrowed. She wore a dark brown toga-style dress, her shoulders covered with a thick pelt. Her blonde hair was combed in a tight bun, and her blue eyes seemed to cut right through us.

"Milady, these are the outsiders," Peyton introduced us. "I do not know why they are here, but I stand by my previous statement. They seek shelter, just as I suspected. I think we should help them." He then smiled at us. "Alara is our town leader. We came here ten years ago, and she was kind enough to grant us amnesty."

We introduced ourselves, one by one, after which Jax and I briefly explained our journey so far, including our stunt at Ragnar Peak. Alara listened to us intently, without any interruptions. The more she found out about what we'd done, the more relaxed she seemed to become in our presence. But she didn't say a word. When she did speak, however, my heart skipped a beat.

"It is an honor to have you all here," she said, her voice soft like honey. "I can assure you that Peyton and his Maras are a part of our family. They do not mind-bend or threaten us. We all live together in harmony."

"You'll have to forgive me, milady, but we've heard that before, back in Azure Heights," Jax replied. Alara smiled.

"Then please, test me, if you wish. You're a Mara; I'm sure you can tell if I've been mind-bent in any way," she said.

Jax gave me a brief sideways glance, nodded, then walked over to her and looked her straight in the eyes. He looked for the usual signs of mind-bending: dilated pupils, a slightly irregular heart-beat, and other discreet symptoms he'd registered over the years.

"Are the Maras holding you here against your will?" he asked, his voice low and husky. That was his mind-bending tone, and it always gave me goosebumps. It was both fearsome and impressive. He'd used it on me a couple of times in the past. I knew exactly how intense he could be.

Alara shook her head with confidence. "I am here of my own volition. We all are."

"Are you aligned with the Exiled Maras of Azure Heights?" Jax asked. He mind-bent her for the truth. Usually, if a person was, in fact, mind-bent by another Mara, Jax could immediately tell. Most of us could, for that matter.

"No. We keep our distance and our lives here a secret. Few daemons or Azure Heights Maras venture into these parts. When they do, they trigger our alarms. We have traps ready for them. We've killed plenty over the centuries. We have protocols in place, which we pass down from generation to generation," Alara explained.

Had she been mind-bent by another Mara, Alara's brain

would've been throbbing in excruciating pain by now. Jax's shoulders dropped as he relaxed. The dark cloud that had gathered over him since we'd spotted Peyton and his Maras had finally and suddenly scattered. He smiled at us.

"Ladies and gentlemen, I believe we have our first genuine instance of Imen and Maras coexisting peacefully, without coercion or mind-bending," he muttered.

We breathed a collective sigh of relief, and Peyton joined Alara's side.

"Milady, can we allow them to stay here tonight?" he asked Alara.

She nodded. "Of course," she replied. "Have them taken to the inn. We haven't had travelers in a long time. And especially not travelers who could help liberate our planet." She then looked at Jax and me. "Whatever you need, we'll get you. We keep a steady supply of food and blood, given our... mixed population. We've learned to use some of the swamp witch spells that Peyton stole from his former superiors in Azure Heights, so we have some herbs and crystals you might find of use, too. And the inn has running water and fireplaces in each room. It will make your stay comfortable."

"Thank you, milady," I said, and bowed before her.

My muscles were throbbing. Exhaustion was finally catching up with me.

"This way," Peyton said, motioning for us to follow him as he walked over to the building to our right—the inn. It wasn't big, but it held a dozen rooms, at least, from what I could tell at first sight.

We followed him inside. The place was open for business. The innkeeper and his daughter greeted us and started taking us to our rooms, in pairs.

"There's also a dining room down here," Peyton said, watching Jax and me as we went upstairs. "You can use it for your group meetings and whatnot. I'm sure you have a lot of planning to do for your next... adventure." He chuckled, then took a seat at the bar, where another Iman served him a cup of fresh blood.

The innkeeper's daughter took us to our room, a splendid and cozy little square with flames already crackling in the fireplace and a small bathroom attached. After we put our bags away and decompressed for a couple of minutes, we made sure that Alles was put in a locked room. Dion insisted on keeping watch over him, and we had no reason to tell him no.

The Imen labored in the kitchen to prepare our dinner, while we cleaned our gear and our weapons, then took advantage of the bathroom facilities. We agreed to sit down after dinner and hash out our extraction plan.

I sank into a tub of hot water, all my muscles slowly relaxing. I breathed out, and, for a few minutes, I felt at peace and carefree. It was a temporary feeling. I knew that. But I'd earned the right to enjoy it. We'd been through a series of physical and psychological ordeals. We needed this breather.

16

HARPER

After dinner, we helped the inn's Imen clear the large, rectangular table in the dining room so we could hold our planning meeting. I felt sated and refreshed on all counts. Fresh blood was flowing through me, I'd syphoned some energy from Blaze and Velnias, and I'd had a long, steaming hot bath. All was sort of well in the universe again. At least for the night.

Peyton joined the conversation, as he was best equipped to provide us with knowledge about access routes to the red garnet mine, which held the secret tunnel that would lead us straight into Azure Heights. The young Mara seemed confused when Jax brought up the mine.

"There's a tunnel there?" he asked. "We thought it was just a collapsed red garnet mine."

Jax, Hansa, Caspian, and I exchanged brief glances. "Have you ever been inside that mine?" Jax asked, frowning slightly.

"Only a few times, for temporary shelter, but I didn't explore it.

Some of its digging tunnels were torn down. I had no reason to go deeper," Peyton replied with a shrug. "Nor did I know about the tunnel. You're saying it goes right into Azure Heights?"

"Yes." Arrah nodded. "The sixth level, to be precise. It hasn't been used in ages, though. They used it to smuggle gems and leathers from Azure Heights, back in the old days."

Peyton nodded slowly, looking at the map that Jax spread out on the table.

"I can take you to the mine, for sure," he said. "It's two miles from the lakes, and it's somewhat secluded. The map doesn't give you an exact location because it's shielded by big rocks and shrubbery."

"Thank you," Jax replied with a nod.

We went over our options, from the least dangerous to the downright reckless and potentially deadly. Of everything each of us proposed, we picked out a hybrid path, of sorts. It required some dirty games and splitting up into several groups.

One thing was for sure: we needed to keep a low profile. For the time being, we had the advantage of being presumed dead, or at least missing, after Ragnar Peak. We all doubted the Maras would anticipate us pulling a hundred-and-eighty-degree turn here and going back to Azure Heights. To anyone else, that would've been suicide.

To us, it was just another day on the job.

We agreed that I'd be on the extraction team. We also agreed we'd keep a low number for ease of movement. Once we reached the sixth level, we needed to find one of the higher-ups in the city to get a location for Lumi.

"Be it torture, persuasion, or a combination of both, it'll be your choice to make," Jax said, looking at me. "The important thing is to find out where they're keeping her."

"I'll do whatever it takes," I replied with a brief nod. "She'll be encased in some kind of charmed meranium room, for sure. The irony of which does not escape me, since she's the author of said charms."

"We'll need another team to extract Cadmus from the prison," Caspian said. "I can't let him rot in there."

"He's right," I agreed. "He helped us out when we needed it the most. The least we could do is get him out of harm's way."

Jax and Hansa both nodded slowly. An hour later, we had a rough plan laid out, with the intention to revisit and polish it in the morning. My stomach tightened a little too much as I thought about the challenge laid out ahead of me. I was putting myself on a tightrope above a lava lake, metaphorically speaking.

It had taken some solid arguments to convince Caspian that I could and would handle my part of the mission. However, even with the meeting over and agreements made as to who would do what, I could see the dark red aura sizzling out of him. It had streaks of dirty yellow. He was still worried.

"We have to think outside the box," Hansa concluded, despite Fiona, Avril, and Scarlett's grumbled protests. "We have to be atypical if we are to succeed. I love you all like you're my children, but this is not just about us anymore. We either go all the way or we give up and surrender. There is no middle path for us."

"We can't afford to squirm or worry about what happens *if*," Jax added firmly, glancing across the table at each of us. "We have to do things they won't expect us to do. Say things they won't expect us to say. They spent a lot of time putting together an elaborate performance to test and trap us. We have to take it a step further and do much worse, if we're to beat them. So, take the rest of the night off. Relax, rest, and make your peace. Tomorrow, we either play them, or we die."

We all nodded eventually, though it would take a while for

everyone to get used to the fact that this time the usual tactics wouldn't fly. We had to get creative.

There was a certain gloom hanging over our shoulders as we looked at each other. But we'd overcome so much already in situations that had been completely out of our control. Our mission to extract Lumi, however, was the one instance where we held all the cards, no matter how ugly or frightening they were.

I was ready to take my chances.

"We'll set out tomorrow evening," Jax said. "As soon as the first moon comes up. We have momentum now; it would be foolish not to use it."

"What about our allies and the sleepers?" Scarlett asked, leaning over the table and staring at the map. "If what Tarsis said is true, they're walking around with unknowing spies, like Alles."

Hansa sighed, then looked at Avril. "Do you have any way of summoning Nevis?"

"I can try, but I have no idea how," she replied with a shrug. "I don't know how the pendant works, or if it works from my end, like the previous one."

"And I cannot communicate with my mother," Pheng-Pheng muttered. "Only the queen communicates to her subjects, and through her subjects. When she does, my eyes are hers, my ears are hers, my lips are hers."

"Listen, maybe they'll reach out to us first. They should, anyway!" I interjected, not willing to let myself get worried over some of the most powerful creatures I'd seen on this planet. "It's been a while since Ragnar Peak came down. Surely they'll be in touch soon, one way or another."

"I agree," Jax replied. "There's nothing we can do from here, anyway."

"Yeah, not with the shield up," Patrik muttered. "Otherwise I would've already reached out to them, but the damn spell is blocking all magic communications, even on a local level, not just Telluris. Believe me, I've tried."

With hearts still heavy, wondering about our odds of success in getting Lumi out and whether our allies were okay, we gradually scattered throughout and around the inn. Some of us looked for some peace and quiet, while others gathered in pairs and little groups to talk some more, or to explore the small island town.

As soon as we walked out into the night, Caspian pulled me into his arms and held me tight, filling me with warmth. Love beamed out of him in hues of gold as he hid his face in my hair, his hot breath tickling my ear.

"No matter what happens, Harper, I am not letting you go. Do you understand me?" he whispered.

I nodded, my eyes tearing up. I put my arms around his neck and pressed my lips against his cheek. He felt rough and scratchy, given his days-old stubble. "I don't want you to let go."

I needed him to hold on and stay strong, to keep me strong, too. I fed on his valor and his strength when mine faltered. Most importantly, it was the thought of exploring this relationship and the prospect of a lifetime loving him that made me muddle through it all.

"Don't you dare let go," I added, trembling in his arms.

17

AVRIL

Heron and I decided to go for a walk around town. The second moon had come up, and the temperature had dropped. The nights seemed chilly here, which made sense, since the city was surrounded by sprawling lakes.

The Imen were few in numbers. I'd counted sixty or so, but they seemed calm and at peace here. Having Peyton and a handful of other Maras keeping watch over them must've helped with the morale, too. The town itself was quiet, the locals gathered at the only bar in the central square.

Small flames flickered in streetlamps—old-fashioned oil burners that gave off a mild but noticeable petroleum-like scent. The nocturnal flowers blooming in the many pots decorating the porches did a good job of countering that smell. The fruit trees were loaded and would soon be ripe. I could only imagine what harvest time looked like here, and how much more beautiful it would be once the people stopped living in fear of daemons and vicious Exiled Maras.

"I know we need to use a different strategy on Azure Heights and all," Heron muttered, "but I still can't help but feel uneasy about what we're going to do."

I let out a long, heavy sigh and slipped my hand into his. The corner of his mouth twitched a little. "It's tough, I agree. But let's face it, they've been two steps ahead of us from day one. This is the first time we've gotten the upper hand, and we can't be gentle or noble with these bastards."

"One more push." Heron scoffed. "One more push till we get Lumi out."

"It's the biggest, most important push. Everything we've done so far has led us to this moment," I replied. "We can hack it. I have all the faith in each of us. Harper was already a veritable soldier before we got here. With what she's had to do and with Caspian by her side, I know... I just know she'll pull through for all of us."

We took one of the side streets leading west, gazing around like wandering tourists—admiring every façade, every window, and every leaf we came across. Heron put his arm around my shoulders, as we continued with our evening promenade.

"We've got our work cut out for us, too." He chuckled softly.

"I wouldn't have had it any other way," I replied with a grin. "Besides, let's face it, we both want to stick it to those snooty Maras. This isn't the first time we're breaking someone out of jail, anyway."

"Right. I wish I had been there when they realized that Demios was missing."

We both laughed. "Oh, man, I'll bet the Rohos were livid!" I said.

Extracting Arrah's brother from the Maras' prison had been

Fiona's task and a great accomplishment for our team, since it had gotten us the cooperation and support of the only Iman who was immune to mind-bending and was a freaking treasure trove of information. On top of that, the thought of annoying the hell out of the Maras had been a welcome bonus.

"Imagine when they see Cadmus missing," I added.

Heron grinned. "Woof, that'll be painful. I mean, for them, Demios was just a measly Iman. Cadmus is a respected and experienced Correction Officer. Caspian's right hand, after all. The Lords could torture him for information or use him as leverage against House Kifo. If we deprive them of their bargaining chip, they'll flip out, for sure."

"Yeah, they're quite extreme, aren't they?"

"You can say that again. I think this whole soul-eating thing has an impact on their sanity," Heron muttered, frowning. "My species aren't as twisted as these fiends. We're quiet, for the most part. Dark and secretive, yes. Manipulative? You bet. I mean, mind-bending. Hello?" He chuckled. "But what the Exiled Maras have been doing... It's messed up. It's destructive and evil to such an extent that it's basically irredeemable."

We reached a round, open courtyard. There was a small, sculpted fountain in the middle, with fresh water trickling down into a stone basin. I liked the sound it made. We sat on the edge, looking out into the distance. The lakes spread out, and the stars flickered on their rippling surface.

It was a clear night, the moons glowing overhead. I rested my head on his shoulder, breathing in his natural scent. I filled my lungs with the idea of him, hoping that it would last me a lifetime —that I would never forget him.

"I honestly can't wait to get Lumi out," Heron murmured. "We'll free her, she'll bring down the stupid shield, GASP will come through and smite the daylights out of these people. And then..."

"We'll get to go back to Calliope and do all that classic dating stuff?" I giggled.

He gripped my chin with his thumb and index finger, gently lifting my head so he could look me in the eyes. I found myself entranced by those jade pools once more, the memory of our night together still fresh and all kinds of wonderful in my mind.

"That and more," he replied, his gaze softening. "So much more."

"Like you said... One more push," I whispered, snaking my hands around his waist. He smiled, then pressed his lips against mine.

I tightened my grip, and he cupped my face and deepened the kiss, making me see all sorts of white lights behind my closed eyelids. Every kiss felt like the first with Heron. There was always the wonder, the powerful impression, the bewilderment and incredible emotion surging through me—all at once.

We were so busy losing ourselves in one another, we didn't even feel the air blow colder. We were already crackling like embers in our embrace. But, at some point, as I welcomed the strokes of his tongue and his gentle, guttural moan against my lips, something felt... off.

Something else was crackling—literally. I paused, my gaze fixed on his and our lips less than an inch apart, as we both listened and noticed the change in the atmosphere. Steam rolled out from our mouths and nostrils. Heron's forehead smoothed, as he was the first to realize what was happening. He groaned with frustration.

I looked down and yelped, then jumped back. Dhaxanian frost had spread on the ground, and it had worked its way up Heron's legs, all the way to his hips, pinning him to the fountain edge. A second later, I was lit up like a firework, angrily looking around for the culprit—whom I knew very well.

"Nevis, you snarky icicle, get your ass out here and face me like the Dhaxanian prince you claim to be!" I shouted.

Heron scoffed, shaking his head slowly. He was remarkably calm, as if he were trying to live through a high-school prank without breaking somebody's neck.

Nevis emerged from the shadows of two neighboring houses, his chin high and his hands behind his back, in his usual "I'm better than you" posture. He smirked, though there was a certain playfulness about his expression that I hadn't seen before.

"Stop trolling my boyfriend," I muttered.

"I'm sorry, stop what?" he replied, his eyebrows raised innocently.

"You wouldn't get it. And if I explained it to you, you'd just find a way to use it to further glorify your childish jabs," I shot back, then pointed at Heron. "Unfreeze him."

Nevis looked at Heron, who gave him a brief, almost respectful nod. *Now I'm confused.*

"How are you not annoyed?" I gasped, glowering at Heron for not being as riled up as me.

He shrugged, while Nevis watched the exchange with mild amusement.

"I think this is what you call a 'guy thing' back in your world," Heron said.

"You spent too much time with Jovi, that's for sure," I retorted, rolling my eyes, then shifted my focus back to Nevis, who tried hard to look serious but was starting to crack up. "Seriously, what are you? Five? Come on, unfreeze him."

"Unfreeze him, what?" He pursed his lips and narrowed his icy blue eyes at me.

Ugh, he can be so infuriating.

"And to think that I was actually worried about you," I muttered. "Unfreeze him, *please.*"

Nevis smirked, then raised his left hand and wiggled his index and middle fingers. The frost keeping Heron in place cracked and snapped, spreading across the ground in iridescent shards.

"Thanks. Your Grace," I added dryly.

"You're welcome," Nevis replied, stifling another chuckle.

I caught a glimpse of Heron and noticed that he, too, was putting in the extra effort not to laugh.

"Oh, my days," I breathed, suddenly enlightened. "You two are somehow besties all of a sudden. Wow. Just... wow." And then I had another minor revelation and narrowed my eyes at Nevis. "Wait, what are you doing here? Where are the others?"

Nevis smiled. "Finally, we're moving on to more important issues, besides you two slobbering all over each other."

"Ew," I shot back, mildly disgusted by his choice of words. He and Heron definitely had the potential to be best friends, though. Even partners in crime. *Oh, no. Two Herons.*

"Is this why you had us wait in the shadows?" Colton growled as he emerged from behind, accompanied by Neha. All of a sudden, I was thrilled to the point where I could easily squeal like a little girl, seeing them alive and well.

Nevis rolled his eyes.

"So you could what, exactly? Torment the poor Mara who bested you for this beautiful creature's heart?" Neha added, her voice soft and sweet as she smiled and winked at me. My cheeks caught fire.

"I'm regretting my decision now. It has backfired spectacularly, since you two decided to claim the moral high ground," Nevis replied bluntly.

Colton chuckled, then gave us a friendly nod. "Sorry it took us so long. We had some... unexpected issues."

Grief flickered across his and Neha's faces. The kind that came with tragic loss. They were trying to seem upbeat and cool, but they couldn't hide it anymore. Something had happened, and it involved death.

I knew that look all too well.

18

HARPER

We were all summoned back to the inn's dining room—and were thrilled to find Neha, Colton, and Nevis standing there, looking over the maps we'd gathered of the gorges and Azure Heights.

Pheng-Pheng slipped past us like a dart and clamped onto her mother in a tight hug, their tails rattling with the joy of reunification. Colton nodded at the massive Hundurr and Rover, who were both obediently sitting on their hind legs just by the door. Nevis kept exchanging glances with Avril and Heron. There was a hilarious dynamic unfolding there, where Avril had suddenly found herself in charge of tempering two sullen teenage boys.

"It's so good to see you all!" Hansa exclaimed, then offered a curt bow.

"I'm thrilled to be able to say the same about you," Colton replied, smiling. "We tracked you with Nevis's help."

"Ah, yes," Avril said, touching the little snowflake pendant hanging around her neck. "We were worried about you. We ran into a group of daemons and Exiled Maras led by a Correction Officer, Tarsis. He said he'd planted spies among the rebel Imen. They don't even know they've been mind-bent into it."

Neha sighed, grief settling on her beautiful face. She held Pheng-Pheng close to her. "We know. We made a clean break from Ragnar Peak, just like we'd planned. We took Wyrran's Imen with us, thinking they'd be safer in our ranks."

"We were ambushed on our way here, but we managed to destroy the hostiles," Nevis added. "Unfortunately, the Imen discovered as spies didn't make it."

"We lost plenty of our own, too," Neha said, her voice trembling, then looked at Pheng-Pheng. "I'm sorry, my darling, but your sisters didn't make it."

Pheng-Pheng gasped, her eyes instantly filled with tears. She tried to keep it together as best as she could, but I could see her pain radiating out of her in deep shades of crimson. It broke my heart to see her like this. Caspian took my hand in his and dropped a kiss on my temple as I watched Neha console her daughter. Pheng-Pheng was all she had left.

"She'll be okay," Caspian whispered. "Pheng-Pheng is a warrior Manticore. It'll take a lot more to bring her down."

"I know," I breathed, "but it still hurts."

Pheng-Pheng wiped her tears, while we listened to Neha, Nevis, and Colton describe their escape and trip to Meredrin. Wyrran had to sit down, too, grief-stricken at the thought of his own people getting some of our allies killed in an attempt to sabotage our rebellion.

"I'm sorry," Wyrran mumbled. "I... I didn't know..."

"You couldn't have. None of us knew," Colton replied. "The Maras are sneaky and resourceful bastards. They're worthy foes,

I'll give them that. What they lack in numbers they certainly make up for in deviousness."

"We all knew that lives would be lost today, one way or another," Neha added. "It's the price we pay for freedom. But retribution will be swift, I promise you that, my darling," she said, looking at Pheng-Pheng.

The young Manticore nodded slowly, then wiped her tears and chose to focus on the maps. Jax and Hansa brought them up to speed with our plan. Nevis listened quietly, then looked at Neha and Colton and put on a devilish smirk.

"Sounds like a good plan," he said. "I think we can make it even better."

"How so?" I asked.

"I can take Queen Neha and Colton with me and summon the remaining Mara Lords," he replied. "Under the pretext of a truce. We'll say we have information about you. I'll have to explain why I've helped you all so far, but it won't be difficult for me to sell that, since I'll emphasize that I've changed my mind. I'll tell them I've seen their coalition armies and not even my Dhaxanians can survive an all-out war."

Hansa and Jax thought about it, while Neha and Colton seemed to agree.

"The purpose would be to keep the Lords busy while Harper and her group handle the extraction, I presume," Colton muttered, looking at Nevis, who replied with a brief nod.

"The Lords won't even see us coming," the Dhaxanian prince said, then nodded at Caia and Blaze. "You two could tail us, invisible, and be ready to intervene if the Lords try something funny. Provided, of course, that your superiors approve it."

"What do you think?" Caia asked Jax and Hansa.

"I think it's reasonable and wise to do that," Jax replied. "But you'll have to be wary of red lenses in Azure Heights, too. Now that the cat's out of the bag, as you Shadians would say, they'll be on the lookout."

"All we need is fifteen minutes in the room with them," Nevis said. "Long enough for Harper's team to find and rescue the swamp witch."

We went over the last few details and agreed to a final, updated plan. Peyton then stepped forward, addressing Neha, Colton, and Nevis.

"You're all welcome to spend the evening in my home, if you wish," he said. "The inn is full, but my house is warm and open to all of you."

Nevis raised an eyebrow, while Avril discreetly rolled her eyes, already suspecting that he was about to say something remarkably pretentious. That's what I was thinking, anyway.

"That's very kind of you," Nevis replied, surprising both Avril and me. "Will there be food?"

Peyton smiled. "Of course, Your Grace," he said, then motioned for the door. "Follow me, please."

As soon as he reached the open doors, he stilled for a second, then ducked as a red-feathered bird shot into the room. Neha gasped, and I froze, as I recognized the creature.

"Ramin," I murmured. The Ekar flew around the room for a few moments, then settled on my shoulder.

Both Pheng-Pheng and Neha smiled. "I see you've made a friend," Neha said.

"This is a surprise," I said, unable to take my eyes off the Ekar. The bird looked at me, its head cocked to the side. "Did you summon him?" I asked Neha.

"No. Ramin came by himself, and it's not like him," Neha replied. "I left him back with the rest of his flock in Akrep. He's never done this before. I guess the fire spirit has taken a liking to you, Harper Hellswan."

I frowned, slightly confused.

"Fire spirit?" I asked.

"Old legends of our people," Pheng-Pheng replied with a shrug. "It's just a story."

"Manticores believe in the spirits of natural elements," Neha explained. "Fire, winds, the earth, the seas and rivers, and so on. It is said that the Ekar is a manifestation of the fire spirit, a way for it to communicate directly with us. Manticores are protected by fire, in a way. It flows through us," she added, raising the tip of her scorpion tail. "And we inject fire into our enemies. We thrive in heat. We are children of the sun."

"And it is also said that the fire spirit may favor a certain person from time to time," Pheng-Pheng continued. "The Ekars are very obedient but not that sociable, which is why Ramin is... different. Mother thinks it's the fire spirit favoring you. I think it's just an old folktale."

Neha chuckled softly. "Yet there he is," she replied, pointing at the Ekar on my shoulder.

I found myself smiling, with the full attention of a strange bird that didn't seem to want to part with me. The Ekar had flown across hundreds of miles to find me—which was probably the most impressive part in all of this. I gently stroked its feathered neck with one finger, and it closed its eyes for a brief moment, enjoying the sign of affection.

"He might come in handy later," Hansa said. "I've rarely seen such an intelligent creature, and I'm sure we will need to send a message somewhere, at some point."

Hansa was right. Having Ramin around could definitely help.

We left the dining room and resumed our bids to relax and enjoy the rest of the evening. We had one hell of a quest ahead of us tomorrow, and I decided to make the best of this night—it could very well be our last. I wasn't giving way to pessimism, but I had to maintain a healthy dose of realism.

Tomorrow would either get us closer to freedom, or it would break us. I had to be ready for both possibilities, and I didn't want to squander a single minute before either came to pass.

19

JAX

I went back to the room and removed the last of my healing patches. I'd gotten hit by several arrows—nothing serious, just painful when they first went in. I washed off the smudges of dried-up paste, checking my torso in the mirror. They were all healed, as per my Mara nature. I only had my Destroyer scars left, but those would never go away. I'd been injured by Destroyers during Azazel's occupation of Eritopia, and I would always carry the marks of those battles with me.

There was hot water in a kettle over the fire in the room. I poured it into the tub, topped it up with cold water, and sank in. All my muscles relaxed. The water wasn't hot, or cold, but the overall feeling was a much-needed respite.

I kept going over the plan and the risks we were taking. Having my "kids" put themselves in danger didn't sit well with me, but I knew that this was our best and only shot to get Lumi out of Azure

Heights. Hansa was right—we needed to think outside the box and do something that neither the Maras nor the daemons would ever expect. *Playing the long game, in a way.*

Once I was done, I wrapped a towel around my waist, waiting for my clothes to dry by the fire. I settled in a chair by the fire and proceeded to sharpen all my blades with a diamond stone. A few minutes later, I finally heard the knock on the door that I'd been waiting for. Hansa came in. Our eyes met.

She didn't bother to keep her succubus nature in check this time. I felt my lips stretch into a smile, trying to figure out what was going on in her head. Those emerald-gold eyes of hers were phenomenal to look into, but they kept everything secret. The inner workings of her mind only slipped out when she allowed it —the tone of her voice, her body language, and the little gestures she thought no one would notice. I'd learned to read her well.

This time, she kept a straight face, but her succubus nature was loose. It made my blood rush and my heart beat faster. I'd never get enough of her. Ever.

"Can I come in?" she asked, standing in front of the closed door.

"You're already in," I replied, then set my blades aside and stood. She drew me to her without any effort.

She chuckled softly as I closed the distance between us. "Everything okay out there?" I asked.

"Yes. Peyton and his Maras are handling the night watch," she said, her gaze clouded, fixed on my chest. The closer I got to her, the hotter I burned. "The others are enjoying the rest of the night however they see fit."

"And how would you like to spend yours, Hansa?"

She looked up at me, and I could hear her heartbeat skipping frantically. It felt incredible to know that I had this effect on her. She breathed deeply, then smiled.

"We don't know how it'll work out tomorrow for us," she said. "It's a gamble. But it's our best shot. Therefore, I'm aware that this could very well be our last night together—"

"Or the first of many," I replied, leaving only a couple of inches between us.

The air thickened, supercharged with energy. I had a feeling I'd see lightning discharge if we touched. There was so much more than attraction between us. I was still in awe of the impact that Hansa had on me. I loved her more than I'd ever loved anyone before. Granted, maybe it always feels like that when you fall for someone. Maybe it always feels like this is it. But with Hansa I knew, without a single doubt, that I would never experience something like this again.

She trailed a finger along my jaw, then moved it lower, down my neck and chest. Her gaze followed it, and I looked down for a second before I went back to searching her face for some hint to her thoughts. My senses were on fire already. Her touch was soft, fluttering across my skin like a butterfly. My stomach tightened as her finger settled on one of the scars on my abdomen. Her brow furrowed, and I found myself one step closer to unraveling. There was so much emotion in those eyes, the complete opposite of how she usually hid behind her warrior façade.

"I thought Maras healed fast, without any traces or scars," she muttered, then looked at me.

"Azazel cursed some of the Destroyer blades," I said. "I had the misfortune of fighting against one. I won, but I took a few souvenirs with me," I added, watching as she found another scar on my chest.

She bit her lower lip, then slowly moved around, her fingers following the ropes of muscle as she found the scars on my back. I'd taken several slashes over my shoulder blades, where three curved lines the length of my palm were left. I stood there, quietly, as I waited for her to say something.

Then the most incredible sensation surged through me. I felt her lips press gently over a shoulder blade scar. A guttural moan escaped my throat as she snaked her arms around my torso and held me tight, her soft form molded against my back. She kissed another scar, then exhaled, her hot breath spreading through my skin like the summer sun.

This was as close as I could ever get to feeling the sunshine on my skin—through Hansa's kisses. I gathered all the strength I had left to keep myself under control. I had to see where she wanted to take this. She kissed me again, and then I heard a zipper slowly come down. I moved my head in a bid to turn it around, but Hansa's husky voice stopped me.

"Don't," she whispered. "Wait."

She planted another kiss, this time between the muscles lining my spine. I shuddered, my skin rippling as she held me tight again, her arms once more slipping around my waist and pulling me into an embrace. My muscles hardened as I felt her skin, her naked body against mine. My brain almost evaporated, my heart throbbing against my ribcage. I covered her hands with mine and surrendered myself to her.

"I love you so much, it hurts," I managed, barely able to speak. A painful knot formed in my throat. There weren't enough words to describe how she made me feel. How helpless and empty I was without her. I still remembered the day we met—the day she showed up with Draven and Serena and challenged my authority. Hansa had made my blood boil and set me on fire almost instantly, from the very beginning.

"Jax, I love you," she murmured, her lips soft against my spine. "We've been through enough already. Whatever comes next, let's face it together. I'm stronger with you."

That was it. That was the end of me—the old me, the Mara who was terrified of commitment, who loathed the idea of getting his heart broken. I'd already told her how I felt. I'd kissed her; I'd felt her in my arms. But this... This was something else entirely. This was Hansa giving herself to me, body and soul, and turning me into a different, better version of myself.

I was undone. I let out a breath, then turned around to face her. There was darkness and depth in her eyes—love. So much of it, I could easily get drunk on it. "I'm nothing without you," I replied, then kissed her.

I put everything I felt into that kiss. Our hearts struggled and echoed in unison as I wrapped my arms around her and reveled in this extraordinary feeling of... her. Every muscle, every inch of soft skin, and every lock of her long, curly black hair was mine tonight and forever. She welcomed me, moaning gently against my mouth as I deepened the kiss and let my fingers dig into her hips.

She brought her hands up and squeezed my shoulders, letting out a throaty sigh as I ran my fingers through her hair and pulled her head back. I trailed kisses down her neck, exploring every curve of her perfect body. Hansa lit up like the moon on Calliope, glowing as my mouth found hers again. We kissed, desperate and hungry for one another.

Months of untold emotions unfolded, and I felt her come apart at the seams as I laid her on the bed and finally claimed her very soul. We made love—it was our first time, but it could very well be our last. We took every minute that we had and turned it into an hour. We loved each other to the point where we'd become one. We both cried as we reached the peak of our union, exploding and scattering across the universe like clouds of stardust.

We sank into the bed, devoid of any notion of the palpable world around us.

"I'm everything with you," I whispered, riding out the ecstasy of her succubus nature.

It was unbelievable. I'd never experienced anything like this. Everything was amplified; every touch made my very core vibrate. I held her close and lavished her with kisses. She was my queen, my goddess... the piece of my soul I never thought I'd find.

20

AVRIL

Heron left to go on patrol with Peyton and his Maras for a while. He wanted to see how they organized and kept Meredrin safe. He promised to be back before midnight. I spent some time warming up by the fire and thinking about our mission tomorrow. Concern gnawed at my stomach. Our part was relatively manageable, but I worried about Harper and her crew. At the same time, I understood why Jax and Hansa had proposed the arrangement we'd all eventually agreed upon. We needed to be decisive and creative if we wanted to win this.

The room suddenly got cold. I pulled my chair closer to the fireplace and added a couple more logs, but it didn't do anything to dissipate the chills running down my spine. It hit me then that this wasn't a natural occurrence.

I got up, then walked over to the door. The closer I got to it, the cooler it felt.

Stifling a smirk, I opened the door and found Nevis standing outside in the hallway, his back to me. He turned around, surprised to see me.

"How did you know I'd—?" he asked, but stopped when he noticed my raised eyebrow and my gaze fixed on the frozen floor beneath his bare feet. "Oh. Sorry. I forget I'm not on Athelathan anymore."

He took a deep breath, and I watched the ice go away. The inn's regular warmth came back, and I stepped back into my room, motioning for him to come in. He offered a polite nod, then stepped inside and closed the door behind him, while I resumed my seat by the fire.

"Is it hard to keep your Dhaxanian nature under control?" I asked, welcoming the heat radiating from the fire.

"No, not at all. It's merely a question of habit," he replied, standing with his hands behind his back. "You're cold by nature as well, aren't you?"

I nodded. "Mhm. But I miss the warmth. It's the one thing we surrender when we become vampires. I don't get to feel the sun on my face anymore, and my body temperature is low. But I do enjoy the fire once in a while. It reminds me of childhood, I guess."

"I understand," Nevis muttered, staring at the crackling flames.

"What brings you here?" I asked.

"Are you really still with the Mara?" Nevis replied, pursing his lips.

I chuckled softly. "Yes, Your Grace. That hasn't changed. I don't think it ever will. I love him, and he loves me. He's an oddball, and he's like a little kid sometimes, but there's a side of him I've seen and fallen for. We're like two pieces of a puzzle. As unexpected as it was for the both of us, we just fit perfectly together."

Nevis let out a sigh, then nodded slowly. "Then I'm here to simply tell you that I'm going to bow out with dignity and grace. I will no longer pursue my ambition to be with you, Avril."

I blinked several times, processing his reply. *A royal to the very end.*

"Thank you, I guess?" I said, then nodded at the spare chair.

He pulled it closer to the fire and took a seat. He kept his back straight, though, as if he were sitting on nails. "I may be cold and perhaps a little too spoiled, but I do understand the concept of love. I accept its implications. You and I are merely a missed opportunity, and I accept that as well. If you love each other, I cannot and will not drive a wedge between you and the loud-mouth," he said.

I giggled. "You're incorrigible, Your Grace."

"Please, call me Nevis," he replied, smiling.

"Nevis, you and the loudmouth have a lot in common, you know. More than you think, in fact."

He looked somewhat offended.

"I highly doubt that," he muttered, then settled his gaze on the fire. "I see what you mean when you say it's nice to feel the warmth once in a while."

"I'm serious. You and Heron are a lot alike. He's royalty where he comes from. He's the brother of a Mara Lord. Should Jax forfeit his position without an heir, Heron will take his place. Granted, Heron has been through plenty of trials and tribulations, but he's an incredible creature. He's got killer comeback lines, just like you. He's intelligent and charming, just like you," I added. Nevis looked at me, smiling. Flattery certainly worked on him. "And he can be a big kid sometimes. Just. Like. You."

Nevis scoffed, making me laugh.

"I'll go ahead and remember the compliments only," he shot back.

"But it makes you who you are!" I replied. "The good, the bad, the hilarious. It makes you—*you*. And, to be honest, had Heron not come into my life the way he did... Had I met you first, I'm sure I would've fallen for you, Nevis. I'm not blind, you know. You're gorgeous. You're royalty. You're powerful and determined. You have principles, and, deep down, you're a good creature."

It was his turn to raise an eyebrow at me.

"As I was saying, a missed opportunity," he muttered. "Thank you for the kind words. I must admit, I'm not here to just bow out gracefully, as my code of honor demands. I'm here to offer my friendship," he added, then gave me a soft smile. "No matter what happens, Avril, I'm here for you. I find you fascinating in every way possible. You're the first creature to stand up to me and defy me. It denotes a strong character, and it's a rare thing to come across in my position. You're fearless. Most people tremble before me."

"Well, your icy nature might have something to do with that," I replied with a grin.

He almost laughed. "True. But I recognize fear when I see it. It's nice to be around someone like you. There's no fear in you, Avril. Not where I'm concerned. I must also admit that I do feel lonely— stuck on Athelathan for so long, unable to leave without starting a war. This crush I have on you will pass, but my affection for you is different. You opened my eyes, and you pushed me to do something I didn't think I could anymore. I stood up for my people. For freedom." He paused, then pointed at the snowflake pendant. "Don't lose that pendant, Avril."

I smiled, touching the snowflake with my fingertips.

"I won't, I promise," I murmured.

He frowned, then put his hand out. "Can I have it for a second?"

I nodded, then handed it over. He brought it up to his lips and whispered something into it. It lit up white for a few seconds, then resumed its pale blue sheen. Nevis then gave it back to me.

"Was that your Dhaxanian... What is it, exactly? Magic?" I asked.

"I suppose, yes. It's not swamp witch magic. It's nothing like that," he replied. "I'm the only one who can use it, anyway. I'm the last of my bloodline, and without an heir, I'll be the only one who can still perform the ancients' rituals."

"Ancients?"

"The first Dhaxanians. My ancestors of royal blood," he explained. "They were long gone before the daemons even took over."

"What about the Dhaxanians you rule over? Can't you find a wife among them so you can continue the royal bloodline?" I asked.

"It doesn't have to be a Dhaxanian, per se," Nevis replied. "My ancestors once married Imen girls, for example. My bloodline doesn't get lost in the mix. On the contrary. I just... I haven't found the right person yet, that's all. I thought it was you, but, you know." He grinned. "Loudmouth and whatnot."

I laughed lightly, then pointed at the pendant. "What did you do with it just now?"

"I added an extra function to it. From now on, I'll not only know where you are at all times, I'll also know if you're experiencing any pain or fear," Nevis said, then stood up. "I'll take my leave now, before the loudmouth comes back and makes a scene."

I shot to my feet and hugged him tight. "Thank you," I whispered in his ear. He faltered, then responded to my embrace and wrapped his arms around me. "The next creature you fall in love with will be the luckiest in this vast universe and beyond, trust me."

"Yes, I'm well aware."

He made me laugh again. We separated, and Nevis walked over to the door and opened it, just as Heron made his way in. They both froze, glowering at one another. Heron looked at me, then at Nevis, then back at me.

"Relax, bloodsucker," Nevis said, his tone flat. "I'm here with a peace offering. An official one, anyway."

"Oh?" Heron replied, crossing his arms.

"I've conceded. I will no longer pursue your girlfriend. But I may still enjoy taunting you once in a while. I find it delectable to rile you up," Nevis declared with a smirk, then turned stone-cold serious. "But if you break her heart, if you make her suffer in any way, I will find you and I will make you suffer through a most slow and painful death."

Heron nodded once, then smiled at me. "You were right. He's not that big of a jerk after all."

Nevis scoffed, then put his hand out. "Truce?"

"Truce," Heron replied, and shook his hand. He stilled, then groaned with frustration as Dhaxanian frost encased his entire arm. "Seriously?"

"You are just a pleasure to pick on," Nevis chuckled, then exhaled sharply. The ice cracked and shattered, and Heron got his arm back. Nevis then looked at me and offered a polite nod. "I shall see you both tomorrow. We have a lot of work ahead of us."

"That we do," I replied, watching him leave.

Heron shook his head in amusement as he closed the door behind him. His gaze softened once it settled on my face. "Good grief, you're beautiful."

I shrugged. "Still the same vampire from a few hours ago."

"Still so beautiful. And smart. And funny. Sorry, I'm being a sentimental blob right now, I know," Heron said, then let out a long and heavy sigh.

"I really hope this isn't about Nevis again," I replied gently. "You really have nothing to worry about, where he's concerned."

"I know," he said, smiling. "I heard everything. Mara hearing, remember?"

I frowned. "You heard everything? Heron Dorchadas, were you eavesdropping?"

"Can't help it. I was coming up the stairs," he replied with a shrug, then closed the distance between us and took me in his arms, covering my face with sweet, soft kisses. "You see a guy walk into your girl's room, you *have* to hear what he has to say."

"I was right, then." I smiled, caressing his face. "You *are* incorrigible."

"Of course," he breathed, tightening his hold on me. "It's why you love me."

I sighed. "I do. I do. Can't help it."

We both laughed, then kissed and took advantage of the rest of the night. We had one hell of a mission ahead of us. There was no better use of our time, given the circumstances. I let myself go in his arms as we chased the stars, wrapped up in each other.

"I love you," he whispered in my ear.

21

FIONA

I stayed behind in the dining room, by myself, poring over the maps and making sure we knew everything there was to know about the access points into Azure Heights. I drew several escape scenarios, too, in case our tunnel was compromised. I remembered enough about the city and its surroundings to work out potential exits from multiple levels.

My stomach churned, constricted with concerns about the mission. This was it. Our greatest challenge. The moment of truth, so to speak. Our chance to save ourselves and thousands of innocent creatures.

I put together about three pages' worth of notes, specifically where terrain characteristics were concerned. With a fae on our detail, we could even look to the eastern side of the mountain, facing the ocean, for a potential exit route. It allowed us to go both up north and down south.

I took several deep breaths, trying to stay focused. My mind kept wandering back to Zane, and I struggled to worry about Azure Heights instead. I couldn't help but scoff at myself. *I'd rather stress over the mission than openly face the fact that I'm in love.* I was nervous, actually, aware that the inevitable would happen—I'd be alone with Zane again, and we'd be unable to stay away from each other. It wasn't this... dynamic between us that worried me, but rather the fear of losing it altogether. I feared that I'd end up falling even deeper for Zane, only to have us torn apart by the daemons and the Exiled Maras.

I didn't even have the courage to say such words out loud.

And I was so absorbed in the maps before me that I didn't even notice Zane standing in the doorway, watching me, until I looked up and nearly jumped out of my skin.

"Crap! You startled me," I gasped.

Gah, he looks hot.

This was it. The moment I'd been sort of dreading. Standing in front of Zane, daemon prince, and working up the courage to tell him how I felt. Admitting my crush not only to him, but to myself, too. Embracing this weird yet sizzling conundrum we'd gotten ourselves into.

Zane gave me a faded half-smile, unable to take his red eyes off me.

"I didn't mean to," he muttered. "You seemed so focused on those maps, I didn't want to interrupt you."

I felt like prey, being stalked by the tall, gorgeous daemon with crimson-colored eyes, long black hair, and tanned skin stretching over ropes of muscle. We were clearly attracted to each other. I was concerned about the fact that what I was feeling for Zane had much more depth than I'd initially thought.

"It's fine," I replied, almost out of breath, and tried to resume my study of the maps.

I couldn't. His eyes drilled holes through me, and it made it very difficult to concentrate. Nevertheless, I didn't want to let him see he had that effect on me. But Zane was annoyingly observant. He stifled a smirk and casually moved around the table, pretending to read the maps as he got closer to me.

"What are you looking at, specifically?" he asked, his voice low and rough, making my skin tingle.

I'm in so much trouble.

"Alternative escape routes, in case something goes wrong," I murmured, barely hearing myself.

My heart thundered in my chest and echoed in my ears. Zane was only a couple of feet away to my right, and I could feel the space between us compress, overloaded with our physical presence.

"Got any good ones?" he replied, giving me a playful wink.

He knew exactly what he was doing. It was written all over his face. He was enjoying this, and he was closing the distance between us on purpose. *What are the odds that he can hear your rampant heartbeat right about now?*

"A couple, yes. Both involve the eastern mountainside and the ocean," I said, then moved a couple of inches back, hoping to regain some of my senses. It worked for about two seconds, before he nonchalantly came closer, pretending to check the maps again. "Plus, the north side is all rocks and wilderness. The south and the west are the worst options, given how they encompass all the levels of the city."

"Mhm, I see," he muttered, then removed another inch of the space between us.

Every cell in my body started to hum in his vicinity. My whole being vibrated, my blood rushed, and my core tightened with the anticipation of another kiss. I wasn't nervous about kissing him again—I was worried about the extent of my need to feel his lips on mine. I wanted him, badly. And my heart cried out for him. That was the scary part.

And he seemed amused, which further fanned my flames and threatened to anger me. Was he a sadist, aware of his effect on me? Or was he just being playful, oblivious to his effect on me? Either way, I was suddenly annoyed that both scenarios were equally possible.

Hey, you fell for a daemon, Fi. This really shouldn't come as a surprise.

"What's wrong, little vampire?" he asked, a seductive grin slitting his face from ear to ear.

All of a sudden, I found myself wondering what his retractable fangs looked like. I'd never seen them before. I reached out to touch his lips, and he stilled. His reaction was surprising, to say the least. I was starting to think he was as nervous as I was about this. Curious to test that theory, I didn't falter, and pressed my fingers against his upper lip. His red eyes twinkled as he realized what I wanted to see.

He kept his mouth open and revealed his fangs. I'd seen other daemons' canines, of course, but Zane's were... different. They measured about two inches in length, and they were elegantly curved. I pressed the pad of my index finger against the tip of his upper left fang and sucked in a breath. It was so sharp, it drew a droplet of blood.

Zane's hand instantly shot up before I could withdraw mine and firmly gripped my wrist. He kissed the tip of my finger and licked the blood off. My entire body turned to liquid fire, and my breath got caught in my throat. I pulled my hand away and took a couple more steps back, but Zane didn't back away. No, he came closer, unwilling to let any room come between us.

I tried to move again, just so I could maybe get half a minute to think about where this was going. It was unbelievably intense, and it both exhilarated and worried me. I'd never felt like this before.

"Do I make you nervous?" he asked, his voice gruff and loaded with the kind of dark energy that could pull my threads and completely disintegrate me.

I'm in so much freakin' trouble!

"I'm fine," I replied, my faux stoicism drawing a chuckle out of him as he withdrew his fangs.

"There's definitely something off here," he said. "Something's changed, because, last time I checked, you and I had already agreed that this..." He gestured between the both of us. "This is real, and it's happening."

I scoffed. "Yeah, so, about that. What exactly is this?" I replied, mimicking his gesture and pointing at the both of us.

He blinked several times, as if confused. "What do you mean?"

"I asked a simple question. What is this? It's real, and it's happening—yeah, I can feel it, duh. But what is it? Because I have no idea what you want from me."

Zane took another step forward, and I had to tilt my head back to look him in the eyes. This was something I had to get used to, given the dramatic height difference. I shuddered, already yearning to feel his arms around me, his massive body close to mine...

"What do *you* want, Fiona?" he muttered, the corner of his mouth twitching.

"I'm not sure it matters much. I'm not from around here," I replied, crossing my arms in one last attempt to maintain some sense of control over the direction in which the conversation was tumbling. "I would like to know what you want. You're the one who kidnapped me in the first place. You're the one who came back for me."

"You came back for me, too," he shot back, raising an eyebrow.

He was getting a little defensive. I may have struck a nerve there, but I didn't give up.

"We don't leave our allies behind, I told you," I said, keeping my chin up.

He scoffed. "So we're back at square one, now?"

"No. I want to know what you want from me. If tomorrow we succeed, and we get Lumi out and we bring GASP over here, what will happen to you and me? Is there an 'us'? Or is this just a fling?" I replied, feeling my heart sink, ever so slowly, into my stomach. I mentally prepared myself for some kind of disappointment.

Zane narrowed his eyes at me, as if trying to figure out what I was thinking.

You and me both, buddy.

"What are you afraid of, Fiona?"

Screw this. If we fail tomorrow, I'll never forgive myself if I don't tell him.

"I'm... I'm afraid this thing between us is just that. A thing. That it won't lead anywhere. And it's making me nervous because I'm in love with you and I don't know what to do with that. I've never felt anything like this before. I don't know the rules or what I'm supposed to do. I mean, don't get me wrong, it's okay if you don't feel the same way, I'm just trying to be open and realistic here. I'm not expecting much, just that I'd really—"

He kissed me, effectively shutting me up. His mouth conquered mine, and I instantly parted my lips to welcome him. He wrapped his arms around me and almost crushed me against his chest. He was hungry and passionate, lighting my senses on fire. A soft moan escaped my throat as he deepened the kiss. All of a sudden, it was smooth and deliciously intense, ravenous and mind-boggling at the same time.

He held the back of my head in one hand, while his other arm coiled tighter around my waist and lifted me off the ground. I was a doll in his hands, and I couldn't get enough of it. He paused for just a moment, so he could look at me, his gaze clouded and dark, and gave me a most radiant smile.

"I'm so relieved to hear you say that," he breathed.

"Really?" I croaked, my heart pounding.

Zane nodded, firmly gripping the back of my neck. "I have a stronger reason to go against my family and my kingdom, knowing you feel the same way about me as I feel about you, Fiona."

Had I not been suspended a few inches above the ground, I would've been floored by his statement, so to speak. Instead, I felt weightless, a mixture of relief and pure joy rushing through me like a river during a monsoon. He dropped a light kiss on my lower lip.

"Makes it easier to commit treason." He smirked.

I'd wholeheartedly wanted to hear him say such things. I'd worried that I was the only one falling—worried that there was nothing in his heart for me, that to him I could very well be just a great fling. Not that there was something wrong with that, but I wanted him to feel the same about me. And he did.

I exhaled deeply, a smile blooming on my face.

"Good," I murmured, then kissed him back.

I took the lead this time, and he didn't mind. I took everything that he had to give me. His natural scent invaded my lungs, a spicy combination of musk and leather. I ran my fingers through the braids and loose strands of his black hair.

Without even realizing it, I found myself gripping his horns. He stilled and opened his eyes, without separating his lips from mine. His gaze locked on mine, and he grunted and leaned onto the dining table, pressing my body against his as he continued the kiss.

Something shifted in the way he touched me. The hand he'd used to hold the back of my neck slowly moved downward, his fingers trailing down my shoulder blade, then my side. They brushed against my curves, then both hands settled on my waist and gripped firmly.

My breath hitched as he sighed, then took me in a most gentle, almost tear-inducing embrace and hid his face in my hair, his hot breath tickling my neck. "I'm serious, Fiona," he whispered, holding me tight. "I'm madly in love with you. I only ask that you understand that I have never... ever felt this way about anyone."

I nodded slowly, resting my hands on his muscular shoulders. He raised his head, his lips reaching my ear. "I will give you this entire kingdom and more, Fiona. And if you don't want it, if you want to go, I will leave everything behind and follow you across the stars."

Tears worked their way up to my eyes as I realized how nervous Zane must've been. In the end, I was the stranger turning his world upside down, knocking over thousands of years of tradition.

"You thought you were nervous about falling in love with me?" he added, with a slight tremor in his voice. "Fiona, I was done from the moment I saw you in that underground prison. I've been living in sheer terror since, haunted by the thought that, when this is all over, you'll leave me behind. And I'll have nothing left. My kingdom is nothing, my privilege is nothing, my whole damn life is nothing without you. You really have no idea how good it feels to know that you love me, because I... I love you."

"Zane," I managed, a tear streaming down my cheek. He was so intense, so dark and wonderful, and so... honest. It completely dismantled me.

He raised his head and frowned, noticing the tear. He kissed my jaw, catching the tear before it dropped, then trailed the tip of his tongue upward to the corner of my eye, where he dropped another kiss. This gesture alone was enough to make me his, forever.

We stayed like that for what felt like an eternity, our arms locked around each other.

"I'm not letting them win, you know," Zane murmured, his lips against mine. "I'm not letting you or your friends get hurt, Fiona, I promise you. I've only just found you, my little vampire. And I'll stop at nothing to see you happy. Am I making myself clear?"

I nodded again, then kissed him.

Crystal clear.

22

HARPER

The evening sky was clear, with two moons now overlooking the lakes and the small town of Meredrin. I spent some time outside, with Neha and Pheng-Pheng, in the main square by a stone fountain. The Ekar climbed on top of the fountain, grooming his feathers in the crystalline stream.

Pheng-Pheng was still reeling from the loss of her sisters, but I could only imagine what Neha was going through, behind that calm and stoic façade. I'd seen glimmers of grief, but the Manticore queen didn't make a habit of displaying her emotions. The one thing I did appreciate about her relationship with Pheng-Pheng was the ease with which they tackled any topic, from the casual to the painfully difficult.

"What were their names?" I asked, watching as Pheng-Pheng settled in her mother's arms, both sitting on the fountain's edge.

"Baylin was my eldest. Ming was the middle child," Neha replied, then stifled a sob. "Pheng-Pheng is my youngest."

"I'm truly sorry for your loss. I know I've said it before, but... I'm sorry," I said, my voice trembling. Pheng-Pheng gave me a weak smile in response, then settled her gaze on her mother's face.

"We'll be okay," the young Manticore said. "They'll never really be gone, in a way. And they died as heroes. Their names will never be forgotten."

Neha nodded slowly, then chuckled softly as she reminisced. "I had so much trouble with Baylin. I nearly died giving birth to her," she said. "I had just become queen. We'd been forced into the Akrep Gorge at the time, and we didn't know if we'd be safe there. I didn't sleep for many nights and days, worried we might be invaded. Having Baylin completely changed my view of the world. Ming and Pheng-Pheng just confirmed it when they were born— precious creatures, blood of my blood. When you lose a child it's... it's like you lose a piece of yourself."

"I can't even begin to imagine what that must feel like," I murmured.

"A chunk of your soul is gone, and you live with the emptiness for the rest of your life," Neha said, her voice broken. "I wish it upon no one."

"Except for the daemon king and the Mara Lords. A life for a life. That's a fair trade," Pheng-Pheng muttered. "Two of his sons for my sisters. No. All of them, Mother. They all deserve to die. They want us dead. Why should we be the nice ones, still? No. All of Shaytan's sons will be cut down."

"Well, Zane's on our side," I replied with a shrug. "Surely you can't wish him dead, too."

"No, he's an exception," she groaned, rolling her eyes. This was her warrior façade on display. Deep down, I knew she was broken and hurting. I could see her emotions clearly. She and Neha were burdened by deep red auras—the kind of raw pain I hoped I'd never experience.

"My darling." Neha smiled, then dropped a kiss on Pheng-Pheng's forehead. "If there's one thing I've learned from all this, it's that life is precious. And if we're looking at a different, better future for our world, we must consider changing our ways to accommodate peace. Otherwise, we will keep going around in this vicious circle. The innocent will die. The evil will bleed. It will just be the same story all over again, but with a different villain."

Pheng-Pheng frowned, then looked up at her mother. "What are you saying? That we should just let the daemons off the hook? They killed your daughters. My sisters!"

"Pheng-Pheng, my sweet, sweet child. Shaytan and the Mara Lords will get what's coming to them, there's no doubt about that. But after it's all done, we need to do better, going forward," Neha explained. "We cannot build a peaceful society if the streets still run red with blood. That's not the kind of future I want for my children."

I let out a sigh, in sincere awe of Neha. "I have to say, the way you're keeping it together is remarkable," I said. "I mean, I understand why, since you still have to lead your people and inspire trust, but still. It's admirable, to say the least."

"You mean for your child, Mother," Pheng-Pheng added. "The kind of future you want for your child. You only have one left."

Neha smiled softly as she first looked at me, then at her daughter. "You're right, Harper Hellswan. I am keeping it together, though it's no easy feat. But I have to. Not just for my people. But also for my *children*. Pheng-Pheng, I wanted to tell you sooner, but today's tragedy made it impossible for me to focus, and—"

"No way!" I gasped, already grinning. I knew exactly what she was going to say. It didn't take a genius, plus there were glimmers of gold and white in her aura—I'd seen them before in the pregnant humans back in The Shade. The glow of a future mother.

"What?" Pheng-Pheng replied, slightly confused.

"I'm with child, my darling," Neha breathed.

"Wait, what?" Pheng-Pheng was stunned.

She jumped back and put several feet between them, just so she could measure her mother from head to toe. She cocked her head to the side and frowned. Neha took a deep breath and elaborated.

"It's Kai's," she said. "In about six full moons, you'll have a little sister. Or brother. We don't know yet."

Pheng-Pheng squealed with joy and hugged her mother tight. They both laughed and cried, while I sat there, tearing up and watching this beautiful, surprising twist in their mother-daughter relationship. I suddenly found myself missing my mom and dad, my stomach churning at the thought of how worried they probably were, unable to get to us. Maybe they didn't even know if I was still alive.

I longed to hold my mom again and feel my father's kiss on the top of my head.

"Mother, I'm... so happy and sad at the same time, I don't know how to explain it," Pheng-Pheng sobbed, resting her head on Neha's bosom. The Manticore queen held her daughter close, smiling softly.

"I know, my love. I'm the same. I'm torn because I will never see two of my children again, but I'm smiling because there's another being growing inside me, another child to love and nurture. I have to stay strong—*we* have to stay strong, my darling, for the little one's sake."

"Does Kai know?" Pheng-Pheng asked.

"And are you and Kai an item or something? I'm still not sure what works and what doesn't in your society," I added.

Neha sighed. "He doesn't know yet. He's out in the gorges now, doing my bidding, preparing the terrain for what will happen once the swamp witch is out of Azure Heights," she said. "The Exiled

Maras will be out for blood, and if anyone is better at ambushes in narrow gorges, it's the Manticores, my darlings. Not even the daemons can withstand our attacks."

"Why haven't you told him yet?" Pheng-Pheng replied.

"I didn't have a chance. I've been working up the courage, but I've yet to find it. I've just buried your sisters, too. It's a little too much for me to worry about," Neha explained, then looked at me —and I could see the helplessness, the pain blaring in her amber eyes. "And no, we're not together. Our traditions would never allow me to take a partner as queen. But I do love Kai. After the girls' fathers died, I didn't think I'd love again."

"I guess love has a funny way of sneaking up on you," I replied with a smirk.

"But I can't have that now. I can't worry about him, and yet I can't help it, either. I'm concerned about his safety, especially out there in the Valley of Screams," Neha muttered. "What's the point of love, anyway, if you can't be with that person?"

"Mother," Pheng-Pheng interjected, somewhat irritated. "You are the queen. You should have the freedom to be with whomever your heart desires."

"It wouldn't be fair if I were the only one with such a privilege, my darling."

"Then give it to everyone. Change the rules. Let everyone be free to be with whomever they want," I replied. "I mean, Hansa was once the Red Tribe Chief, back on Calliope. The succubi had strict rules, too. They were segregated by gender and only sought the males, the incubi, to have children. They kept the females in their tribes, and they sent the males to their fathers. And it was okay for a long time. But then everything changed. The overlord was taken down. There was freedom again."

Neha listened carefully, seemingly curious. "And now?"

"And now Hansa is free. She never thought she'd be with

anyone ever again either, but then Jax came along, and, well, they're together. And, despite our circumstances here, they're happy. But all the succubi were given the same benefits. And it worked. We embrace change when it brings freedom and joy. They set new rules; they established new traditions—more inclusive ones, that allow the succubi to raise both males and females, to have wholesome families and to experience a different, better life," I said.

"A happy society is a prosperous society, isn't it?" Pheng-Pheng asked, looking at her mother.

The Manticore queen kissed her daughter's temple.

"Yes, it is," Neha replied.

A couple of minutes went by in silence. I thought about Kai for a second.

"You should tell Kai, you know," I muttered.

"I will, as soon as I see him again," Neha said, then glanced up at the moons. "If I see him again."

My heart thudded. I was reminded of what lay ahead of us tomorrow. Neha was right. There was a big "if" in front of us. It could all work out, or it could lead to our end on Neraka. Either way, I could tell Neha was regretful for not having spoken to Kai about the pregnancy sooner.

And I didn't want to feel that way about anything, especially where Caspian was concerned. I didn't want us to go into Azure Heights without having done and said everything we needed to do and say. I didn't want the morning to come and for me not to experience the full potential of my relationship with Caspian.

This was a now or never kind of thing, and I suddenly longed to see Caspian.

To be with him.

23

SCARLETT

P atrik and I retreated to our room shortly after the meeting. As soon as I closed the door and turned around, he took me in his arms and held me like that for a while, without saying anything. He hid his face in the warm space between my head and shoulder, exhaling deeply as his heart thundered against my chest.

I knew what this was about. Our perilous journey aside, Patrik was still reeling from the Death Claw tackle back at Ragnar Peak.

"I know I've said this before, but I feel the need to say it again," he murmured, slowly raising his head, his lips brushing against my ear. "I'm just over the moon to see you in one piece. I would like to kindly ask that you don't give your enemies, feral or otherwise, the opportunity to take you down like that Death Claw did ever again."

"And I know I've said *this* before, but I obviously have to say it again," I replied, giggling. "I simply didn't want the beast to hurt you or our defense. I can take one hell of a beating, Patrik, and still pull myself back together. It's in my nature, as a vampire. You, on the other hand—"

"Don't throw this back at me," he said, smirking as he looked at me. "I'm not reprimanding you, Scarlett. It's not my place." His steely blue gaze then darkened, as he remembered that whole scene. "I just... I had flashbacks of Kyana's dead body when I saw you tangled with that Death Claw. For a split second, I thought that was it. That I'd lost you, too. I'm selfish, I know. But I think I've earned that after what I went through."

"You most certainly did," I replied, cupping his face as I dropped a soft kiss on his lips.

"You nearly broke my heart again." He sighed.

I traced the contour of his dark eyebrows with my fingertips, then sank my hands into his curly black hair. Patrik smiled, his hands resting on the small of my back.

"I need you to have a little bit more faith in me, Patrik," I said. "I would never be reckless with my own life. And if I am to leave this world, it certainly won't be because of a mindless Death Claw. I know little to nothing about Kyana, but I'm sure she was an incredible creature. However, she wasn't a trained GASP agent."

Patrik chuckled softly, biting his lower lip. "I am a terrible Druid, you know that? I should give you more credit."

"Damn straight," I replied, then kissed him, deeply and with every ounce of love that blossomed in my heart whenever he looked at me.

Patrik was a fascinating enigma. On one hand, he was one of the strongest, most seasoned Druids I'd ever met. His ambition and resilience carried echoes of Derek's own fierce character, yet, at the same time, there was this sliver of fragility, this open wound that may never heal. It made Patrik the amazing person I'd inadvertently fallen for.

He didn't deny or hide his vulnerability. No, he embraced it. He voiced his concerns and wasn't afraid to show me how much he needed me in his life. And that was rare. Most guys usually went for the tall, dark, handsome, and mysterious persona, the tough nut that almost never cracked.

Patrik was an exception to the norm, and that just made me fall even deeper in love with him. In the end, it was his honesty that truly got to me. Well, that and those baby blues.

He paused for a second, enough to look at me and smile again. "In my defense, this is simply my fear of losing you," he said. "I feel helpless when I watch you fighting, anyway. I would never let anything happen to you, of course, but given your speed and strength, I often feel like all I can do is just stand back and watch. When you come out of a fight still alive, it's like I'm born again. And when you fall, it's like the sky comes crashing down."

"I think this has to do with the way in which you and I actually got together," I replied, feeling my cheeks catch fire as I remembered the first time I'd kissed him. It seemed like ages ago, although it had only been a handful of days. "We found each other in the middle of an atrocity. There's danger at every corner, and almost everybody on this planet wants a piece of us, Patrik. But Neraka will not be the end of us. I've got plans for this relationship."

Patrik grinned, a playful twinkle settling in his eyes. He brought a hand up and pressed his thumb against my lower lip. I instinctively kissed it, and he tightened his other arm around my waist and pulled me closer. I felt soft, like molten wax, against his muscular frame.

"Oh, you have plans, now?" he quipped, raising an eyebrow. "Might I ask what it is you intend to do with me, Miss Novak?"

"I was thinking the usual," I replied, rolling my eyes. "Dinner, long walks on the beach, exploring a new planet, fighting off a bunch of rebel incubi on Tenebris... You know, the basic stuff."

Patrik then pulled the hair tie out of my ponytail and let my hair loose. He ran his fingers through it, following its flow as it cascaded down my back. There was this look of adoration almost lighting him up from the inside as he admired me with my hair down. He inched forward and covered the side of my neck with wet, hot kisses, and he continued to comb my hair with his fingers.

It knocked the air out of my lungs. I pressed my body against his, feeling the hard muscles beneath his shirt against my curves. I moaned gently when he nipped my skin, his teeth grazing me softly and sending billions of electrical currents through my body.

"Anything else you had in mind?" he muttered, then caught my earlobe between his lips and suckled. My breath hitched, and I instinctively wrapped my arms around his torso, hanging on for dear life as he ripped me from the clutches of reality.

"I can't formulate a coherent thought at this point in time, I'm sorry," I breathed.

He stilled, then raised his head to look at me.

"We're getting out of here, one way or another, Scarlett," he said. "I was caged and enslaved once. It's not happening again. Most importantly, I will not allow you to go through anything like that. Ever."

I nodded, then put my arms around his neck and pulled myself up to kiss him. He instantly lowered his head and met me halfway, his mouth crashing against mine in a hungry and passionate kiss. The taste of him alone could cause a lifelong addiction—and, as I was a vampire, that pretty much encompassed an eternity of loving him.

A heartbreaking growl emerged from outside. We both froze, then opened our eyes and stared at each other as we listened. A series of whimpers followed. Something was happening out in the inn's backyard.

We rushed to the window and looked outside. I gasped.

"Oh, wow," Patrik muttered.

Hundurr and Rover were out there. Rover lay on his belly, watching Hundurr as he writhed in sheer agony. His muscles throbbed, and his bones cracked as he stretched and fought against his pit wolf form.

"Is he—"

"Yes, yes, he is," Patrik replied before I could ask the full question. "He's trying to break out of his pit wolf curse!"

"How do you... Have you seen him do it before?" I asked, briefly looking at Patrik before shifting my focus back to Hundurr.

The pit wolf struggled in a lot of pain, but he was halfway through, recovering some of his humanoid form. There was even a patch of reddish hair growing on his back as part of the process. Rover stayed close, watching with interest and sympathy, occasionally letting out a supportive whimper, as if telling Hundurr that he could do it, that he could beat this.

"I take full responsibility," Patrik said, the corner of his mouth twitching as he watched Hundurr.

"How? I mean, did you know he could do it?"

"Not really. Neither did he. But, then again, I once thought I'd be a Destroyer forever, but Vita came along and forced me back to my Druid roots," Patrik explained. "All I did was take Hundurr aside. I told him about it. There's no harm in trying, right?"

I shook my head, unable to take my eyes off Hundurr. "Absolutely not. I'm amazed he's even tried it. Do you think he'll make it?"

He shrugged, then chuckled softly. "I did my best to incentivize him. Scarlett, you and I both know that he's crazy about you, even in that pit wolf body."

"Well... I guess, yeah," I replied, blushing. "But I—"

"It's okay. I know." He gave me a brief and understanding glance. "Your heart's mine, Scarlett. I'm not giving it back unless you ask me. But I told Hundurr that he would at least stand a better chance of trying to win your affection if he regained his Adlet form."

"Oh..." I murmured.

I was both stunned and impressed. Hundurr was incredibly close to shifting back. But he caved. He exhaled sharply and collapsed, his pit wolf body rippling back to full size. Rover nuzzled and licked his face, as if comforting him. Hundurr was too exhausted to even move, poor soul.

"He'll get there soon enough," Patrik said, then put his arm around my shoulders and held me close. "He's a strong creature."

I looked up at Patrik, in genuine awe of him. He never ceased to amaze me. There was always another layer, a part of him that further proved what an incredible spirit he had. Of course he'd spurred Hundurr into fighting to get his original form back. Patrik was the living example of the struggle and the victory against an evil curse.

There was no one better to teach and support Hundurr in breaking free.

I rested my head on Patrik's shoulder, feeling my heart swell with everything I felt for him. "You know, I'm the luckiest vampire across all known dimensions," I whispered.

"I'm guessing that has to do with me?"

"Duh," I replied, then laughed when he took me in his arms and sat us both in an armchair in front of the fireplace, where flames crackled playfully.

I settled in his lap, curled up with his arms around me. We had our greatest challenge yet ahead of us tomorrow, but, for one more night, I could relax in Patrik's embrace and marvel at how wonderful we were... at what amazing things could happen between us once we got Lumi and our freedom back.

24

HARPER

After my talk with Pheng-Pheng and Neha, I went back to the inn. Ramin was given a space in the lobby area downstairs, nestled beneath a potted tree with seeds and fresh water. I stopped by to check up on the Ekar, then made my way back to the room.

It was nice and warm, the fire burning and casting its amber glow over the plastered walls. I rummaged through the dresser and found a large bath towel, then went into the bathroom to wash up.

My mind wandered back to Caspian. I was going to take one hell of a chance tomorrow with our infiltration mission, but getting Lumi back was worth it. I had no intention of spending another week in fear, trapped on this planet. Most importantly, I wanted to save Caspian, to free him of his blood oath and his horrible people. He deserved a better life.

In a way, I needed him more than he needed me. I had GASP behind me, and I was determined to restore the freedom and the dignity of all Nerakians, but I felt empty without Caspian. Somewhere along this perilous journey, he'd become an essential part of my existence. He needed me and my people to defeat the daemons and the Exiled Maras, but I needed him to breathe again.

Is this what true love feels like?

I thought about my mom and dad, and their bonded souls. They were a part of each other. Together they were one. Caspian had already become an integral part of me. The thought was scary, given the speed with which we'd fallen for each other. However, it also filled my heart with excitement, the anticipation of an endless future with him by my side.

Caspian was the last thing on my mind whenever I closed my eyes. As soon as I woke up, I thought of him. I breathed a sigh of relief when I felt his arms around me. His strength fortified me; it gave the extra kick in the pants I needed to shatter any obstacle in our path. And the way he looked at me... I felt like the most important creature in the universe. And I was all his.

I couldn't help but chuckle as I came out of the bathroom, wrapped up in my towel and remembering my previous stance on relationships. I'd thought it would take a long time for me to actually consider one. I wanted it, of course, but the timing had felt off. Then, I'd laid eyes on Caspian, and something had instantly shifted inside me.

I stilled at the sight of Caspian sitting on the edge of the bed.

"Hey," I murmured. "Everything okay?"

He looked up at me. There was something in the air between us. He seemed different, somehow. Dark and mysterious, like the first time we'd met, but with none of the chills. He wasn't cold at all, in fact. Fires burned in his jade eyes as his gaze settled on my face, his brows slightly furrowed.

"I need to tell you something," he said, his voice low and husky, "and I need you to not try and stop me."

I nodded slowly, feeling my pulse speed up.

"I was out with Peyton and his Maras for a while, as you know," he started. "I know him, it turns out. I wasn't sure when we first met them, but I remembered the day he ran off. There were dozens of them, in fact. Not all of them survived, because the Lords sent out Correction Officers to hunt them down," he added, his skin gradually reddening.

His blood oath was starting to burn through him, and I instantly moved forward. He raised a hand to stop me, then took a deep breath and continued, braving the developing burns as he told me about times which he'd been forbidden through swamp witch magic to talk about.

"I helped Peyton and his crew escape," he said, grunting from the pain. "His group wasn't the first for whom I'd secured passage out of Azure Heights. The Lords caught me, though. They gave me two options: imprisonment until I died from having my soul eaten or taking the blood oath and proving that I could still be loyal to the city."

He gasped from the pain, red blotches covering his face, his neck and hands. He inhaled and exhaled several times, giving the blood oath some time to withdraw before he spoke again. My stomach churned as I watched him suffer in his effort to tell me something. I had a feeling it was something that meant a lot to him and he could no longer keep to himself, blood oath be damned.

I stood there, my hands balled into fists, fingernails digging into my palms.

"At first, I regretted my choice," he muttered. "I watched innocent creatures getting dragged away, tossed into the underground prison and fed on by daemons and Maras alike. I watched the life drained from them. Their blood sucked out. Their souls gone. I couldn't do anything against my people. I held on, though, hoping the day would come when I would either stop this insanity or finally die."

He stood up, panting, as the burns worsened. "I felt lost. Then you came along, Harper... and I hated myself even more for not being able to tell you the truth."

"Please stop," I gasped, tears burning my eyes. I just couldn't take it anymore. The sight of him in pain tore me apart. It broke my heart, over and over, and I hated myself for being so helpless before his blood oath. "Stop hurting yourself like this."

Caspian gave me a soft smile, and his burns started to fade away. "It doesn't hurt as much as the thought of not having lived through it all, up until the moment I met you. Harper, this is what I'm trying to say," he said, grunting as he pointed at the symbol carved behind his ear. "I no longer regret my choice to take the blood oath. It allowed me to live so I could be with you."

He sighed, then gave himself a minute, as his burns healed. I was stunned, unable to look away. My brain refused to function, but I tried to register what he'd said. All this pain he'd put himself through, just to tell me that he didn't regret anything anymore because... because he'd met me.

Tears streamed down my cheeks, my heart aching and burning, as I finally understood what this was. This was love, in its purest form, taking over my body and my soul, etching Caspian into every fiber of my being. I was nothing without him.

"I love you, Harper," Caspian said, his voice trembling and raw with emotion.

I could see it, too, as the red aura of pain around him blossomed into an almost ethereal gold. It felt as though I was looking at the sun, its warm rays caressing my face.

"Caspian..." I managed, barely recognizing my own voice.

"I mean it," he replied, then took a couple of steps forward and closed the distance between us. "I love you, Harper Hellswan. This whole world can be destroyed or saved tomorrow. I don't care. It doesn't change this single moment in time, or anything that has led up to it. I love you. I was lost and bound to a curse, until I found you and realized that... that there's still hope for me. That I have something more to fight for. It's one thing to resist and conspire to save your people, and something else entirely to fight to keep the love of your life. The energy I get from you, Harper, it's... it's irreplaceable."

I shuddered, as he gently brought his hands up, his thumbs brushing along the length of my arms. Even through the towel's layer of plush cotton, his touch sparked thunderstorms beneath my skin. He wiped my tears with his knuckles, without saying another word. He just gazed at me, while I lost myself in those dark jade pools.

"I didn't expect any of this to happen... yet, here we are," I whispered, my heart galloping and my blood rushing from my head, leaving me a little bit drowsy. "I love you, Caspian. I love you so much it hurts, and it scares the hell out of me, but, at the same time, it makes me want to turn this entire planet inside out, if that's what it'll take for me to be with you, to feel you—"

Caspian kissed me, shutting me up in an instant.

The golden light of his aura somehow enveloped me, warming me up from the inside. It felt so strange but so, so incredible.

"You're the only good thing in my life, Harper," he breathed, then put his arms around me and squeezed me tight, trailing kisses down the side of my neck. His lips tickled me, my core ignited as I ran my fingers through his short black hair and tried my best to stay upright.

His aura almost blinded me. I closed my eyes, breathing him in, as my hands traveled down his chest, then unbuttoned his shirt. His muscles were hard, twitching nervously under my touch. The feel of his skin on mine was something simply out of this world.

His mouth claimed mine, deepening the kiss. We were both consumed by a whirlwind of emotions, feeding off one another, passionate and desperate to feel everything.

"I love you," I whispered against his lips.

He stilled, then looked at me, the shadow of a smile flickering across his gorgeous face. The firelight played with his features, creating a dramatic contrast of almost black shadows and amber glimmers, his sharp jaw and the blade of his nose beautifully outlined.

His hands rested on my waist. His pupils were dilated, like black holes swallowing the jade universe in his eyes. With shaky hands, I managed to take his shirt off completely, discarding it on the floor.

"Be mine, Harper," he said, gently cupping my face with his hand.

I leaned into it, unable to catch my breath. My heart threatened to explode, my entire body humming and my soul yearning to feel his. The sentry side of me begged for release, for the ultimate union. I needed him so much it hurt.

"Caspian, if we do this... I'm a sentry, you might—"

He kissed me again, this time with ravaging hunger. My lower lip got caught between his lips, and he suckled softly, coaxing a moan from my throat. I shivered in his grip. His fingers slowly pulled the towel up to my hips.

"I don't care, Harper. I want to be with you, in every way possible."

He breathed out as he pulled the towel off me completely. All of a sudden, I was naked, every cell in my body vibrating as Caspian took his time to worship me. "You are perfect," he whispered, then scooped me up in his arms and laid me on the bed.

I sank into the layers of fur on top of the mattress, my heart pounding as I watched him slip out of his boots and pants. He climbed into bed, then covered me with his muscular frame. His weight pinned me down as he kissed me, deeply, leaning onto one elbow.

He used his other hand to trace my every curve, leaving blazing trails behind. His mouth made love to mine first, his fingers exploring everything in their path. We lost ourselves in the night and in the stars and in the three moons rising somewhere above the inn.

Caspian was made for loving me. I could tell from the way he touched me, relishing every sensation. As he claimed me, we established a rhythm, following the frantic beats in our chests, our bodies molded together as we melted and abandoned ourselves to this single, most perfect moment. Caspian made love to me, kissing me all over and whispering the sweetest words in my ear.

I held on, my heart pounding as we ascended higher into existence, beyond the night's sky, beyond the fabric of time and space. We rode the midnight winds, we sailed the endless seas, and we felt the sand under our feet—a thousand emotions at once, crashing into us like turbulent waves. And we loved every second of it.

"Hold me tight," Caspian murmured, then put my arms around his neck.

I did as he asked, and he took me higher and farther away from the present. His arms slipped around my waist as he moved deeper and demanded my consciousness. My sentry senses unraveled, I cried out his name, and our souls finally fused in a bright flash of white light.

A second was stretched into a million years as Caspian made love to me, over and over. My name settled on his lips as he kissed me, as if kissing me was his only chance at survival. Colors splashed before my very eyes as we surrendered to each other, body and soul, heart and mind.

I couldn't get enough of all the love he had to give me. His lips tasted like honeysuckle and spices. His hot breath sent ripples through my skin. And I could feel everything he felt.

This is it.

Caspian stilled for a second, staring at me. I could see entire galaxies unfolding in his eyes. Fascination and adoration settled on his face as he caressed mine. "Harper, this is... this is incredible."

"I can feel you." I nodded slowly.

He frowned gently, clutching his chest. "I feel you. It hurts so good," he whispered, his flushed lips stretching into a lascivious smile. "You're simply unbelievable, my love."

"We're linked like this forever, Caspian," I replied softly. "No one... nothing can tear us apart."

We kissed once more. This time, we took our sweet time to enjoy all the new sensations that came from having our souls eternally bound to one another. The night was still young, the fire crackling, and our senses stretching across the whole world, somehow.

"I never thought I could experience something like this," he said, holding me tight and rolling us over in bed.

"Making love to a sentry?" I breathed, winding up on top of him.

"No. Loving you. It's... It's indescribable," he replied, his hands quietly moving up my thighs and settling on my hips.

It was my turn to take control. I kissed him, greedy and possessive, and I felt us both ignite once more. He parted his lips and welcomed me. My tongue worked his in languishing circles, until he grunted and flooded my senses with his. I was coming into my own as a sentry. Opening up to someone like this was truly a sublime experience.

"Love me like you do," Caspian breathed.

I did. I loved him until we were both reduced to wisps of

energy, two stars colliding in the vast universe. Tomorrow was still very far away, as we collapsed into each other, our souls and limbs entwined.

Inseparable and unbreakable.

Eternally existing as one.

25

CAIA

Out of all the rooms in the inn, Blaze and I got the smallest one, with a double bed crammed against a wall. It was nice and cozy, but it left little room for actual movement. Of course, no one paid attention to room sizes when they were assigned. Frankly, even in that moment, it was the least of our worries.

"So, we're sharing the bed, then," I muttered, as I came out of the cramped bathroom after changing into a long cotton nightgown.

Blaze stilled at the foot of the bed, awkwardly clutching a pair of linen slacks over his chest. He nodded slowly, and I chuckled, moving aside so he could go into the bathroom and change as well.

My temperature was way up just from being in the same room with him. Sleeping together was going to be sweet torture. I climbed into bed and settled under the fluffy comforter. The pillows were fantastic. It had been a while since I'd experienced comfort. Not since the Broken Bow Inn, back in Azure Heights. It was literally one of the few good things I could count in that place.

"I think we're luckier than Rush and Amina, though," Blaze said from behind the bathroom door.

"Why do you say that?"

"Well, they're sharing a room with Ryker and Laughlan. I think we have it easy," Blaze replied.

"Yeah, nothing like two chatty Druids to spend the night with." I giggled.

My heart skipped a beat when he came out. The linen slacks hung loosely around his beautifully sculpted waist, with every single muscle of his glorious torso in full view. My cheeks burned as I struggled to look away and failed miserably.

But there was something about his expression that felt... wrong. He was upset by something, and he was trying very hard to hide it. It had become impossible for him to keep anything from me. Ever since we'd come to Neraka, we'd rarely been apart. For Pete's sake, we'd even been abducted together.

"What's wrong?" I asked, frowning slightly as he stood in the middle of the room, staring at me.

He took a deep breath, then let it out as his muscular shoulders dropped.

Focus, Caia.

"I hate being vulnerable," he replied.

"Where's this coming from?"

I was a little confused. At the same time, I still had a hard time coming to terms with the fact that we were about to share a bed again. It was becoming increasingly difficult to focus when we were so close to each other.

"We're going into Mara territory tomorrow," he said. "I don't ever want to be mind-bent again, Caia. If we run into Rewa... If we're discovered, you know she'll want me to finish what I started the last time."

It hit me then. He was in a lot of emotional pain, still. He'd just gotten over almost killing me the last time we'd confronted Rewa and the other Lords. He didn't want to go through it again. My heart inflated like a balloon, realizing how deep his pain must've run. He'd never meant it, but he'd hurt me under Rewa's influence, and it tormented him.

I tossed the covers aside and slid across the bed. He froze, a flurry of emotions swirling in his midnight-blue eyes. I gave him a soft smile, then caught his hand and pulled him closer.

Blaze didn't know what to do, but he didn't object to my gesture, either. As strong and as imposing as he could be, the dragon was incredibly soft on the inside—at least where I was concerned. I knew I was his weakness. And yes, it worried me too that the Rewa episode might happen again, but under no circumstances was I going to let Blaze falter because of that. We all took risks in this mission, some more than others.

"This is our challenge, Blaze," I said, putting my arms around his waist.

He held his breath as I pulled him close. His frame was huge compared to my pixie size, and that somehow made my blood rush even faster. I had a lot of fire in me, but there was something about Blaze that made me feel tiny and vulnerable in his arms, in the weirdest, most wonderful way.

Blaze looked into my eyes, his arms slowly coming around in a possessive embrace. Celibacy oath or not, he clearly felt the same way about me. It was written all over his handsome, square-jawed face, despite his noble restraint.

"We'll be invisible, and we'll be careful," I added. "Also, we won't look directly at them. And we won't give them the opportunity to mind-bend either of us. We'll strike fast and hard if they catch us."

He nodded, a smile briefly flickering over his lips.

"I don't get why we can't just kill them while we're there," Blaze replied, then let out a heavy sigh.

"Because killing them would be easy," I said. "They deserve to be punished. They deserve to suffer for everything they did and everything else they're going to do. Death would be the easy way out. If we have no other choice, then yes, of course, we'll burn the assholes to a crisp. But otherwise, you and I both know that they're looking at a world of pain once we restore Neraka's freedom."

He chuckled, shaking his head.

"Good grief, you are an evil mastermind," he quipped.

"I think we're both rotten to the core when it comes to defending each other," I replied, my voice dropping. I was telling the truth, to my surprise. There was nothing I wouldn't do to keep him safe. And I'd already seen what Blaze was willing to do to protect me. Daemons, Death Claws, Exiled Maras, and pit wolves had already perished in his flames.

"We are," he muttered. "I've told you before, and I will say it again, Caia. I will burn this whole place down for you."

"That's just so... cruel when taken out of context. And yet so hot," I replied, then gripped the back of his neck and pulled myself up so I could kiss him.

His lips crushed mine, his tongue demanded access, and I exhaled softly as he tightened his embrace, pressing me against his chest.

Blaze burned hot on the inside. We both did, for that matter. Our reactions to one another were deliciously similar. There was passion between us, and there was this awkward budding romance. I secretly hoped we could take things to another level, as

I became more and more convinced that I'd truly fallen in love with him.

The one thing that motivated me to be so daring whenever we were alone, was knowing that he felt the same way. He'd gathered the courage to tell me how he felt, back in the library refuge, and I understood exactly how serious he was about us. I'd gotten to see sides of him that had convinced me of his seriousness where matters of the heart were involved. The fact that he'd been raised by Heath further added to my conviction. Blaze was a most noble creature and took his feelings seriously.

He wouldn't have said a thing, had he not meant it. Especially since he was still very much under a celibacy oath. Dammit.

I relished the feel of his skin against my fingertips as our kiss threatened to get out of control. We were both aching for each other, but more than anything, I wanted to ease his mind regarding the Maras. It chipped away at his confidence, and I needed my dragon in full force tomorrow. Our lives depended on it.

"Blaze," I breathed against his lips, suddenly illuminated. I had an idea. "Of course... Why didn't I think about it before?"

Blaze panted, trying to regain his senses. We were both out of air, our hearts pounding and our bodies blazing, but we had to get hold of ourselves. I had a really good idea.

"What is it?" he asked, his gaze still clouded, catching a shade of indigo as he looked at me.

"I think I know how to fix that mind-bending problem. Hold on," I replied, then jumped out of bed and rushed out of the room. "Wait there!"

I went straight to Rush and Amina's room, then feverishly knocked on their door. I listened to the footsteps shuffling inside. Amina opened for me. She looked tired, stifling a yawn with her hand.

"Oh, I'm sorry, I woke you up," I gasped.

"No, no. I doubt Rush and I will get much sleep tonight," Amina muttered, then stepped aside to show me inside their room. She pointed at the window, where Ryker and Laughlan had taken over a small table, experimenting with various crystals and powders, igniting them in small stone bowls.

They were testing explosives in tiny quantities, with an occasional pop.

Rush sat on the edge of the bed, watching the Druids with a sullen expression.

"I take it you're still adjusting to the four of you sharing the room, huh?" I muttered. "Can I come in?"

Amina nodded with a warm smile, then closed the door behind me. Ryker and Laughlan were so absorbed in their chemical formulations, they didn't even notice me come in. Rush, however, stood and offered a curt bow, and I responded with a smile.

"I'm here to talk to you guys, actually," I said, my gaze shifting between Rush and Amina.

They motioned for me to take a seat by the fire. I settled in one of the armchairs, facing them.

"Of course," Amina replied. "How can we assist you?"

"Well, it's a bit of a longshot, but you might actually have some idea, since you're older than Jax and Heron. I'm hoping you might know more about mind-bending and how to prevent it. I don't know, I guess I'm thinking you may have more experience in the subject. Jax and Heron have no solution to stopping Maras from mind-bending us."

"Ah," Rush replied, nodding. "I honestly don't have a good answer, I'm afraid."

"It's all about eye contact," Amina offered with a shrug. "You could do your best to look away. I hear Jax can do a lot more with his wards present, but he's a chilling exception. The rest of us rely on looking into a person's eyes in order to influence them."

I felt a little deflated. "I see."

"You know, I've always had a theory about mind-bending," Laughlan interjected, narrowing his eyes and pursing his lips, as if rummaging through his memory for that precious little snippet of information.

"Oh? Pray tell!" I replied. "With Blaze and I going into Azure Heights tomorrow, I want us to be covered, in case anything goes wrong. Last time, they got hold of Blaze and I almost died, so... hoping to prevent that," I added, wearing a flat grin.

Laughlan nodded. "Yes. Well, I was thinking about covering the eyes with something," he said. "I've seen glass prohibiting a Mara from mind-bending another creature once, a *very* long time ago. It's not a known fact, however. I wouldn't be surprised if the Maras themselves weren't aware. There are barely a handful of Eritopians who wear lenses to improve their eyesight, while the Maras tend to stay away from other societies, in general. So they haven't had many opportunities to try it."

"Okay, that could work out!" I said, scratching the back of my head. "But if we're caught wearing any kind of glasses or lenses, they could very well remove them before they mind-bend us. I doubt that'll help, unless..." My voice trailed off, as another idea made its way to the surface. "Lenses. Contact lenses. Yes."

Laughlan and Ryker looked at each other, then frowned, shifting their focus back to me.

"What are contact lenses?" Ryker asked.

"Back on Earth, where I was born and raised, there are many humans with eyesight problems, especially as they grow older. They use glasses," I explained, "but they also wear lenses. Tiny little things, made of a material called plastic, or even rigid gas. They're soft and malleable, and don't break like glass would. Thing is, they wear them over their eyes, literally," I said, then pointed at my iris.

Both Druids stilled, their eyes wide with both surprise and realization.

Ryker shot to his feet, a grin splitting his face. "I know exactly what we can use for something like that," he breathed, then rushed out of the room.

Laughlan opened his mouth to shout after him but gave up and gave me a warm smile instead. I felt hope blossoming in my chest. If the Druids could do this for Blaze and me, it would pretty much secure our safety against the Maras, going forward. And that was one hell of a game changer.

"Come back in the morning, little fae," Laughlan said. "Ryker and I will work on something tonight. I imagine he's out to fetch whatever material he saw that would be useful for these... contact lenses."

"And Rush and I can run some tests with them," Amina said.

"Yes, one of the Druids can wear them, and we can try to mind-bend him," Rush added. "Make sure they work."

I was overwhelmed with gratitude at this point. I hugged them all, one by one, unable to wipe the broad smile from my face.

"Thank you all so much," I murmured. "I'll see you in the morning then!"

I went back to our single room and found Blaze in bed. He wasn't moving.

He'd already fallen asleep.

26

CAIA

Blaze was exhausted—and who could blame him? He'd spent half the day in dragon form, fighting off daemons and Death Claws up on Ragnar Peak. He'd gotten shot with a giant arrow, and he'd had the scare of his life when the tower collapsed, thinking I'd died.

The memories of that battle came rushing back, and I suddenly felt the urge to cuddle him.

Light on my feet, I locked the door behind me and slipped under the covers. He had his back to me, his large frame poking through the comforter like a mountain. I gently put an arm around his waist and spooned him. I was so tiny by comparison, it made me grin.

I didn't pay attention to his breathing until I got close, realizing that he wasn't sleeping at all. His heart boomed in his chest, and he was very much awake. His hand covered mine as it settled on his abdomen.

"Are you going to tell me what that was about?" he muttered.

His voice was low and rough, making my spine tingle. *Oh, this is going to be a long night.*

"We may not have to worry about mind-bending," I replied. "I gave the Druids an assignment. They seem to love a good challenge so, you know, I figured it was worth a shot."

He sighed, then abandoned my embrace and sat up.

"I think it's best if I sleep downstairs," he said. "I saw a sofa in the lounge area."

"Really? There's no need to punish your back when we can just share a bed," I murmured. "I mean, we've done it before."

Blaze gave me a sideways glance, and I felt my pulse stutter. His midnight blues were darker than ever, distant lights twinkling in there—resonating with my own desire for him. But I was selfish. I wanted to sleep in his arms before we made our way back into Azure Heights.

"Caia, I'm not... I'm still under a celibacy oath," he breathed.

I frowned. "We're just sleeping. I'm beyond respectful of your vows, Blaze. I know to keep my hands to myself." I chuckled. "Come on, don't be stubborn. We're just sharing a bed. There's no point in you sleeping downstairs when there's some room up here."

"I am not worried about you keeping your hands off me," Blaze replied. "I'm worried about my ability to keep *my* hands off *you*. I'm afraid I'll sabotage myself and break the oath. It's a highly respected tradition among the members of my species."

I sat up, suddenly irritated. "You know what? Maybe it's a stupid tradition," I said. "Maybe you should consider changing it. I mean, you've proven your strength and resilience over and over since we've been here. Everything you've been through over the past couple of days alone should be worth at least one celibacy vow."

"You know it doesn't work like that," he grumbled.

"Okay," I replied. "I actually have a solution I think you might appreciate," I said, stifling a smirk.

He looked at me, his brow furrowed. "What might that be?"

"Let's get back to bed and sleep. And if either of us gets out of line, I can just bring up Rewa." I chuckled. "I mean, she was always an excellent wedge, don't you think?"

Blaze thought about it for a couple of seconds, then scoffed and climbed back into bed, pulling the comforter over the both of us. "I think Rewa is what Jovi would refer to as a 'boner killer'."

We both laughed wholeheartedly. Blaze pulled me into his arms, and we cuddled beneath the covers. I raised my head and kissed him, softly. He exhaled, his gaze clouded but his tone mildly reprimanding. "You're not making this easy, Caia."

"That was just an innocent goodnight kiss, Blaze. We're going to see Rewa tomorrow, for sure. I would at least like to sleep in your arms tonight before that," I muttered, then rested my head on his broad chest.

I listened to his heartbeat for a while, as he held me close and ran his fingers through my hair.

"We'll have to be careful tomorrow," he said.

"I know. I promise I won't go off script and reduce her to ashes," I grumbled, relaxing in his embrace, his body heat enveloping me and disrupting gravity itself.

"It's actually this fiery side of you that makes it difficult for me to respect my celibacy oath." Blaze scoffed, dropping a kiss on the top of my head.

"I can't shut it down, darling. But I can keep mentioning Rewa instead."

A couple of minutes went by as we settled and got comfortable with simply holding each other. It was a significant challenge, since we could both hear each other's frantic heartbeats. Self-control was key, however, no matter what lay ahead. If we couldn't keep ourselves in check, then we certainly couldn't pull anything off tomorrow in Azure Heights.

Giving in to our impulses could spell doom, not just for Blaze and me, but also for the rest of our team. As disconnected as our budding relationship was from the Nerakian mission, it was a good test of our resolve. I was falling hard and fast for the dragon, and he felt the same. It was the one thought that gave me the strength and patience to pull myself back whenever we caught fire.

"When we go back to The Shade, I'll talk to my father," Blaze said, his voice barely audible.

"About what?"

"What do you think?"

"Oh, the oath," I replied, then breathed out and locked my arms around his waist. His hand came up to caress my face, his knuckles gently brushing along my jawline. It made my heart sing —a midnight lullaby that spread through my thoughts and added weight to my eyelids.

"I don't know what to do, Caia, but I do know that now isn't the time to worry about it," he murmured. "I'd rather focus on making sure those bastards don't win, so we can get back to The Shade and *then* address my celibacy vow."

"I completely understand," I whispered, feeling myself slowly drift away.

Just as I surrendered, allowing the darkness to swallow me, his voice rippled through the nothingness preceding my dreams. "I love you."

I wanted to open my mouth and say something, but I was already submerged in a dream. A shapeless mystery which I'd yet to untangle or understand. Voices hummed around me. Smudges of color streaked across my field of vision. I followed the stream of my subconscious, wishing I could shout it from the bottom of my lungs, so he could hear me in his dreams.

I love you, Blaze.

27

HARPER

*T*his is bliss.

I opened my eyes, ever so slowly, as if worried that nothing that had happened during last night was real. That Caspian wasn't really there, and I was stuck in some cage in the depths of a daemon city. But he was. He lay on his back, keeping me close with one arm.

This was the epitome of love for me—this fluttering moment in time, where Caspian and I were together, bonded in every possible way. Our union went beyond the realm of the physical. My heart soared as I admired every inch of him, until my gaze found his, and I realized that I didn't want to leave this place.

We'll have to. At some point.

He gave me a lazy smile, then kissed me deeply. We hummed in marvelous unison, our souls attuned to one another. "It's the most wonderful thing to wake up next to you," he said, then rolled us over until he pinned me under his body. "Good morning, sunshine," he added.

"This is incredible," I breathed against his lips, bathing in the golden light of his aura. "I can feel what you feel on top of everything I'm already feeling."

He paused to look at me, his jade eyes filled with love. "I can feel you, too. I can see what you feel. I see the gold aura you're wearing, much like what you described seeing in me." He sighed, shaking his head slowly. "You were still figuring out what each color meant at the time. Do you know now?"

I nodded, running my fingernails up both sides of his torso. He groaned softly, the jade pools beneath his black eyelashes suddenly darkening. His golden aura burst even brighter, mingled with streaks of hot white.

"It's love, Lord Kifo. Gold is love. White... I think is desire," I muttered.

He grinned, then chewed his lower lip as he pulled the bedcovers away and tossed them on the floor, leaving us both naked.

"Good grief, Miss Hellswan, you are positively glowing like the sun this morning."

There was a hint of playfulness in his tone that did things to me. My blood rushed, my heart throbbing. "I could easily blame you for that," I whispered, tracing the contour of his lips with one fingertip.

"I take full responsibility, you extraordinary creature," he replied, then kissed me passionately.

Before we started this fire, however, I wondered how our union had affected him. I caught his face in my hands and gently pushed him away—just a couple of inches, so I could see his face.

"How are you feeling?" I asked, my brow slightly furrowed.

Caspian blinked several times, then smiled, as if finally

catching up with the conversation. We were both spiraling into a delicious daze with every second that passed.

"Different," he replied. "My soul is bound to yours for life, Harper. I can feel everything you feel, and... and it's the most incredible experience. I never thought I'd ever live through something like this. Also, this," he added, then stared at the empty glass on the nightstand.

I heard his subtle grunt, then watched a faint pulse ripple out of him. It knocked the glass onto the floor. It didn't break, landing on the carpet with a thud. I gasped, then smiled at him.

"Was... Was that a barrier?" I croaked.

He nodded. "I think so. I've been trying it out for the past hour," he said, then pointed at several other objects he'd managed to knock off nearby furniture and onto the floor—a vase, a picture frame, and a molten candle.

We both laughed, utterly entranced by this new development.

"I think you're becoming a Mara-sentry of sorts," I replied, beaming at him. "The first of your kind."

"I don't care if I grow an extra head, too, as long as I'm with you, Harper," Caspian murmured, then suddenly turned serious. "Please, don't dump me if I grow a second head. I'd be lost without you."

I stifled a chuckle, then resumed my new favorite activity— caressing his gorgeous face, my fingers tracing the sharp contours of his high cheekbones. "I'm even more into you now than I was before." I giggled like a teenage girl, my cheeks flaring as he dropped kisses down my neck.

"This is forever, Harper," he said, slightly amused. "I really hope you're not easily bored. Otherwise, I'm screwed."

We laughed again, rolling over onto our sides.

"I'm a lifetime deal, Caspian," I replied, planting a soft kiss on his lips.

He smiled. "Good," he whispered, and then all the joy seemed to drain out of him, as he remembered what still lay ahead of us. "If anything goes wrong tonight, we may not get another chance to be like this."

"Don't say that—"

He shushed me gently, pressing two fingers against my lips as he tightened his hold on me. "Yes, I know, we're shooting for victory and whatnot, but let's be realistic. There is still a chance we won't succeed. I just want you to know that... if we fail, if we lose tonight... I'm thankful to have had these moments with you, Miss Hellswan. I now have a piece of you, a sliver of your precious soul inside me, in a way. It gives me energy and strength like nothing I've experienced before. So, allow me to further enjoy you... *us*, this morning, until someone knocks on our door and drags us back to reality."

Tears glazed my eyes, and I pressed my lips tight in an attempt to stop myself from crying. I didn't think such happiness existed. I almost felt guilty for even experiencing something like this in the middle of our Nerakian mess. But I wouldn't have changed anything from what had already happened.

Every secret that had come unraveled, every stolen glance, every drop of blood we'd shed, and every risk we'd taken in our fight for liberation—it had all led to this singular, absolutely perfect moment, when it was just me and him. Forever compressed in one night and one lazy morning.

Caspian lowered his head to kiss me, but stilled, his lips barely an inch from mine, when we heard a knock on the door. We waited, quietly, as if conspiring to keep quiet and wait until whoever that was would leave so we could resume our lovemaking. I desperately needed more of him, and he could barely hold himself back at this point.

The second knock made me sigh.

"Who is it?" I called out, my gaze fixed on Caspian.

"It's Caia. I need to show you guys something downstairs!" she said from the other side of the door. I couldn't resist an eyeroll.

A couple of moments passed. My heart sank, dragged to the bottom by disappointment. The universe was cruel, and this was my reminder.

"I'll meet you all in the dining hall in about half an hour, forty-five minutes, okay?" Caia continued.

Hope blossomed in my chest, a thousand thrills lighting me up from the inside. It was truly mesmerizing to see and feel myself through Caspian like this. Everything we experienced was shared. The closer we were to one another, the harder it was to recognize ourselves as individuals.

"That's perfect," Caspian replied, raising his voice. "We'll see you there!"

"Okay, cool!" she replied.

I was willing to bet that she was smiling, without using my True Sight. I peeked through the door and chuckled at the sight of her leaving, a huge grin on her face. As soon as she went down the stairs, Caspian regained control of the situation and pulled me to him, loving me with everything he had.

I surrendered to him, body and soul, and regretted nothing, as we made love and gave ourselves a few more minutes of sheer bliss.

28

HARPER

The whole group was gathered in the dining room by the time Caspian and I made our way downstairs. I briefly scanned the group, reading emotions where possible. There was grief coming from the Manticore mother-daughter pair, and concern and determination from Colton and Nevis, as well as the Druids. There was love glowing through Hansa as she stood next to Jax. And there was hope, a colorful ribbon, coming out of Caia, who stood next to Blaze and motioned for Ryker and Laughlan to come forward.

A lot had happened last night, and not just between Caspian and me. There were plenty of stolen glances and flickers of loving smiles fluttering across the room—enough to tell me that the dynamic had shifted significantly between the pairs involved. Seeing Hansa and Jax so close had a warming effect on my heart. They both deserved another shot at happiness, even if it only lasted for one night.

We're shooting for longer here, though, I reminded myself.

Dion, Peyton, Wyrran, and Arrah were also present, while Alles was still locked in the room upstairs, for his own safety. We'd already agreed to leave him here with Wyrran to watch over him, as Dion was needed on our Azure Heights detail. He was one of the few Imen who knew the city, and Jax had already tested and confirmed that Dion had never been mind-bent like Alles.

"So I had a talk with Rush, Amina, Ryker, and Laughlan last night about possible ways to prevent Maras from mind-bending the likes of Blaze and me," Caia said. "Given that we're vulnerable to it and cannot afford a single mistake in the mission at hand, I started thinking about eye contact—the only way in which Maras can mind-bend someone."

Blaze listened intently, clearly curious. Judging by the anticipation building up inside me, Caia had yet to reveal the Druids' findings to anyone.

"The use of my wards is an obvious exception to the rule, of course," Jax replied. "But yes, Caia, you are correct in your assessment. Maras need to look into a creature's eyes for the mind-bending to have a full effect. But we have yet to figure out a way to stop that. I do know of a couple of instances from long ago where glasses were used to render mind-bending useless," he added, then put on a boyish smirk. "But we never really looked into it, nor did we try to find out if it was an absolute fact. As Maras, we're not really into publicizing ways to stop our mind-bending."

Heron chuckled. "That would've cost us a war or two."

"I totally get it," Caia replied, "but this time it's different. The times have changed, and our circumstances require that we use whatever method we have available to protect ourselves from the Exiled Maras. Thing is, even if we had glasses available, it wouldn't work with these jerks. If Blaze and I get caught while covering

Nevis, Neha, and Colton, they'll take our glasses off and mind-bend us. They're not stupid."

"True," Caspian replied, intrigued. "So what do you propose?"

Caspian was a bundle of emotions, all tucked beneath his dark, mysterious façade. It was a privilege to have access to it all, to feel it, thread by thread, as if flowing through me. The one thing he looked forward to the most was revenge. Nobody wanted to bring down the Mara Lords more than Caspian.

"Back on Earth, humans use contact lenses to help them see better," Caia said, prompting all of us Shadians to instantly nod in agreement.

"Yes! Completely undetectable," Avril chimed in, then pouted. "But we don't have anything like that here. Contact lenses are made of special plastics, from what I remember."

"That's correct, but..." Caia replied, then nodded at Ryker, who took a step forward and placed a small porcelain plate on the table.

There was a pink liquid in the middle of the dish, where four small, pale blue, semi-transparent lenses were set. "There are several species of algae growing in the surrounding lakes that can be used instead," Ryker explained. "Based on Caia's description of the earthly contact lenses and the purpose they served, I figured the algae would be best to experiment with. I processed a few leaves with a couple of bonding crystals and anti-inflammatory powders at high temperatures, until I was able to produce lenses like these," he added, pointing at the plate.

"We then tried them on ourselves," Laughlan continued, unable to wipe the satisfied grin off his face. "I devised the pink liquid as a natural lubricant, with calming essences extracted from local flowers. We dipped the lenses, then wore them throughout the night. The color difference is barely noticeable, especially if the wearer has blue eyes, so they are quite discreet. And we experienced no irritation or discomfort whatsoever. So, as far as wearing these is concerned, we've got you covered."

"But do they work?" Jax replied with a frown.

Laughlan smirked. "Well, we put them to the test, thanks to Rush and Amina, who were more than happy to assist."

Both Rush and Amina smiled, then shrugged. "They do work," Rush confirmed.

"We tried from different distances, we went full Mara on them, but we were not able to mind-bend them," Amina added. "I believe we officially have a means to stop mind-bending."

"Although, like Jax said earlier, we also advise that we keep this limited to this group," Rush said. "The last thing we want is other species and potential hostiles knowing they can use such gimmicks. And I'm not just talking about Neraka here."

"We're on the same page here, worry not," Hansa replied. "We're all well aware that peaceful Maras use mind-bending responsibly. Their ability is essential during investigations. GASP would never divulge this information unless hostile Maras were involved, as is the case here."

"Oh, we also added a bit of Druid protection magic to these bad boys," Ryker said, "to help preserve them for as long as possible before they need to be removed."

Blaze was stunned, lighting up like a little kid in an amusement park after he was told he could try all the rides—even the ones he was too young to go on.

"Can I try them on?" he asked, moving closer to the plate.

"By all means," Laughlan replied. "In fact, let's do a brief demonstration. Jax, please do us a favor and mind-bend our good dragon here."

Jax stilled, his gaze darting between Blaze and Laughlan. He then looked at Blaze with questioning eyes, demanding his approval. "Are you sure?" Jax muttered. Blaze smiled and nodded enthusiastically. Jax's eyes glimmered gold as he unleashed his power over the dragon. "Blaze, I need you to jump three times on one foot, then three times on the other."

Blaze's expression went blank as he obeyed the command and jumped thrice on each foot. Ryker and Laughlan exchanged glances, crossing their arms and nodding in unison. These two could bring down an entire planet if left to their own devices. I liked them.

"Okay, Jax, can you confirm that Blaze responded fully to your mind-bending?" Laughlan then asked.

"I can definitely confirm," Jax replied. "All the signs are there. Blaze, as we already knew, is susceptible to mind-bending."

"Good," Laughlan muttered, then motioned for Blaze to put on the lenses. Blaze caught one on his index finger, then carefully placed it over his iris. He took a deep breath, then proceeded to apply the other. We all watched, the excitement vibrating throughout the entire dining room.

It was one thing to have Rush and Amina tell us it worked, and something else entirely to see it with our own eyes. Blaze blinked several times as he adjusted to the contacts.

"These feel a little weird," he murmured. "I mean, I'm comfortable wearing them, just not used to them."

"Mhm. Jax, please, try mind-bending our good dragon here again," Laughlan said.

Jax nodded, his eyes glimmering gold again as he shifted his focus onto Blaze. "Blaze, I need you to jump three times on one foot, then three times on the other."

A couple of moments passed, until Blaze chuckled. "You know, without the actual mind-bending, you guys sound pretty funny when you try to order us around," he replied.

"Blaze, I order you to jump," Jax insisted, his voice gruff and his gaze incredibly intense, as he stepped forward and amplified his mind-bending.

Blaze crossed his arms, grinning defiantly. "Holy crap, these things actually work." He chuckled, sincerely relieved.

Even Jax was pleased, the shadow of a smile rushing across his face. Caia moved closer and put her arms around Blaze's waist, beaming with joy.

"There we go. Problem solved!" She giggled.

Blaze lovingly cupped her face in his palms, then kissed her softly, leaving the rest of us out of breath. "Thank you, Caia, for making this happen."

Caia blushed, suddenly tiny and shrugging, then pointed at the Druids.

"It wouldn't have been possible without them," she said.

Hansa smiled. "Darling, it's your spirit of initiative that gave us a defense method against the Exiled Maras. Your determination and your resourcefulness. After all, you looked all the way back to your planet for a way to protect our dragon and our team. It says a lot about you."

We all nodded in agreement. I was so proud of Caia and her dedication. With creatures like her on board, we definitely had a winning hand.

Heron narrowed his eyes and pursed his lips.

"I thought you were on a celibacy vow or something," he quipped.

Blaze frowned, tearing his puppy eyes off Caia and shifting his gaze to Heron. "Yeah, and?"

"Well, are you sure you two should even be kissing?" Heron replied, grinning mischievously. Avril nudged him with her elbow, but he didn't quit, stifling a chuckle.

Behind them, Nevis stared at Blaze and Caia, a faint smile stretching his lips. His aura was pale, in a multitude of colors—

quite difficult to interpret, compared to other species. There was something curious about him, something I'd yet to put my finger on, triggered by the persistence with which he stared at the contact lenses on the plate.

I figured it had something to do with protecting his Dhaxanians from the Exiled Maras. It didn't seem like a bad idea, given their history.

"You worry about yourself, pipsqueak," Blaze shot back, then wrapped his arms around Caia and held her close, surprising not just her, but also the rest of the room. I'd spotted the feelings buzzing between them already. I knew that this was just the dragon's way of making it official.

"You're lucky you're a big-ass dragon. Otherwise I would've had a better comeback," Heron muttered, feigning disgruntlement.

They all chuckled, and I took a step back and briefly scanned every member of our group. The day had started out well, in a way. Having something to protect our dragon from the Exiled Maras was a huge step forward. It certainly boosted the collective morale.

We had one hell of a mission ahead of us. The least we could do was head into it with clear heads and full hearts. We were on the right track.

W e spent the rest of the day preparing for the mission. With our weapons, invisibility spells, and supplies ready, we gathered back into the dining room for a final roundup. Jax and Hansa checked the maps once more, as Fiona showed them the potential escape routes on the eastern side of the mountain on which Azure Heights had been built.

Zane and Velnias exchanged ideas for disabling Correction Officers as discreetly as possible, while Nevis, Colton, and Neha went over their scenario for the Mara Lords.

Ramin, Harper's faithful new companion, sat on the branches of a potted tree in the corner, watching everything intently. Harper had told me about Neha's stories regarding the fire spirit, and how it would sometimes communicate through the Ekars. I wondered if that was the fire spirit of Neraka watching us through the Ekar's eyes.

"Ramin should stay here," Pheng-Pheng suggested. "Given where we're going and what we're about to do."

"Oh, absolutely," Harper agreed, then lowered her head to be on the same level with Ramin. "I need you to stay in the inn for now," she said to the fiery red bird. "I'll need your help later down the line," she added, then straightened her back and gave Pheng-Pheng a sideways glance. "I wonder if he understands *everything* we say."

Pheng-Pheng shrugged. "I wouldn't be surprised. He's a smart one, well above the average for his species."

The Ekar wasn't exactly a point of focus for her, given the circumstances. I could see the pain flickering in Pheng-Pheng's eyes. There was still so much of it stiffening her frame and clutching her heart. I almost felt it myself.

"Listen, I can see you're in a lot of pain, and I'm sorry. For what it's worth, I think it'll get better with time," I said to her, giving her shoulder a soft squeeze. "I don't know what it feels like right now, and I hope I never do, but I do know that time dulls everything in the end."

"Except love," Pheng-Pheng replied, putting on a weak smile. "My love for my sisters will never go away."

"And it never should," I agreed. "We'll make them pay, I promise."

"Oh, I know we will," she shot back with a cold grin.

Hansa cleared her throat, signaling the rest of us to pay attention.

"Okay, so, here we are," she said. "This is it. The moment we've been fighting for since we found out about this wretched alliance between the daemons and the Exiled Maras, and the extent to which they're willing to go in order to sustain their sickening addiction to souls."

"We're clear on the teams, as per our previous discussions," Jax continued, crossing his arms and looking at each of us with a mixture of pride and encouragement. "Harper, Caspian, Fiona, Zane, Pheng-Pheng, and Arrah will lead Lumi's extraction. You know what you all have to do. Do not derail or delay the plan in any way. Every second counts, from the moment we enter the city."

Harper looked at Caspian, then Pheng-Pheng, Fiona, Zane, and Arrah. They nodded at each other, not needing words to confirm that they were clearly a tight crew, and that they would stop at nothing to get the swamp witch out of Azure Heights. My stomach churned at the thought of what trial lay ahead for Harper, in particular, but I pushed the fear back down to the bottom of my consciousness, refusing to let it bother me.

Caspian rested a hand on the small of Harper's back. She'd also told me about the previous night, including Caspian's newly developed sentry abilities. He could feel everything she felt now. I also knew how nervous she was about her task, wondering how good she was at keeping that under control. The last thing she would've wanted was to let him think she was having any second thoughts. It had taken plenty of talking to get him on board with this in the first place. From the look on his face, he was still mostly okay with it.

"Yes, we're clear on orders and protocols," Harper replied, keeping her chin high and slowly descending into soldier mode. She had this clean-cut expression I'd learned to recognize; a signal that she was detaching herself from the emotional side of things and transforming into the "Cool Cucumber" we'd learned to both fear and admire. It was the single most important feature she'd picked up from her father, Tejus—that ability to clear her head and go into the war zone with razor-sharp focus.

"Good. Hansa, Dion, and I will guard the tunnel exit in Azure Heights," Jax said. "We'll make sure no one comes around, by accident or otherwise. Since the door will be unlocked once we come through, we can't risk any curious Maras or Imen popping by," he added, then pointed at the exit on the map. "This will also be our gathering point. Once everyone does what they've been tasked with, we'll meet back here. Clear?"

We all nodded this time.

"Hundurr and Rover will guard the tunnel entrance with Vesta," Hansa said. "We'll need this part of our access route into Azure Heights protected. Should the worst-case scenario happen, should we fail in any way, Vesta will make sure no hostiles come through and track anyone back to Meredrin. The town must be protected at all costs."

Peyton stepped forward, one hand resting on his sword handle. "I'll take two of my Maras and keep her company. The rest will continue to guard the town on a prolonged watch, as discussed."

"Thank you, Peyton," Hansa replied, then looked at Vesta. "No matter what happens, you must protect the delegation. Even if we fail to come back, you must find another way to get the swamp witch out. As soon as that shield comes down, there's absolutely no doubt in my mind that GASP will bring in troops to rescue us. Someone will need to make sure they know what happened, if... if we're gone," she added, her voice trembling slightly.

"Rest assured, I've got you covered," Vesta said.

Idris and Rayna stood behind her. "Count on us for anything," Idris added. "You gave us our lives back. We'll make sure that Lumi gets out, one way or another."

"Okay, but let's focus on us actually succeeding in this mission, because you people are bumming me out," I interjected, checking the maps. "I'll take Heron, Scarlett, Patrik, and Velnias through the lower half of the city for our side of the mission. We've got the explosives and spells ready to rig, and we know the way into the prison already. We'll handle Cadmus's extraction."

Velnias crossed his arms, narrowing his eyes at the map.

"If we get an extra minute in there, I'd like to try and get a couple of Maras out of there," he muttered. "Friends of mine, pacifists themselves. They'll come in handy for stage two of the plan."

Hansa thought about it for a second, then nodded. "But only if you have the time. Otherwise, we'll have to make do with the fighters we already have on our side," she replied, then looked at Nevis, Neha, and Colton. "You three will pay an unannounced visit to the Mara Lords. I presume you'll know when to make your entrance, ensuring they're all together, including Rewa, in Darius's absence. Caia and Blaze will cover your backs, invisible and now protected by their anti-bending lenses."

"That is correct," Nevis replied. "We'll keep them busy for fifteen minutes. Neha, Colton, and I have already agreed on what to tell them."

"Okay, just make sure you don't screw us in the process," Heron muttered. I nudged him and gave him a meaningful frown. He chuckled in response.

Nevis, on the other hand, seemed equally amused. "Rest assured, if I wanted to get my hands on Avril, I wouldn't betray this entire alliance to do it. I may be extreme, but even I have my limits."

Hansa clicked her teeth, discreetly pulling us all back to the main conversation.

"Everyone else will stay in Meredrin," she said. "Wyrran will watch over Alles, and the rest of the delegation will prepare for stage two—both scenarios. Whether we fail or succeed, it will be up to you to help us complete this quest and get Lumi out."

Neha cleared her throat. "Our people are also stationed in the gorges, and by 'our people', I mean all of us—rogue Imen, Adlets, Manticores, and Dhaxanians," she replied, smiling softly at the delegation members. "Whatever you need, you can rely on our troops. We have Ekars in place to send messages, and I believe

Wyrran has his own scouts to send into the Valley of Screams. All this, of course, is if we fail to return."

"However, I trust we will all be back in one piece," Nevis retorted, slightly irritated. Something told me he didn't tolerate the prospect of failure much. Yet another thing he and Heron had in common. They even scoffed almost simultaneously whenever the worst-case scenario was even brought up. "I have no intention of dying at the hands of bloodsucking bastards."

"Oh, trust me, we are on the same page," Jax replied with a firm nod. "We're all getting out of this alive. Am I clear?" he asked, looking at all of us.

The agreement was vocal and in perfect unison, a resounding *Yes*.

"We leave in ten," Hansa said. "Get ready."

Tension gathered in my shoulders as I leaned against the dining table. I was already ready and fully geared up. I'd even put my backpack on. Heron moved closer to me, leaving only an inch between our bodies. My core buzzed, my heart delighted by the vicinity.

"Are you okay?" he asked, lowering his voice as he carefully analyzed my expression.

"Yeah. Just bracing myself for what comes next," I replied, resting a hand on his chest. "Stage one is scary enough as it is, based on what we all agreed to do. We *have* to make it to stage two, though."

He pressed his lips against my forehead. "I know. We'll get through it," he said. "This is a secret extraction. We're not causing a ruckus this time. We know the city already, unlike our previous... adventures. We know that city almost inside out, in fact. And, besides, with you by my side? I told you, I'll take on the whole freakin' planet."

I chuckled softly, then raised my chin so I could kiss him. His lips were sweet and soft, like midsummer roses at dusk. He filled me with the energy I needed to get through this.

"Remember, I've got a lot of dating to do with you," he added, wearing a playful smirk.

"I think I just puked a little in my mouth," Nevis interjected with the grace of a pachyderm in a china shop, his tone ice-cold and flat.

Heron and I both rolled our eyes, then scowled at him. Nevis raised an eyebrow in response.

"Your finesse is beyond reproach," Heron shot back.

Nevis shrugged, stifling a grin. "Perhaps keep the nauseatingly sweet couples' crap for the bedroom, loudmouth," he retorted. "It'll make it easier to be around you two. Even if I weren't partial to Avril, I'd still be a little sick."

Heron scoffed. This was their new favorite pastime. Poking one another, then deliberating on who had the sickest burns. They'd gone from rivals to weird friends almost overnight, and I was both amused and somewhat horrified by their bromance.

"You're lucky my girlfriend likes you. Otherwise I would've made more of an effort to make you eat your words," Heron replied.

"And you're lucky I tolerate you. Otherwise you would've been turned into an icicle decoration for my bedroom mantelpiece," Nevis said dryly.

"Ooh, burn," I whispered, then burst into laughter.

I let it all out, doubling over, thankful to have such crazy, incredible people in my life. I needed the chuckle. It fed my soul as we delved into our quest to rescue the one creature who could get us back home. Sure, we wanted to free Neraka, but the selfish part of me was simply eager to go back to our worlds.

I want to go home so badly.

30

HARPER

With our backpacks loaded and our shields mounted on top, we prepared for the two-mile trip to the abandoned red garnet mine. The sun was about to set, streaks of pink and flaming orange cutting across the sky. I put my hood, mask, and goggles on. I'd no longer need them by the time we reached Azure Heights. The plan was to get there in the evening, when there was less activity from the resident Imen, and thus less to worry about in case of combat.

Vesta hugged both her parents tight, swallowing back tears as they said their farewells.

"You come back to us, you hear me?" Idris said, his voice trembling as he kissed his daughter's forehead.

Vesta nodded, giving them both a weak smile. She then joined our group, and Peyton led us out of Meredrin. We used the boats this time, to conserve energy. The small vessels cut across the rippling lake waters. I looked back and watched the delegation,

Sienna, Tobiah, and our hosts stay behind. Hundurr and Rover swam along, surprisingly agile. They had impressive stamina, considering the distance they had to cover through the water. Vesta and Caia were ready to assist them if they needed help, though.

"We'll be at the mine in less than an hour," Peyton said, rowing with smooth, controlled movements.

We used the small canals connecting the lakes to get across and reach the southwestern edge of the region. Leaving the boats tied to a small jetty hidden beneath sprawling greenery, we made our way on foot for the rest of the short journey.

"Are you sure about leaving Sienna and Tobiah back there?" Caia asked Hansa.

Hansa replied with a brief nod. "If anything happens to us, the town and the delegation will be protected," she said. "They'll need all the help they can get if rescuing Lumi ends up falling on their shoulders. The same goes for a sudden ambush of any kind."

"Which is why we're taking this short trip the old-fashioned way," Peyton added as he led the way toward a large mound covered in thick shrubs and gnarled old trees. "The smaller our imprint on this area, the slimmer the chances that daemons might pick up a scent or trail our footsteps back to the lakes."

"Is that it?" I asked, pointing at the wooded hill.

"Yes. The mine is at the base. The tree crowns keep it out of sight," Peyton replied.

The closer we got, the clearer we saw how easy it could be for someone to miss it if they walked past it. The mine entrance was partially collapsed, nestled between curling trees with thick and heavy crowns. From certain angles, there was nothing there that could invite the thought of a mine, or any kind of shelter, for that matter—other than the trees, of course.

"Few know of its existence in these parts of Neraka," Peyton continued. "This was one of the first mines used to extract red garnet, back when the Maras first came here. It's known to have collapsed, but the workers didn't have a clue as to how much of it actually became inaccessible."

"What do you mean?" Hansa asked.

"Well, the entire tunnel didn't cave in. Just a hundred or so yards of it," Peyton explained. "My Maras and I once explored the above-ground length of the tunnel. We drilled holes here and there, just to see if there were parts of the passageways that we could still use. After a couple of weeks of digging and mapping, we were able to figure out that the collapse itself only covers about a hundred and twenty yards, at most."

"Shouldn't we just dig in from where the tunnel is clear again, then?" I asked. "Instead of working our way through the mine?"

"Strategically speaking, it wouldn't work to our advantage," Peyton replied. "It is, in fact, easier if your Druid or one of your fae clears the collapsed tunnel directly. It will take less time, as well, and it will keep our access route secret. Digging on the surface anywhere beyond the hill would leave the tunnel open to discovery."

"There are daemons and probably Correction Officers roaming these parts of the land, now," Jax muttered. "Especially after our stunt at Ragnar Peak."

"Absolutely," Peyton smirked, then pointed at the entrance. I had to use my True Sight to see the opening, framed with dark wood beams. "There. We'll go through there."

"Harper, how are we looking, position-wise?" Hansa asked me, just as we reached the mine entrance.

I looked around again, using my True Sight.

"Pleased to confirm we've got zero hostiles on a three-mile radius at this point," I replied. "There is *some* movement on the far west side, but it's getting farther away, beyond my scope."

"Perfect," Peyton muttered, then went first into the mine.

One by one, we followed. As I took my hood and goggles off, I quickly adjusted to the pitch black surrounding us. This was just the first pocket of the mine, with three possible offshoots—three narrow, rectangular tunnel openings.

The walls wore a faint red shimmer here and there, remnants of raw red garnet deposits.

"You'll go this way," Peyton said, pointing at the tunnel opening to the left. "The other two lead deeper and into the north. This one goes south."

Vesta settled on a large rock by the entrance, clicking her teeth at Hundurr and Rover.

"Come on, fellas. Looks like we'll be here a while." She chuckled.

The pit wolves sniffed around and stayed back. Hundurr kept his red gaze focused on the outside, while Rover sat on his hind legs next to Vesta, looking at us with big, curious eyes.

"You look after Vesta and wait for us here, okay?" Scarlett addressed Hundurr.

He groaned, as if unhappy with the order, but eventually huffed and lay down as a sign of submission. Scarlett gave him and Rover a quick scratch behind the ears.

"Don't worry, Scarlett," Vesta said, "we get the boring side of the mission. Hundurr and Rover can hunt something nearby if they get hungry. Or bored."

Scarlett chuckled softly, then Hansa gave Vesta a gentle shoulder squeeze.

"Keep your eyes open," Hansa said. "If any hostiles come through from the tunnels, it's up to you, the Maras and the pit wolves to stop them from getting out. The same goes for fiends coming in from the outside, looking to use the tunnels."

Vesta offered a firm nod in response.

"Be careful," the fae murmured.

Hansa turned around to face us and motioned for Arrah to go deeper into the mine.

"Let's go," she said. "Your turn to guide us, Arrah."

We made our way down through the narrow shaft, using the carved steps. I welcomed the tranquil darkness enveloping us as we reached the collapsed part of the tunnel. Faced with a wall of crushed stones, we stood back, and Caia and Patrik worked together to unblock the passageway. After all, Caia was a fae—she could manipulate all the natural elements, though fire was her strong suit. In this case, she focused on her ability to work the earth.

Caspian held my hand, and we exchanged glances. My nerves were already stretched thin, and we hadn't even reached Azure Heights yet. Caspian was equally on edge. I gave him a soft, reassuring smile. The warm, golden light of his love filled me to the brim, easing the tension and reminding me of what was at stake here.

I rejected failure as an option.

31

AVRIL

It took Caia and Patrik less than an hour to ease our access through the tunnel. The move was a joint effort to shift and drill through large slabs of stone, using her earth elemental abilities and a plethora of Druid spells. They were, of course, assisted by Velnias, Zane, and Fiona, who used their strength to remove the stone clutter.

We made our way through the narrow passageway that resulted from their teamwork. We had a smooth trip ahead, keeping a steady but rapid pace. Harper used her True Sight along the way, looking at the terrain above. We passed several small groups of daemons and Exiled Maras searching the northern edge of the Valley of Screams for us.

By the time we reached the gorges, hostile activities increased.

"Fifty daemons and twenty Correction Officers directly above us," Harper muttered, keeping her voice low. "Headed west now."

We kept quiet for most of the journey, in case anyone had their

ears aimed at the ground. The daemons were well aware of potential tunnels running beneath the gorges, so it stood to reason that
we should keep a low profile so as not to alert them to our
presence.

"A good daemon scout could track us above ground, if they
hear us," Zane said.

The tunnel itself ran in a straight line beneath the ravines. At
some point, I caught a whiff of moss and heard water running
above. We were directly under a river flowing into the plains.
Going through my memories of the Maras' city, the green fields
surrounding it, and the rivers snaking toward the eastern ocean,
compared to where we'd come from, I had a pretty good idea as to
where we were.

By the time we reached the plains, I knew our location with
great accuracy. If given a map, I could even point us out—invisible
dots sneaking in from the northeast, directly under the southern-
most of three rivers crossing the fields toward the ocean.

"We have two miles left," Arrah said. "How's it looking
up there?"

Harper used her True Sight again, then smirked. "It's clear.
There's movement farther down, but they're more than a
mile away."

"Perfect. We can run till we reach the mountain," Hansa
replied.

Arrah gave her a brief glance over the shoulder, then nodded
and started running. We dashed after her, shooting through the
tunnel.

Less than half an hour later, we reached the mountain base.
Harper looked up, frowning as she scanned the area.

"The first moon is up," she muttered. "There's more activity on the lower levels, particularly on the first, second, and third. Imen are going home now. Correction Officers are out in pairs and groups of four. Some are wearing red lenses, as we'd suspected."

"How many red lenses do you see?" I asked.

"One per group. Some don't wear them, though. The fifth and sixth levels are heavily guarded, from what I can see, but I don't remember exactly what's in each of the buildings they're posted in front of."

"Any daemons?" Velnias replied.

"I don't see any from here," Harper said. "However, there are several buildings with meranium coating. I'm not able to tell which is the one we're looking for."

Hansa cursed under her breath. "We'll need to find someone who can tell us, like we expected."

"Yeah, I, too, was hoping for an easy one on Lumi's location." Harper sighed.

Jax pursed his lips, then looked at Caspian.

"Lord Kifo, do you think a superior Correction Officer might know? Nod or blink once," he said.

Caspian thought about it for a moment, then nodded and instantly cringed from a burning sensation. That blood oath was such a pain.

"Any of the Mara Lords' family members and lieutenants might know, as well," Zane replied. "Like Vincent, for example. I'm sure Fiona would love to catch up with him," he added, chuckling softly.

Fiona smirked. "Absolutely."

Hansa took a deep breath, then nodded slowly.

"All right," she said. "Let's head up, then, and scope out our exit area first."

We kept going as the tunnel began its ascension through the mountain.

"Crap, this part of the tunnel is coated with meranium," Harper muttered. "I can't see past it."

"Then be prepared for anything once we reach the top," Jax whispered.

The tunnel got narrower as we passed the middle levels of the city. There were carved steps for us to use, along with numerous swamp witch inscriptions on the stone walls. I ran my fingers over them as we continued our climb.

"What are these supposed to do?" I asked.

"Protection for the tunnel," Arrah replied, panting from her climb. "This is one of the few tunnels that no one left in Azure Heights knows about. All the rebels who've used it before have either fled or died. They went to a lot of trouble to keep this route hidden, just in case a day like this might come."

The tunnel ended at a small square door. We all stopped behind Arrah, listening carefully to the world beyond the meranium walls. My nostrils flared as I tried to catch as many foreign scents as possible, in a bid to identify hostiles outside.

"The door's made of meranium, too," Harper whispered, frowning.

"And charmed," Arrah added, then produced a pair of thin metal tools, which she used to pick the lock. We all watched in silence, somewhat befuddled. Picking up on the question we all wanted to ask, Arrah smirked. "Only a handful of the rebels had a key to this," she murmured. "Like I said, this tunnel was super secured. I never got a key because I never saw the last Iman who had it after he ran away last year. But I can still pick a lock."

"Yeah, that's what I'm wondering. When and how did you learn to do that?" I replied, my voice low.

She shrugged. "I had to get around the city without being noticed," she muttered. "Plus, the Rohos kept a lot of documents under lock and key in their mansion. I was a curious child."

I stifled a chuckle. She successfully unlocked the door, put her tools away, and prepared her crossbow. We'd laced all our short arrows with Pheng-Pheng's venom, to quickly and discreetly disable any hostiles coming our way, prior to killing them.

Arrah opened the door slowly, keeping the crossbow aimed through the increasing crack. Moonlight came through, along with a gust of cool mountain air. She briefly glanced at us, then nodded and slipped out of the tunnel.

We followed in silence, then closed the door behind us. It was fitted with a stone mask on top of its meranium plating, perfectly blending into the stone wall of the mountain and facing the back garden of some rich Mara on the sixth level.

I heard Jax mutter a curse under his breath as we all looked around. We'd made it into Azure Heights, only none of us had known exactly where the tunnel would lead, other than the general proximity of the sixth level. We'd gotten the level right, but we were all standing in the middle of a gorgeous flower garden behind a white marble mansion—two floors of noble grandeur, with forged iron decorative details and a plethora of garden sculptures poking out of the sea of fragrant flowers.

We all quickly ate our first batch of invisibility paste and put on our red garnet lenses. A minute later, we were all just faint ripples in the air.

"Get ready to deploy," Hansa whispered. "Dion, Jax, and I will wait for you here."

We split up as per our initial plan, headed for the front of the house, when footsteps made us freeze. I held my breath as a male Mara walked into the garden, frowning and looking around. He'd heard something, for sure. He sniffed the air, visibly concerned.

My team was first on the stone path in front of the Mara, with Harper's group behind us, and Hansa, Jax, and Dion at the back, by the hidden tunnel door. I looked over at Heron, who didn't let the

Mara out of his sight. He gave me a brief look, then slowly drew his sword.

"Who's there?" the Mara asked, his voice low and rough.

He seemed relatively young, though it was impossible for me to ascertain a possible age, given his species. But he was on edge. He fumbled through his coat pocket and produced a red lens. My heart skipped a beat and my stomach tightened as I quickly realized that we were in the backyard of a well-to-do Exiled Mara who knew we could very well be in this part of town, using invisibility spells. He'd been briefed.

Heron didn't give him a chance to put the lens on, though.

He dashed across the stone path and put his blade up to the elegantly dressed fiend's throat. The Mara stilled and gasped. The sword pressed against his pale skin. He instantly put his hands up in a defensive gesture.

"Please don't hurt me," he whimpered.

I couldn't help but scoff.

"Where are they keeping the swamp witch?" Heron hissed.

The Mara trembled, his expression morphing from one of shock to one of horror. "I don't know, I swear! They don't tell us."

"What if I don't believe you?" Heron replied.

I looked around, checking our team's expressions. Nobody seemed to believe the Exiled Mara, and everyone was ready to intervene, if needed. The tension was high.

"I'm telling the truth. I'm just a magistrate," the Mara replied. "I'm not in the inner circle. I don't know where they're keeping her!"

He reached for his sword, but that was a foolish move. Heron was infinitely faster. A split second later, the Exiled Mara's head rolled into a nearby flowerbed. Scarlett rushed to get his body, while Patrik grabbed the head. They hid them behind a gazebo, beneath a rich layer of crimson flowers.

Hansa exhaled sharply.

"Clearly, they're taking precautions," she whispered. "This doesn't change the mission, of course. Do what you have to do. Be careful. And may the Daughters be with you, every step of the way."

We all nodded and headed out of the garden.

This was it. The moment we'd been mentally preparing for over the past week. Our make-or-break moment.

Our way out of here.

32

HARPER

A rrah, Caspian, Pheng-Pheng, Fiona, Zane, and I moved through the sixth level of Azure Heights, while Avril and the others made their way down into the prison, and Blaze and Caia tailed our trio of rebel-allied leaders. The city was on alert, with Correction Officers wearing red lenses at every corner.

It made it difficult for us to sneak around, but we managed to stay out of sight. The numerous alleys and narrow spaces between neighboring buildings helped a lot.

The Exiled Maras were out enjoying the fresh evening air. The taverns and cafes were open, the terraces loaded with nobles sipping on blood. This time, however, something was horribly wrong with the picture, and it took a lot of self-control to stop myself from going out and beheading each and every one of these bastards.

There were plenty of Maras drinking blood from crystal glasses, but some had Imen sitting on their knees at a few tables, mind-bent and docile as their overlords fed directly from open wounds on their necks and wrists. The Maras draining the Imen grinned and giggled, their mouths smeared with fresh blood, as they exchanged gossip and pleasantries.

It made my stomach churn.

Caspian squeezed my hand and offered me an understanding look, then nodded at the end of the alley to our left. My breath hitched at the sight of Amalia, Emilian's daughter and heir to House Obara. My blood boiled as I remembered how overly fond she was of Caspian, despite her claim that they were just friends.

She was escorted by two Correction Officers walking toward the dead end. There was a small but pretty-looking house there, with flowerpots and lights flickering in the wall-mounted fixtures. She went inside, while the COs waited by the door, looking around occasionally.

We moved in, hidden in a small nook between two houses. I used my True Sight to keep an eye on the COs and to see what Amalia was up to inside. I stilled at the sight of her walking into the living room and sinking her fangs into the throat of a young Iman girl. Her parents cried as they tried to stop her, but Amalia hissed and mind-bent them into submission. They were forced to watch as she fed on their daughter.

"Imen live in these parts, I see," I murmured, then looked at Caspian. He nodded. Fiona, Pheng-Pheng, and Zane looked at me, slightly confused.

The only one who knew what I was watching and could also speak up was Arrah. "They breed them in this neighborhood," she whispered. "They're mind-bent into thinking they're well-to-do, and they run good businesses on this level. They're just populating the Maras' feeding ground. But they're dying out, still. There used to be hundreds of them here."

"I'm counting a few dozen in this quarter, at most." I scoffed, scanning the area briefly.

Each house lining the alley was home to a family of just three or four Imen.

"This is where the richest of Maras come to feed," Arrah explained.

"I think I'm going to be sick," Fiona groaned, shaking her head in disgust.

"I wish I could bring my entire nest here," Pheng-Pheng muttered. "We'd have the Maras on the ground in excruciating pain in a matter of minutes."

"Yeah, but they've got red lenses and swamp witch magic on their side," Zane reminded her with a raised eyebrow. "You wouldn't get to do as much damage as you'd like."

Pheng-Pheng sighed, her shoulders dropping with disappointment. "I know..."

"Is this what it's always been like?" I asked Arrah, still coping with what I was watching unfold before my very eyes. She nodded, and the sadness in her pale green eyes made my heart hurt.

I looked around again, noticing that Amalia was still in the house, taking her sweet time with the poor Iman girl. It had to stop, and we needed to find out where they were keeping Lumi. Two birds, one sword.

I walked out of our hiding place, prompting the rest of my team to follow me.

"What are you doing?" Caspian whispered.

"We need information, and your bitch of an ex-girlfriend needs to stop feeding on Imen children," I hissed. "We're going in."

I expected opposition, but all I got was the sound of a crossbow clicking behind me. An arrow shot past Caspian and me and lodged into the throat of one of the COs. Arrah quickly reloaded and released the second one, just as the other CO put on his red lens and spotted us.

"She was never my girlfriend," Caspian muttered, then rushed down the alley and pulled one of the COs out of sight, dumping his poisoned body behind a large potted hydrangea-like bush.

Zane tossed the other one on top, as if he were just a ragdoll.

"They're done for," the daemon prince said, then smirked at me. "You've got spunk. I like you."

I looked at Caspian, wearing a playful half-smile. "Just teasing," I whispered. "But I still hate her guts."

"By all means, then," Caspian replied, motioning for me to go inside the house.

I opened the door slowly, followed by the others. Upon reaching the living room, I resisted the sudden urge to wretch at the sight of the gruesome scene before me.

The Imen parents were forced to kneel, while Amalia suckled on the Iman girl's neck. The poor creature was turning pale. Her mother and father were still and stone-faced, their eyes blank and glassy.

"You know, if you keep killing your food like this, you'll wipe out the whole pantry by winter," I said, gritting my teeth as I stepped into the living room.

Amalia froze, then looked up, visibly confused. Her mouth and chin were covered in blood, further pushing my boundaries. I was a vampire; I understood feeding on someone for sustenance, but my species had made progress. And so had the Maras back on Calliope. Amalia and her people's habits were absolutely disgusting—especially since she'd chosen to feed on the young daughter. She could've at least gone for one of the parents.

She slipped a pair of red lens glasses on her nose, then sneered at me, baring her bloody fangs.

"What a surprise," she said, her voice annoyingly sweet for my turbulent state of mind. She beamed at the sight of Caspian standing right behind me. "Caspian, my love! You've come back!"

I scoffed, rolling my eyes and drawing my swords. "You must be joking," I replied.

Amalia raised an eyebrow at the others, slightly disgusted. She completely ignored me. "Caspian, my darling, since when do you hang out with these fiends? They're the worst of the worst."

"Amalia, the jig's up," I said, drawing her attention. I pointed a sword at her. "Step away from the Iman girl and tell us where you're keeping the swamp witch."

She grinned, licking her lips, then slowly stood up. The Iman girl slouched to the side, unconscious, blood dripping from the open wound on her neck. Fiona rushed to her, moving around the armchair so she wouldn't get too close to Amalia, who watched her with narrowed eyes.

Fiona applied healing potion to the Iman girl's neck, then bit into her wrist and pushed it against her purplish lips. "Drink, sweetie. It'll help you heal faster," she murmured. The girl moaned and started drinking.

"I really dislike having my dinner plans foiled," Amalia said, her tone flat.

"I really dislike seeing you, in general, and yet here we are," I shot back. "Now, talk. Where's Lumi?"

Amalia raised her eyebrows in surprise, then chuckled. "I see you've done your homework."

"I've done a lot more than that since we last met," I replied.

"Caspian, my love, you look a bit... smitten," she said, shifting her focus to him. "I take it she's spread her legs already?"

That set me off a little too fast. I shot forward and brought my sword down, but Amalia dodged it gracefully. She produced a long knife from the folds of her pale blue dress and tried to cut me with it.

I blocked her hit, then engaged in a double-blade attack. She whipped out a second knife, making me wonder what kind of arsenal she'd stashed in that dress of hers.

"If she takes out a catapult from under there, I'm going to be pissed," Zane muttered.

Had I not been darting left and right, fighting Amalia, I would've laughed. She was good, though. I had to give her credit. Light on her feet and extremely agile, she avoided my hits and came back with twice the fury. Although she only had two long knives, she still managed to cut me.

I hissed from the pain but brought a sword down in a diagonal slash. She caught the blade with her knives crossed, then kicked me in the stomach. I grunted and slid back a couple of feet, surprised to find myself panting. She was making me do all the hard work.

"I'm going to cut you down, eventually," I said. "Talk, Amalia, and I will spare you."

She giggled, as if I'd just told her a great joke. "Don't be ridiculous. You're food. I don't talk to food," she replied, then gave Caspian a warm smile. "My love, we used to be so close. You used to come to me every night with flowers and fresh blood. Now you're hanging out with our meals? Honey... I miss you. Come back, and I promise I'll have Daddy spare you."

"You lost me the moment you chose this sick, dark path, Amalia," Caspian replied bluntly. "And that was a very long time ago."

Amalia processed his words, then put on a contemptuous smirk. "Always a weakling, huh? I actually thought you and I could be together. We still could, provided you grow a spine, Caspian. We could inherit this city!"

"Where's Lumi?" Caspian hissed.

None of us had the time for her delusional nonsense. It made my heart swell three times its usual size as I heard him verbally cut into her like that. I had no reason to doubt his love for me, but I had every reason to despise her for what she'd done to him. She was as guilty as the Lords, forcing him into his blood oath and killing so many innocent creatures just to satisfy their thirst for blood and their addiction to souls.

"I would rather die than tell you anything!" Amalia snarled, finally infuriated.

"You don't have to tell me twice," I scoffed, then moved to attack her again.

Caspian beat me to it. He darted ahead and reached her first. She didn't see it coming.

His blade pierced her chest in a firm, upward thrust. The tip went out through her upper back. He held her in place as she whimpered from the shock and the pain. Her eyes nearly popped out, her mouth gaping as blood poured out of her throat.

It didn't take long for internal bleeding to wreak havoc inside her body.

"Caspian..." she breathed.

"Tell me where Lumi is," he muttered, his eyes fixed on hers, his expression carved out of marble. His skin reddened slightly as he was discussing swamp witch issues in our presence, but he didn't let the blood oath stop him this time.

"We could've been together," she managed, both hands clutching the blade.

"Tell me where you're keeping her!" Caspian raised his voice.

I moved closer to get a better look, hoping I might offer Amalia a chance at pain relief in return for information. Caspian's sword wasn't going to kill her, but it was causing her sheer agony—which she struggled to keep to herself.

"I told you... I would... rather *die*!"

"*Tell me!*" Caspian snarled, valiantly ignoring his burns.

I froze, noticing a gold glimmer in his jade eyes. Was he trying to mind-bend her? It wouldn't work on another Mara—but then I saw her expression change. The pain went away, and blankness took over.

"Oh, wow," I muttered, utterly shocked, my gaze darting between Amalia and Caspian.

"Tell me where they're keeping Lumi." Caspian repeated his request, this time his voice lower, a little off, even. Different.

"She's in the Palisade Building," Amalia said. "I don't know what room, but that's where they're keeping her."

Caspian gasped, surprised by his own ability. His burns healed quickly. He pulled his sword out and stepped back, blinking rapidly as he tried to figure out what was going on. I recognized the confusion. I'd once been like that, unsure of my own power, asking myself "Did I just do that?".

Amalia shook her head and took advantage of that sliver of regained consciousness to try to stab him, but I cut her head off in one swift and unforgiving hit. She collapsed on the hardwood floor, blood pooling beneath her.

Caspian stared at her, then at me, as Zane, Pheng-Pheng, Fiona, and Arrah came around.

"I'm sorry, Caspian," I said softly. "I had to kill her. You know that, right?"

"She's been dead to me for years," he replied, though I could feel his sadness. It was the kind of dull pain one felt when losing an old friend—the one he hadn't seen in years, hoping she'd turned her life around and saddened to see she'd only gotten worse, in a way. Only in this case, he'd watched her decay, unable to stop her.

"What the hell just happened?" Fiona breathed, staring at Caspian. "How'd you get her to tell you? She was ready to die for it!"

"Mind-bending doesn't work on Maras," Caspian replied, genuinely in awe of himself. He shook his head slowly, then looked at me. "How *did* I do that?"

I offered him a warm and reassuring smile. "I don't think that was your mind-bending," I said. "I think that was your inner-sentry manifesting. Mind control."

He was even more confused, as were the others. "Sentry mind control doesn't work on Maras," he muttered, frowning.

"Maybe it works because *you're* a Mara, yourself," I said, shrugging. "It's literally the only explanation I have. This... This has no precedent whatsoever."

Fiona chuckled softly. "I take it you two took your relationship to the next level."

My face burned. Caspian put on a childish smile that didn't help either.

Zane laughed lightly, then pointed at the Imen.

"All this aside, you might want to mind-bend these critters into cleaning this mess up and forgetting what they saw," he said. "Lord Obara will want answers and heads to roll."

It hit me then—the gravity of what we'd just done. My blood ran cold. Amalia had obviously deserved it, but I'd nearly forgotten whose daughter she was. Emilian was going to have our heads, if given the chance.

"Actually, I think we need to hide her body, too," I murmured. "If anyone finds her while we're still in town, there will be a riot."

Zane nodded, then dragged Amalia out of sight and into one of the nearby rooms, collecting her head along the way. His self-control and lack of squeamishness were downright impressive. I was still training my stomach to control its impulses, despite the number of kills I'd accumulated on Neraka.

Taking a life was never easy.

Caspian looked at me. "I know where the Palisade is," he said.

"We should go," he added, then turned and mind-bent the Iman family into cleaning all the blood from the floor, staying out of the room where Zane had stashed Amalia's body, and forgetting we were ever there.

Zane came back, hands on his hips and smiling like a kid on a school trip.

"Okay, ready to go?" he asked, weirdly serene.

"You're enjoying this a little too much, don't you think?" Fiona remarked, raising an eyebrow.

"Took the words right out of my mouth," I muttered.

Zane grinned. "I've been rooting for this day for a while now," he replied with an innocent shrug. "I've seen Amalia before, and I get the feeling you ladies thought this was the worst thing she's ever done. Let me tell you, though, it's not. Losing her head was an easy way out for..." He feigned her feminine, ladylike voice and speaking mannerisms. "Amalia, future Lady of House Obara."

Caspian scoffed, the corner of his mouth twitching.

"Judging by the look on your face, I'll go ahead and assume Zane's right," I said to him.

He gave me a weak smile and a single blink, then motioned for the door. "Let's go. Time's not on our side."

He went out first, and we followed.

The alley was dark and quiet as we made our way through the back streets of the sixth level and headed for the Palisade. We didn't know what floor Lumi was on or what room she was in, but we knew the building. It was a great start.

One step closer to our freedom.

33

CAIA

We kept a close but safe distance from Nevis, Neha, and Colton as they snuck up to the top level of Azure Heights. They'd only ingested a small amount of invisibility paste, enough to keep them covered until they entered Emilian's mansion through the back door.

The seventh level was secured with at least twenty Correction Officers outside. One in five was wearing a red lens. It took additional efforts to get past them undetected, but we managed to follow Nevis and the others into the mansion.

There was a dinner party taking place on the ground floor, with maybe a dozen attendees. We waited in a secluded area of the service kitchen, until Nevis, Colton, and Neha's invisibility spells wore off. It only took about five minutes, during which time Colton knocked out any Imen coming in to retrieve more crystal glasses for the Exiled Maras' dinner.

We could hear them talking and laughing in the dining room.

Once they were visible again, our allies walked right in. Nevis had no time for pleasantries with the attending Correction Officers, encasing them in Dhaxanian frost and leaving them to slowly suffocate until they were left unconscious.

Blaze and I kept to the side, behind a decorative panel made of colored gems mounted on a copper-like structure. The scene we witnessed made my stomach turn itself inside out. The Lords and their guests were feeding off live Imen, who were mind-bent into submission.

Emilian was busy consuming the soul of an Iman elder, the bright white wisps escaping from an open neck wound and slipping between the Mara Lord's lips.

Everyone stilled at the sight of Nevis, who put on a grimace of disgust.

"Good grief, you Maras are loathsome," he muttered.

The remaining Correction Officers lunged at him, but Neha and Colton were quick to disable them. Neha was unbelievably fast, her tail stinging left and right until ten COs had collapsed on the floor. Colton used a crossbow loaded with poison-tipped arrows to take down the other five.

In a matter of seconds, Emilian, Rowan, Farrah, Rewa, and three other Maras were left speechless, stunned as they stared at Nevis. Their Imen subjects were catatonic, slumped on the floor, slowly bleeding out. I wanted to help, but Blaze gripped my wrist firmly, as if making sure I didn't go off on my own. I couldn't blame him, and I knew he sympathized with my discomfort at this point. We both wanted to help, but the lives of five Imen were going to be wasted anyway if we revealed ourselves and hindered the mission.

There wasn't enough GASP training in the world to prepare me for what we'd seen and experienced on Neraka so far. I was still adjusting.

"What are you doing here?" Emilian asked, his tone flat and his brow furrowed. "What are you all doing here?"

"The better question to ask is who your friends are, Nevis?" Rowan chimed in, narrowing her eyes at Neha and Colton. "I smell a filthy dog and a Manticore. I didn't know the bugs still lived outside the daemon prisons."

Neha smirked, but allowed Nevis to take the lead.

"Relax, we're here to talk," the Dhaxanian prince replied.

Emilian scoffed and pulled the linen tablecloth off, revealing a swamp witch symbol. He muttered a spell under his breath but failed to touch the symbol, as Nevis shot out a pellet of Dhaxanian ice and covered the entire table section, making it impossible for Emilian to complete his spell.

"Don't be foolish," Nevis said. "Just hear me out."

"Why? After the stunts you pulled against Shaytan's people?" Emilian spat, obviously infuriated. "I heard about your shenanigans, Nevis! Not nice!"

"First of all, you will address me as 'Your Grace'," Nevis shot back, his tone sending chills down my spine. "I've been nothing but respectful to you, and whatever issues I may have with Shaytan, they're between me and him, and do not concern you. Second, I've got a problem with the outsiders," he added.

"Oh, really? After you kept them away from Shaytan's soldiers?" Farrah scoffed, crossing her arms.

Nevis raised an eyebrow at her. "Milady, if you don't know the full story, you should keep that beautiful mouth shut before I freeze it. I doubt you look good with purple lips," he said, then shifted his focus back to Emilian. "Now, don't get all riled up. You'll pop a vein. Yes, I helped the outsiders, but I did it with a purpose. I wanted to find out exactly what they were up to. I'll admit, I was intrigued at first, but I sincerely doubt they'll be able to pull it off."

Emilian's interest was piqued. "What are they trying to pull off?"

"I thought you were smarter than this, Emilian," Nevis replied with a dry chuckle. "Obviously, they're after the swamp witch. They were able to put two and two together. They know she's here, in the city."

Emilian and the other Maras exchanged nervous glances.

"Point is," Neha interjected, "we'd rather fortify our alliance with you than help the outsiders. They are doomed to fail. They lack the numbers, and we're done getting our people killed to oppose you and the daemons."

"We'd like to propose a new alliance," Nevis added.

"And what alliance is that?" Rewa asked, pursing her lips.

She was as obnoxious as ever—even more so now, as she tried to look and sound like her father. She reminded me of an evil fairytale queen, wearing an all-black dress with gold embroidery on the sleeves. It also covered her head, on which she'd mounted a delicate gold crown. It was overkill, in my opinion. It made her look like an evil nun of sorts.

"There are Adlets and Manticores willing to sign a truce, along with the Dhaxanians," Nevis replied. "All we want is a couple of territories. We'll give you a number of our younglings, once a year, for you to feed on. We're willing to sacrifice a few for the good of the many. In return, we'll help you defeat the outsiders before they get anywhere near the witch."

"Or! And hear me out here... You all swear your allegiance, and we promise to kill you all fast, instead of feeding on you slowly, over the course of millennia," Emilian retorted with a grin.

"Or my friends and I just walk out of here and let the outsiders get their hands on the swamp witch. Seeing how inclined you Maras are toward arrogant stupidity, they might actually stand a chance against you, after all," Nevis said with a straight face.

Emilian shook his head slowly. "Why should I trust you? You've already tried to screw with Shaytan. And that alone will cost you dearly."

"If I were you, I wouldn't get too lovey-dovey with Shaytan," Nevis replied. "The daemon king won't let your friend, Darius, come back to Azure Heights. He's afraid you'll find out about his phenomenal failure to capture the outsiders."

Rewa shot to her feet. She was furious. "Excuse me?!"

"Darius is no longer staying in Infernis voluntarily," Nevis said. "I have eyes and ears all over Neraka, little Mara. Infernis has taken a serious hit and will take a while to recover. Draconis has fallen. The surviving pacifists and Druid delegation are on the loose. Ragnar Peak was destroyed, as well. Shaytan and his daemons aren't as strong as you think. My guess is they fooled you with their numbers, not their brains."

"Had you not given them swamp witch magic, *you* would've been the dominant species on Neraka, not them," Colton said, the shadow of a smile crossing his face.

Emilian, Rowan, Farrah, and Rewa looked at each other over the course of a few seconds. Then Emilian smirked at Nevis.

"What are you trying to say?" he asked.

"As long as you bloodsuckers have the swamp witch, the outsiders will never prevail. And neither will the daemons," Nevis replied. "Cut off Shaytan's access to swamp witch magic. Get her to give you some serious warfare spells. Then watch the daemons fall. All you need to do is get the outsiders first."

Rewa cursed under her breath, losing her composure slightly. I was thoroughly enjoying the view.

"How dare Shaytan keep my father hostage? That's unacceptable! Emilian, we need to do something!" she snarled.

"I just gave you a good idea," Nevis interjected, playing the facilitator.

"Hold on, hold on," Emilian replied, trying to get his thoughts organized into a coherent response, but Rewa didn't give him time. She wasn't just infuriated; she was downright infuriating to everyone in the room, judging by the other Lords' rolling eyes.

"No! No, we need to get my father back!" Rewa growled, then pointed a furious finger at Nevis. "And you need to prove your loyalty! You've screwed Shaytan over already. We can't have that here!"

A moment passed in absolute silence. Nevis put on a half-smile, his hands casually resting behind his back.

"Harper Hellswan is on her way to snatch the swamp witch as we speak," he said. "I don't know if she's already in the city, but I know for a fact it's happening tonight. If I were you, I'd double the security around your witch."

A gasp escaped Rowan's throat as she looked at Nevis in disbelief. "How do *you* know?"

"I told you, I'm resourceful," Nevis replied with a shrug, then snapped his fingers and defrosted one of Emilian's Correction Officers. The guard fell to his knees, coughing and wheezing as he regained his consciousness and staggered back to his feet.

Emilian let out a subtle grunt, then motioned for the CO to leave. "Go warn the Palisade," he said. "Harper Hellswan is somewhere in the city, looking for our prime asset. Double... No, triple security."

The CO nodded and rushed out of the mansion. Emilian sneered at Nevis.

"This had better not be a ruse," Rewa hissed.

Nevis sighed. "Forgive me, I don't speak 'imbecile', so please refrain from addressing me," he replied dryly. "As far as I'm concerned, Darius still rules over House Xunn. I don't recognize your authority."

Rewa scoffed and opened her mouth to respond, but Emilian

raised his hand, motioning for her to keep quiet. He then raised an eyebrow at Nevis.

"Fine," the Mara Lord said. "Now what?"

"Oh, I'm not done yet." Nevis chuckled softly, prompting both Neha and Colton to frown at him, somewhat confused. My stomach suddenly tightened. Something was off. "We have company," he added, then snapped his fingers.

Before either Blaze or I could do anything, we found ourselves immersed in Dhaxanian frost. I froze, almost instantly, up to my neck.

"No!" Blaze cried out, grunting and struggling against the ice, to no avail.

The Mara Lords were stunned. Rewa grabbed a pitcher of water and spilled it over our heads, revealing Blaze and me. She squealed at the sight of him, prompting me to groan and struggle even harder against my restraints.

Neha and Colton were livid but said nothing.

I glowered at Nevis, my heart breaking into a thousand little pieces as the concept of our doom crept up on me. "Why? Why would you do this? Why?!"

"There you have it, Emilian," Nevis said, ignoring me completely. "A fae and a dragon. I imagine that's enough for you to start drafting a truce with us."

He then gave me a brief glance, and I suddenly stilled. He winked.

Oh, crap. He changed the script. He's going off script, but... Wait, he's not exactly throwing us to the wolves here. He hasn't told them about our anti-mind-bending lenses.

As it all fell into place, I got a better idea of what he was planning. That smirk I'd seen on him earlier in the morning, when the Druids presented the lenses, finally made sense.

I looked at Blaze and nodded briefly, while Rewa jumped

around us, giddy like a little girl at Christmas. She'd gotten one hell of a present this time.

"My frost will keep them both in place," Nevis added. "Your dragon can't... go dragon while in it. You're welcome."

Blaze stared at me, in genuine disbelief, as he listened to their exchange.

"Whatever you do, pretend they can mind-bend you," I whispered to him.

"What?" He was utterly shocked.

When Rewa came and caressed his face, however, he instantly understood what I'd meant. We were in for a rough ride, but under no circumstances could we let them figure out we'd found a way to bypass their mind-bending.

Nevis, as devious as he was for not telling us, had a plan. Whatever it was, Blaze and I were going to make it happen. I ignored the pang in my stomach when Rewa took off his red garnet lens, which he no longer needed anyway, since we were both visible.

"You've come back to me, Blaze!" She giggled, then covered his face with short kisses.

I rolled my eyes, fighting to keep my gag reflex under control. The part about Harper's presence in the city had been part of our plan from the beginning. It had taken a lot of effort to convince Caspian to agree to it, too. But giving our presence away had not been discussed at all.

It made me angry, but not as much as watching Rewa slobbering all over Blaze.

Nevis snapped his fingers and removed the frost from the Correction Officers. One by one, they got back up, coughing and recovering their breaths.

"Go fetch a pair of charmed cuffs from my study," Emilian ordered one of them, then pointed at another CO. "And you, prepare one of the rooms for our new guests."

The Correction Officers dispersed, and Emilian continued to give orders for our accommodation. Rewa came in front of me, grinning like the vicious banshee that she was.

"Thank you so much for bringing Blaze over," she sneered. "I guess you realized he's better off with me. Don't worry, he's my plaything now. I'll take care of him from now on."

"You *are* sick," I muttered. "In the head, I mean. Sick in the head."

"Oh, and I promise I'll make you watch," she replied, then moved back in front of Blaze.

"No, what are you doing?" I breathed, my eyes widening as she gripped his chin between her index finger and thumb.

She used her mind-bending ability on him. "Blaze, darling, how about you kiss me?"

It took a lot of self-control for Blaze to pretend he was under her influence. It took a lot more for me not to scream when he pressed his lips against her. She opened her mouth and deepened the kiss, gripping his head as she moaned with delight. Rewa had her tongue stuck down my dragon's throat, and I had to put up with it.

"Your gesture of goodwill has been duly noted," Emilian said to Nevis. "I'll draw up the papers and have them ready for you to sign tomorrow."

Nevis smirked, while Colton and Neha were forced to keep playing along, though both of them were visibly disgusted by the unexpected turn of events. Nevis had kept all this to himself, and it made me extremely mad. At the same time, I had to keep my head clear and stay on high alert. Had he truly aimed to betray us, he would've definitely mentioned the contact lenses.

"Like I said, you're welcome," Nevis replied. "Just make sure you keep your end of the deal," he added, then turned to Rewa, who was still busy making out with Blaze, much to my dismay.

"Oh, and make sure the dragon stays in one piece. Shaytan has plans for him."

"Shaytan can find himself another dragon," Rewa spat.

"Agreed. Shaytan won't be getting anywhere near Blaze," Emilian replied. "He's done enough, and he will not prevail. I will have a talk with him about Darius, too. I won't stand for any of this nonsense. Besides, you have a point. The swamp witch is ours."

Emilian grinned, while Rowan and Farrah came closer to get a better look at Blaze and me, unable to move and unable to burn them to a crisp.

"We'll be on our way then," Nevis said. "And return tomorrow to sign the treaty."

"Just keep your distance from the outsiders," Emilian commanded. "I'll handle them once and for all."

Nevis shrugged, then left through the back door, accompanied by Neha and Colton.

"Fine by me," he muttered as he left Blaze and me behind, snapping his fingers just at the CO's came back with the charmed cuffs. As soon as the Dhaxanian frost shattered, they restrained us —the charms made it impossible for us to use our fire abilities, and we were already too outnumbered to initiate close combat.

Emilian smiled as soon as his gaze settled on me. He looked as though he'd just been reunited with an old friend, in a way. He wore none of the psycho allure that Rewa so proudly displayed.

"Good to have you back, Caia, Blaze," he said softly. "We'll take good care of you from now on."

I scoffed. "You'll drain our blood and eat our souls, you mean."

Rewa chuckled, then kissed Blaze again, just to spite me. My dragon was seething, but his self-control was truly something incredible to behold. *Guess that celibacy oath really does work to keep him emotionally and physically restrained.*

"Well, yes, that too," Emilian replied.

There was no return from this point forward. Whatever lay ahead, Blaze and I had to be ready for it. As long as they couldn't mind-bend us, we stood a chance. Whatever Nevis had planned, it had to be good. All Blaze and I had to do was act.

One look at Rewa, and bile threatened to burn through my throat.

Gah, this is going to be so, so difficult.

34

FIONA

The Palisade was a beautiful building, designed like most of Azure Heights's landmarks, with a sumptuous marble façade, pale beige roof tiles, and an abundance of floral accents on every French-style window. Had it not been for the heavily armed Correction Officers guarding the main entrance, I would've said this was the place where all the great parties happened—the kind that offered expensive drinks and weirdly named hors d'oeuvres.

We snuck around the back, then spent a few minutes waiting for the service entrance to clear. Iman servants buzzed around, emptying metal bins into the large trashcans at the far end of the backyard. There were two Correction Officers stationed by the door, busy conversing. They occasionally sneered at the Imen, who avoided eye contact with the Maras, their expressions pale and fearful.

It broke my heart to see them like this.

"The Palisade is a luxury hotel of sorts," Caspian explained.

"The rooms are used by Maras for romantic encounters of all kinds, in and outside official relationships."

Zane scoffed. "They're also used as a prime feeding ground," he muttered. "They bring up young Imen, both male and female, for the noble Maras willing to pay higher prices in gold. Caspian can't tell you anything about that, unfortunately."

I looked at Caspian, who shook his head in disgust. "The Maras running this establishment specialize and trade in seduction… and secrets. They know most of the inner workings of the Lords, and they're paid very well to keep their mouths shut and eavesdrop whenever there's a special guest visiting."

"And by 'special' he means daemons," Zane added with a faint smirk. "My species isn't immune to the Maras' charms, as you've already seen."

He meant Tobiah and Sienna. It didn't strike me as odd or unexpected. Harper was a hybrid, too, the fruit of love between different species. The laws of physical attraction transcended natural boundaries—not to mention love. Love was unstoppable. It took one look at Zane for me to reinforce that belief.

"What do you see?" I asked Harper.

She used her True Sight to scan the entire building, from top to bottom. "I can't see beneath the ground floor or in several of the upper-level rooms," she murmured. "I'm guessing meranium and swamp witch charms for protection and concealment, but—wait." She frowned, narrowing her eyes as if to get a better look. A grin slit her face as she turned her head to look at me. "Found your old friend, Vincent."

My blood instantly simmered. Zane and I exchanged glances before he shifted his focus to the two Exiled Maras at the back door.

"Okay then, let's speed this along," he said, then took out his crossbow and loaded it with a poisoned arrow. I did the same with mine, as we needed to strike fast and disable both guards before either could make a sound and alert the others.

We shot them simultaneously. The short arrows, laced with Pheng-Pheng's venom, got lodged in the Correction Officers' necks. They both stilled, clutching their throats, then collapsed as the poison worked its way through their bloodstreams.

The coast was clear. We shot out from our hiding place on the edge of the backyard and rushed inside. We slipped between Imen servants along the corridor. They were almost catatonic, mind-bent into absolute submission as they went about their chores, without even noticing the air ripples around them.

We followed Harper up to the first floor, sneaking past several Correction Officers. I breathed a sigh of relief when we got out of sight again, since some of the Maras were wearing red lenses. It took extra work and planning to move from one area to another without detection, but we managed to infiltrate the western corridor in the end.

Harper stopped in front of a door—one of the many on that level, all luxury bedrooms used for carnal pleasure and other, more heinous activities, according to Zane. Harper motioned for us to move behind her. Once we were on that side, we were able to eavesdrop on Vincent and what sounded like a female Mara with a sensual, husky voice.

"Come on, Mel, you know you want to." Vincent's voice could be heard coming from the room.

Mel's mocking laughter rippled through the corridor. "Oh, darling, you think too highly of yourself," she replied dryly.

"What, my money isn't good enough for you?" Vincent spat. "You're the best of all the ladies working tonight, and I only play with the best."

I resisted the urge to puke, realizing what the conversation was about. I squirmed instead, mouthing an "Ew!" at Zane, who stifled a grin as we kept listening. Harper shook her head slowly, while Caspian, Pheng-Pheng, and Arrah rolled their eyes.

"That's just so... lame," Harper whispered.

"Vincent, there isn't enough gold on this planet to get you in my bed," Mel retorted. I heard the subtle jingle of jewelry tossed on a soft surface—perhaps the bed.

"Not even these beauties?" Vincent asked, sounding a little too needy for anyone's taste. Mel laughed again. "Come on, Mel, I need some stress relief, and you're the only one who can give it to me."

"No, darling, I'm not the only one who can give it to you. I'm the only one who won't waste a single minute of my time in your company. I've made my feelings about you clear many times before. What part of 'Never in a thousand years' did you not understand?"

Harper and I looked at each other and covered our mouths, struggling not to laugh out loud.

"I'll take what I want then!" Vincent growled. "I'm done being nice! I'm a Roho, dammit!"

Mel gasped, and something made of glass broke, followed by the muffled sounds of a struggle and muttered curses. Zane groaned, and I squeezed his arm, understanding his urge to storm in there.

We all jumped back and froze when the door burst open and Vincent stumbled out of the room, his lip split and bleeding, his dapper velvet suit ruffled and torn at the seams.

"Seriously?" he cried out, scowling at the female Mara still inside the room.

A purse filled with gold coins and jewels was thrown out, smacking Vincent right in the face.

"And stay out!" Mel shouted, and slammed the door shut.

Vincent scoffed, then licked the blood from the corner of his mouth and collected the purse and its spilled contents from the floor.

"Ungrateful fiend," he muttered.

With pride utterly shredded and a bag full of gold and jewels that the Palisade's best Mara lady rejected, Vincent sighed and made his way downstairs. Only then did I realize that we were all grinning.

We followed him to the ground floor, keeping a safe distance and staying behind potted trees, unsuspecting Imen servants, and whatever pieces of lobby furniture we could use to avoid detection. Vincent made a sharp turn left after the reception desk and went all the way to the end of a narrow corridor. We stopped on the corner, watching him quietly as he looked around, making sure no one saw him, then lifted the corner of a picture frame.

We all recognized the click—a hidden mechanism revealing a secret door. A rectangular piece of the wall dislodged and opened inward. Vincent slipped through, then closed the secret door behind him.

With my heart racing, I rushed over there, with the others right behind me.

I stopped in front of the picture frame, then looked at Harper.

"You said you can't see below this level, right?" I asked, my voice low. She nodded in response. "Can you see past this wall?"

She tried, then shook her head. The entire wall section was protectively coated with meranium. I took a deep breath and lifted the picture corner, like Vincent had done before me. Secret door clicked, then opened slowly. I pushed it all the way in, discovering a set of stairs leading into the basement.

There wasn't much light coming from below, with the exception of a few flickering wall sconces at the bottom of the stairs.

We descended into the basement level and spotted Vincent chatting with one of the guards positioned in front of a room at the end of the hallway. Harper took a minute to assess the entire area, then frowned.

"It's all meranium and carved symbols beneath the wallpaper," she muttered, then nodded ahead. "There are multiple corridors, though."

The main hallway had several doors on both sides. Every forty feet or so, it opened into different corridors, all lit by the same kind of amber-colored wall sconces.

"This whole level could very well be a secret maze of rooms and hallways," I whispered.

Vincent nodded at the guard, then went inside the room, closing the door behind him. I spotted the red lens on the Correction Officer's tunic, mounted on a slim chain.

"We need to disable him first, then check where the others might be," Zane said. "Let me handle this."

He stepped into the hallway and headed straight for the guard, looking left and right through every corridor as he advanced. The CO must have seen the air rippling or caught a glimpse of Zane's red eyes, as he reached for his red lens. Zane was faster, though, and shot him with a poisoned arrow, then caught him under his arm before he could collapse and make a noise. He held the Mara up like a lifeless doll as the poison disabled his nervous system, then motioned for the rest of us to come through.

He put his index finger up to his lips. I nodded and joined him first, followed by Harper, Caspian, Pheng-Pheng, and Arrah. We caught glimpses of other COs stationed along the adjacent corridors, staring blankly at the walls in front of them. I counted about twenty of them scattered across the level.

We stood by the door, listening in. I put my ear against the keyhole. Two seconds later, my heart nearly stopped. I looked up at Harper and noticed her stunned expression. She could hear it, too.

Jax's voice.

"Don't worry, Draven, we're good so far," Jax said. "We're organizing another search party tomorrow. No sign of the missing Maras, either."

Something was horribly off here. We'd left Jax behind with Hansa and Dion, back at the tunnel exit. Yet it sounded like him. It sent chills down my spine and ravaged my stomach, as I tried to make sense of what was going on.

Caspian frowned, then sighed audibly. It got our attention. He was angry, pressing his lips with frustration. He knew what was in that room—I could see it in his eyes. Judging by the wide-eyed expression on Harper's face, she realized it, too. Caspian's blood oath prevented him from speaking.

Harper grunted, then pushed the door open.

We stormed inside and came to a screeching halt, shocked by what awaited.

It was a simple, cubic room with meranium walls, covered in swamp witch symbols. But that wasn't the highlight of the entire scene—far from it. On the floor, in the middle of the room, was a large Druid circle, with a variety of crystals, herbs, and powders strategically positioned along the chalk drawing, which glowed white.

Right at the center was a contraption of some kind, resembling an old phone—specifically the first type ever invented, with a bell-shaped receiver and a makeshift microphone, made from a combination of metals and soft wood casing. It was positioned on a small table with shelves underneath, where a plethora of glowing, multicolored crystals were stacked, each connected to the faux phone through hundreds of black and white wires.

Every inch of that table was scribbled with swamp witch symbols. In front of it was a stool, on which Vincent sat, holding the receiver to his ear. He saw the air ripple in front of him and spoke through the microphone.

"Sure, we'll talk again soon," he said, in Jax's voice.

I froze, watching as he put the receiver back on its hook and pressed a button on the faux phone's base. He removed a small black pellet from his throat, carefully placing it on the table next to the strange contraption.

He put on his red lens with trembling fingers, then scoffed.

"Took you long enough to find this place," he muttered in his usual voice.

My stomach dropped as I understood what was going on here. Why we hadn't seen any sign of GASP whatsoever. How the Exiled Maras had kept our people away, even when we couldn't reach out to them.

These bloodsucking, soul-eating bastards had been pretending to be us, somehow tapping into the Telluris spell and using that weird combination of Druid and swamp witch magic to communicate with Draven, back on Calliope. The shield kept us from reaching out to our people, but the Exiled Maras had found a way to keep our people at bay, letting them think they were talking to *us*.

Oh, so many questions came surging through my head, all at once, as my temperature spiked, and rage threatened to burst through me like a devastating firestorm.

This was, by far, the most despicable of all the tricks employed by the Exiled Maras to get away with their nefarious plans.

35

HARPER

My muscles stiffened at the sight before me.

It cost us dearly, because I didn't register Vincent's sudden movement as he trashed the phone-like contraption with his foot. It fell apart in just one blow.

"No!" I gasped, watching the crystals shatter against the floor, chunks of wood and metal pieces scattering across, wires tangling around like spilled entrails. The Druid circle glow faded when one of the bowls of powder and herb mixture got knocked over.

Vincent snickered as he shot to his feet. He reached for the short sword mounted on his belt, but I beat him to it. He'd done enough damage already. One of my blades reached his throat before he could take his out. His fingers froze, clutching the handle.

The color drained from his cheeks.

"You bastard," I hissed. "What's this all about?"

Vincent smirked, checking each of us out. "How nice to see you again, Miss Hellswan. Fiona, darling, what are you doing with that oaf? You really don't know how to choose your company, do you?"

"Said the guy who just got rejected by a Mara who's literally paid to say yes," Fiona shot back, gritting her teeth. She pointed at the pile of tech and magical paraphernalia on the floor. "What the hell was that? How did you make your voice sound like Jax's? Were you talking to *our* Draven just now? Is this how you've been keeping GASP at bay?"

"Oh, sweetheart, had you only stayed by my side," Vincent replied, a grin cutting his face from ear to ear. "I would've taken care of you."

"You would've taken care of me?" Fiona scoffed, then nodded at Pheng-Pheng. "Let's see you take care of yourself, first!"

Before he could even react, Pheng-Pheng darted behind him, stung him with her scorpion tail, then stepped back and came around to face him again. Vincent stilled, holding the side of his neck. Slowly but surely, his veins blackened as the venom started spreading through his body. I lowered my blade and moved away.

"I used a smaller dose," Pheng-Pheng muttered. "It'll take him out slower, but it will still burn and cause agonizing pain."

"Fantastic!" Fiona quipped, then rammed her fist into his face.

Vincent dropped onto one knee, spitting blood, but Fiona wasn't done. None of us intervened. She deserved this much, after his theatrics and key role in the Exiled Maras' plots. In fact, after what we'd just discovered here, we all deserved a shot at dismembering Vincent.

Fiona grabbed him by the shirt and dragged him back up, then slammed him into the wall.

He struggled against her hold, but his limbs weakened as the venom took over. He squirmed and whimpered from the pain, breaking out in a cold sweat.

"Tell us what's going on here, Vincent, and I'll end it faster,"

Fiona hissed. "Or I'll just leave you here to writhe in agony until, eventually, you lose your head. I can make time to watch you die, you filthy piece of—"

"It's a spell!" Vincent croaked.

"What kind of spell?" I asked. "I see a Druid circle and a bunch of swamp witch symbols. Explain yourself!"

Vincent moaned from the pain. "We tortured the Druids, forced a couple of spells out of them a while back, on top of what we got from the swamp witch. It's a hijacking spell... The shield around Neraka stops communications and access. This spell, however, captures incoming signals and spells, including Telluris. It's... It's a combination of both types of magic."

"What does it do?" Fiona replied, pushing him harder against the wall.

Zane stifled a grin, crossing his arms and watching the entire scene unfold. Arrah and Pheng-Pheng stood between us, with Caspian to my right. He wore a permanent frown, a muscle ticking in his jaw. As long as there was tension and frustration burning through him, I knew we'd yet to get everything we could out of Vincent.

"It picks up Telluris transmissions, among other things," Vincent explained, panting. "Oh, it hurts so much..."

"Talk!" Fiona snapped, then drew her sword and pushed it against his throat.

Vincent started sobbing. "It's... It's a trick! We've been using it to make your people think you're okay. Whenever GASP tries to reach out to you, we intervene. We use voice-changing charms to pretend we're one of you, whoever Draven's calling out to. It's kept them at bay for a long time."

"Why would you do that? If the shield keeps everybody out, why go to this effort?" I asked, somewhat confused. I repositioned the new puzzle pieces in my mind and tried to make sense of the full picture.

"We didn't have the shield up when you first arrived," Vincent croaked. "We didn't know how long it would take to get the swamp witch to write the formulas down. And then, after it went up, we weren't sure it would be enough to keep your people away long enough for us to play out the whole lie. We have a script we're working with, stages of the story, to draw GASP in and get them to send a specific number of creatures to look for us. This was well planned from the very beginning, down to the last detail. This was one of the first things we put together to make sure GASP didn't come looking for you too soon."

Fiona, Zane, Caspian, and I looked at each other, finally understanding the complexity of the Exiled Maras' elaborate plan to not only trap us here, but to get more of our people to come without igniting a full-scale invasion of Eritopian and GASP forces.

"Wishful thinking, friend, because you really underestimated these fine ladies," Zane chuckled, no longer able to hold back.

Despite the pain surging through his body, Vincent found the strength to sneer at him, then noticed Arrah. "You... Arrah, right? You were a servant in our house," he muttered, narrowing his eyes as he remembered her. "Yes, I remember you," he added, then tried to mind-bend her. "Be a darling and get the Manticore's tail. I need the second sting."

Arrah smirked, crossing her arms.

Vincent didn't see that coming, judging by his face. He was genuinely confused.

"I'm immune to your mind-bending, you sniveling dirtbag," Arrah retorted.

"Hah!" Vincent gasped, suddenly enlightened. "I didn't think it was true, not even when Mother said it out loud."

Arrah frowned. "What are you talking about?"

"I should've paid more attention to the details," Vincent muttered. "You've been pretending to be mind-bent all along, haven't you?" Arrah's silence was his answer. "Then it's true. My father did spawn a bastard with your mother. That wench…"

Fiona pushed the blade deeper, drawing blood. "Mind your manners, you tool."

"What are you implying?" I asked him, then noticed the glimmer of realization in Arrah's eyes.

"I should've seen it. The color of your eyes… The strong will… I'd thought my mother had mind-bent the willfulness out of you, but you're immune. You're half Mara, darling. You're my half-sister." Vincent chuckled, then coughed, the venom gradually disabling his organs.

"That… I don't get it," Arrah murmured.

We'd speculated about this before, but she hadn't been keen to address it. Now, she had no choice.

"You're immune to mind-bending, and your mother was a little too close to my father!" Vincent spat. "He wanted to get out of here, you know. I mean, we knew about his affair with your mother, but we didn't think it would produce any offspring. He wanted to take her away, along with you, Sienna, and that idiot brother of yours. Mother made sure that never happened," he added, then scowled at Arrah. "I wasn't on board with watching my father die. I've always blamed your mother for it. Boy, did I laugh when we tossed Demios in prison and made your mother disappear."

"You kept me around the house, thinking you could mind-bend me into submission," Arrah replied, putting two and two together. "That's why you were always so jovial and accommodating whenever our paths crossed. You knew what you and your mother had done, and you both enjoyed watching me toil around the house, thinking 'look at the poor Iman girl, she has no idea what we did'… right?"

Vincent smirked.

"Well, joke's on you, then," Fiona replied dryly. "You're down here with us, and rest assured, we won't stop until you're all dead or in chains."

"Who came up with this... contraption?" Zane asked, crouching to pick up the broken pieces and get a better look. "I've never seen anything like this before. I mean, I knew you people had tricks up your sleeves to keep the Eritopians out, but this... this is a whole new level of skill."

Vincent shuddered, now losing control over his limbs altogether. His skin was paper-white, black veins streaking across like spiderwebs.

"Mother... She came up with the idea," he replied. "She spent months torturing the swamp witch to get something out of her. After a few weeks and a couple of failed attempts, she managed to put this together," he added, nodding at the shattered pieces on the floor. "Calliope doesn't even know you're all done for."

"Put it back together," I said. "Fix it. Make it work, and we'll spare you."

My heart drummed hard. If we could reach out to Draven through this spell hybrid, we could finish this even quicker than we'd anticipated. We'd still have to get Lumi out, but we'd also have people already on the way until we brought the shield down.

Vincent sneered, and I knew, deep down, what it meant.

"I can't," he said. "Only Mother knows how to do it."

"Dammit." I scoffed, pinching the bridge of my nose.

"Where are you keeping Lumi?" Fiona asked, moving on to the most important part of our mission. "We know she's in here, but which room?"

"You'll kill me anyway. Why should I make it easy for you?" Vincent shot back.

"We'll make it easy for you in return," I said, bringing both of my swords up for him to see. He sighed, then shook his head.

"Not worth it. Not if you kill me."

Fiona exhaled sharply, then rolled her eyes. "Fine. We'll spare you. You'll spend the rest of your life in a cage, then."

Vincent gave her a playful wink, then grimaced from an incoming seizure, his whole body shaking and his jaw clenching from the pain.

"Tick tock, Vincent," I replied.

"Take... Take the first corridor on the left as you get out of here. Go to the end, turn right. There's another corridor there. At the end. *By the gods*, this hurts too much!" Vincent managed, sweat dripping down his face. "There's a door at the end. The frame is different from the others. It's covered in swamp witch warding symbols. You can't miss it; it's guarded by two daemons and two COs."

He started choking, gasping for air. Fiona released him. He fell to his knees, reaching out for her as she stepped back.

"Now... Help me..." he breathed.

I knew exactly what Fiona was going to say. I was thinking it, too, and, although it wasn't in our nature, I was totally on board with it.

"You deserve to die in pain," Fiona replied. "And I'm okay with watching until you can't take it anymore."

Vincent summoned the last bit of strength he had left, utterly enraged. "You liar! You filthy little liar! My mother will kill you all! If you kill me, she'll skin you alive! She'll flay you and have you for dinner! She'll eat your soul and feed your entrails to the pit wolves! You'll suffer for this! You bitch! You'll—"

Zane grabbed him by the hair and cut his head off with one swift slash of his rapier.

We all stilled, watching his body collapse. Zane dropped his head—we watched it roll on the floor and settle in the middle of the Druid chalk circle.

"Sorry, I couldn't take the yapping anymore," Zane replied with a shrug. "His own mother never liked him much, actually. Rowan Roho is a despicable Lady, and she is cursed with an endless lifetime of disappointment. A rebel daughter. An incompetent son. No magic trick in the world will change the outcome for her."

A couple of moments passed in awkward silence, until Fiona sighed, putting her swords away and crossing her arms.

"Well, she only has a rebel daughter now," she muttered.

And Sienna would rather chop her own head off at this point than come back under her mother's evil thumb. I breathed deeply, then gently nudged Caspian.

"Are you okay?" I asked.

"Let's go," he said, quite sullen.

He was in a foul mood, and I couldn't really blame him. It made my stomach churn, though. I didn't like seeing him like this; however, time wasn't on our side. But we finally had a precise location for Lumi.

36

FIONA

We left the room behind and followed Vincent's instructions. On the first corridor to the left, there were three guards stationed at three different doors. Our guess was that they were keeping something or someone in each of the rooms they'd been assigned to, but we had no time to check.

Pheng-Pheng and Zane went ahead. The Manticore disabled one Correction Officer with her scorpion sting, then cut his head off to silence him.

Zane darted toward the second Correction Officer, who spotted his fallen partner and drew his sword. He had barely managed that before Zane cut him down with one swift slash.

The third one put his red lens on and reached for a whistle hanging from his neck. Harper reached him with lightning speed and drove both swords into his chest. He gasped, blood gurgling out of his mouth. His wide eyes were fixed on her, glassy with sheer horror, as she pulled her swords back then cut his head off.

We left the dead COs behind and reached the end of the corridor. Around the corner to the right it was clear all the way to the end, where, as per Vincent's description, there were two Correction Officers on both sides of a large meranium door. The air rippled in two spots nearby, prompting us to put our red lenses on and spot the two daemon guards shuffling back and forth.

The door was different indeed. It had been lined with a copper frame and riddled with swamp witch symbol engravings. Even the doorknob was marked.

Harper took a deep breath.

"I'll go first," she whispered, then quickly kissed Caspian and ran out to tackle the daemons and Maras guarding Lumi's door.

"Wait," Caspian breathed, then rushed after her.

We followed.

A hiss made us stop. Caspian froze, just five feet ahead of us. Harper had ten feet on him already when she stilled.

Water sprayed out from tiny holes in the ceiling above us.

"Crap," I muttered, then drew my sword.

Our cover was blown. The water canceled our invisibility spell and revealed us.

The Correction Officers were the first to spot us. Their blades screeched as they left their scabbards and the Maras moved toward us, but the daemons stepped in and held them back. Emilian Obara showed up from around the corner, joining the guards.

"Oh, no," Arrah murmured.

Emilian smirked at the sight of Harper, who drew her swords and came at him. Emilian snapped his fingers, and a thin sheet of glass shot out from the wall—she bumped into it. Access through that corridor was blocked.

We ran toward her. My pulse raced.

Emilian snapped his fingers again, and another sheet of glass came between us and Harper.

"No!" Caspian growled.

He tried to break the glass, but he couldn't even crack it. Harper looked at us, her eyes wide and her breath heavy. She rammed the hilt of one sword into the glass sheet in front of her, but nothing happened. She tried again. Just an unbearable clang.

Shivers ran down my spine. Emilian chuckled from across the corridor. He was definitely enjoying this. The jerk.

I made my way in front of the group and punched the glass. Nothing. I couldn't get through. We all tried—fists, swords, arrows, knees... everything. We couldn't break it.

Harper was trapped in the corridor between two sheets of weirdly unbreakable glass and two closed doors on both sides. She tried to open one, then the other, but they didn't budge. They were locked.

"Harper!" Caspian shouted, banging his fists against the glass.

He was livid, angrily hitting the barrier, unable to get through. Harper looked at him—and I could see the pain in her eyes.

"This was a little too easy," Emilian said.

The COs and daemons stood by his side, smirking at us. We looked like fools, struggling to get Harper out of there. Emilian was in his element down here, and I looked forward to wiping that smile off his face.

My blood curdled as the alarm blared through the building.

"Dammit!" I cursed under my breath, briefly looking over my shoulder.

It was a loud, ear-piercing noise, high-pitched and nasal, like a firetruck siren on steroids. It made me cringe.

"Harper! No!" Caspian shouted, still fighting against the glass sheet.

The door suddenly opened to her right. I froze. "Uh-oh."

A Correction Officer came out and stabbed her in the neck with a metallic syringe, before she could even react.

"Harper!" Caspian lost it, banging and kicking at that glass sheet, as Harper's eyes rolled back in her head.

The CO caught her in his arms and took her inside the room, slamming the door behind them. Zane pulled Caspian back. "Come on, we have to get out!"

"No! Harper! They got her! This... I can't do this! No!" Caspian was devastated.

It tore me apart on the inside, but Zane was right. I could already hear the boots on the ground. We ran back down the corridor and went straight ahead, instead of taking the first left turn to head back. As soon as we got out of the sprinklers' coverage, we swallowed more invisibility paste and kept a low profile behind a corner, watching several Correction Officers come through from the other side.

We vanished, one by one. Caspian was pale and ready to bring down the entire Palisade, but we had to regroup. We had to go back and stick to the plan. Otherwise it was all for nothing.

Emilian pointed in our relative direction, prompting the COs to come our way.

"Let's go," Zane whispered. "Follow me."

We darted through the hallways, taking a series of left and right turns to avoid the clusters of COs looking for us. They had red lenses on, so our best bet was to sneak out before they could spot us.

Caspian cursed under his breath as we turned left into another corridor. Boots rumbled all around us, but not in immediate sight.

"We know where to find her," Zane muttered. "Hang in there, my friend. We'll get her back."

"I... I didn't expect this."

"We'll get her back," I reiterated Zane's point.

Correction Officers spotted us from the back, just as we reached the main hallway. That secret staircase was our only way out, and it had yet to be inundated by incoming Maras. We ran as fast as we could, shooting down the hallway with COs hot on our tail.

We couldn't get ourselves captured, too. It wasn't part of the plan.

37

AVRIL

We infiltrated the prison stealthily, bypassing the guards as we made our way through the bottom level. The tunnel gates were down, with at least an hour left until daemon chow time. It ate away at me to not be able to do anything for the prisoners, since most of them were, in fact, innocent Imen and Maras who had been resisting Azure Heights and Shaytan's dirty alliance.

The Exiled Maras didn't pay much attention to prison security at this point. Their main concern was to guard the swamp witch, so the lower levels of the city and the prison itself weren't as heavily secured as the top side.

It worked in our favor, as we'd already planted all the explosive charges and charms that Patrik and the other Druids had prepared for this mission. Levels one, two, and three were fully loaded and ready to go for part two of our mission.

For now, however, we still had to get part one out of the way.

Velnias took the lead on this particular venture. We followed and provided backup if needed.

"I've come to this place more times than I can count," he whispered as we advanced through the bottom level of the giant, cylinder-shaped prison. "I picked up high value prisoners for Draconis from here."

We were invisible, with our red lenses on, just in case. We'd allowed the Exiled Maras to surprise us before in different circumstances—we'd learned our lesson by now.

Velnias bolted toward a pair of Correction Officers doing their rounds. He instantly decapitated one, then grabbed the other by the throat and rammed him through the bars of an empty cell. The metal bent under the COs mangled body, and he grunted, then wheezed from the impact.

"Where's Cadmus?" Velnias hissed.

"Oh, wow, he does not play around," I muttered, keeping a hand on my sword as I looked up and around. We were in a blind spot for the time being, as the other guards were on the upper levels. Velnias had certainly picked the right time for this.

Consider me officially impressed.

The Correction Officer pointed directly above with a shaking hand. "Up... First level. Cell 20."

"Most kind of you, thanks," Velnias replied bluntly, then cut his head off.

Heron and I stared at each other for a second, not knowing whether we should be horrified or in awe of his badassery. Scarlett and Patrik covered our backs as we stayed behind Velnias and made our way up to the first level.

We found the cell in a matter of seconds, following the numbers mounted above each compartment. Cadmus sat on the floor in a dark corner, his head down.

"Cadmus," I whispered, moving next to Velnias, who fiddled

with his lockpicking tools. The High Warden had an arsenal of small metal picks for precisely this kind of operation, and he kept them in a leather pouch attached to his belt.

Cadmus's head shot up. He frowned, noticing the air rippling in front of him.

I tossed a red lens into the cell. He was quick to grab it and put it on. He immediately beamed at the sight of us, then stilled when he saw Velnias and what he was doing.

"I'd like to say I'm happy to see you're all okay, but how did you get a daemon to do your bidding?" Cadmus muttered.

Velnias scoffed, shaking his head. "Typical Mara grunt. Thinks we're puppets," he muttered. "I'm here of my own volition, Cadmus. Unlike you."

Cadmus smirked. "I know you. You're a High Warden in Draconis. I've—" He stopped himself as burns blossomed on his face in blotches of red.

"Blood oath," I murmured.

Cadmus raised his eyebrows at me. "Yeah, we know. We know everything," I replied. "We've been busy since we last saw you, Cadmus," I added, then tossed a small satchel of invisibility paste at him. "But we can catch up later. Let's get you out of here first."

He checked the satchel and smirked. "You kids are impressive."

"And you, good sir, are a free Mara," Velnias replied, and finally opened the cage door, sliding it to the side.

Cadmus jumped to his feet and ingested the invisibility paste. A few seconds later, he shimmered out of sight. "Thank you for the rescue," he muttered. "Is Caspian okay?"

"We certainly hope so. He's upstairs looking for Lumi," I replied.

He froze, as if we'd given him the worst news possible. That didn't sit well with me.

"What?" I asked.

"I can't say. I'm sorry." He sighed, then turned his head to the side, showing me his blood oath symbol and reminding me of how much he actually knew, but couldn't tell.

"We'll frown about this later," Velnias hissed, then gently nudged us both to get moving.

We headed back down the stairs when a whistle blew across the hall. I groaned, my ears hurting from the high-pitched noise. Correction Officers had spotted us from the other side. There were six of them.

"Dammit, move!" Velnias muttered, then rushed down the stairs and headed back to the secret door through which we'd come through.

Within seconds, however, more Correction Officers emerged from the top-level offices, their boots thundering down the metal stairs. We fought our way through, tackling a group of ten COs, with more coming in from behind. We hacked and slashed, left and right.

I even gave Cadmus one of my knives—he only needed it for one hit, before he disabled a CO and took his sword away. Even with an extra fighter on the team, it wasn't enough. Patrik employed his blue fireball spells, too, but we were still outnumbered, as more Correction Officers swarmed down the stairs and converged on our location.

"I saw this coming, but I totally underestimated the numbers," Heron muttered, then dodged a sword hit, swerved to the left, and ran his blade through the CO's neck. Seconds later, the Mara's head rolled on the stone floor.

"I'm not surprised, honestly," Scarlett replied. "This isn't the first time we've dived in head first, anyway."

She then flashed between two COs and delivered a flurry of sword hits with her hyper speed, then decapitated them both in one three-hundred-and-sixty-degree turn. She was truly an artist —of the bloodiest kind.

Velnias took the brunt of the attacks, still, tackling multiple opponents at once. The daemon definitely had game, unafraid to fight up to four COs at once. Despite his considerable size and muscular mass, Velnias was extremely agile and light on his feet.

"You go ahead. I'll catch up," he breathed, then cut the head off a Mara.

More COs came down, while bodies gathered at our feet.

"No, we're not leaving you behind," I shot back, then killed another guard.

"Don't be stupid! I can handle myself. Take Cadmus and complete the mission!" he growled at me. It sent shivers down my spine.

Patrik released another fireball, the blue flames consuming two COs at once.

"He's right, we need to go before more of them come down," the Druid said.

I groaned with frustration, then backed away from the scuffle, accompanied by Cadmus and the rest of my team. Patrik left the COs with a blistering souvenir—a cluster of five exploding fire-balls—while Velnias roared and kept the remaining dozen busy.

An alarm went off, blaring throughout the prison.

"Go!" Velnias shouted. "Go now!"

We had no choice at this point.

I shot up the service stairs and slipped through the crack in the stone wall. It was a narrow little passageway that led to a hidden tunnel, connecting the prison to the second level. We'd never used it before. We hadn't even known about it until Velnias showed us the way.

My stomach twisted itself up in a painful knot as we got out of the prison and reached the second level of Azure Heights. Echoes of the prison alarm rose from below, prompting nearby Correction Officers to rush to the other side of the second level, where one of the main access routes was.

We hid behind some greenery, watching them go.

For the first time, I found myself praying to all the possible forces in the universe. *Please, please let Velnias come out of there alive and in one piece.*

"He knows where to find us, babe," Heron whispered, then motioned to the upper city levels. "We need to go."

I exhaled and darted up the stairs with the rest of our crew.

Mission accomplished. Casualties: none. Missing in action? *One. For now.*

38

HANSA

We could hear voices and scuffles nearby. Something was going on in the city—and we knew exactly what that something was.

Dion paced up and down the stone path in the garden, while Jax and I stood by the secret tunnel door, occasionally glancing at each other. Our nerves were frayed as we waited for the kids to come back. There was a dull pain settling in my stomach. I'd been so stressed, I'd forgotten to eat during the day. It was finally catching up with me.

"Should they be this noisy?" Dion asked, looking at us.

"It depends on which group is making the mess, at this point," Jax replied with a shrug. "We all knew they might have to fight their way out of there. Just have your weapon ready, Dion."

"I still don't feel completely comfortable with the plan," I muttered. "I mean, I know I suggested most of it, but... I don't know. It feels bad."

"As it should," Jax said, giving me a gentle smile. "It just shows you have a conscience. But this calls for tough choices, and we had to make them. Otherwise, we'll never get out of here."

I sighed. "I know."

"It will work out," Jax added. "I trust our team with my life."

The way he said it made me smile. The strength in Jax was definitely part of the reason I'd fallen so hard for him. He often played the role of the realist, but I could see the glimmers of hope in his jade eyes. We'd all made our bed. One way or another, we were going to sleep in it until we brought that shield down.

Avril, Heron, Scarlett, and Patrik were the first to return, rushing into the garden with Cadmus. I frowned, counting the figures.

"Wait, where's Velnias?" I asked.

"He stayed back to help us escape," Avril replied, her eyes glassy with tears and her voice trembling. I felt as though I'd been punched in the gut.

"He knows where to find us, provided he makes it out of there," Patrik added. "I trust they won't kill him. They need every soul they can feed on, even if it's from a traitor to the kingdom."

Avril rolled her eyes. "Yeah, not making me feel any better."

Jax shook Cadmus's hand. "Good to have you back," he said to Caspian's lieutenant. "Were you followed? We're hearing noises out there. What happened in the prison?"

"Getting Cadmus out of his cell was the easy part," Heron explained, his hand clutching Avril's. "One of the COs spotted us, though. There are lots of red lenses in this place!"

"We fought our way out, but there were too many of them piling up on us," Scarlett added. "Velnias gave us the window we needed to get Cadmus out. I doubt we were followed up here, though. I think the ruckus we caused downstairs is one of the reasons why there's all this commotion outside. There's a large number of COs running down to the prison now."

"I'll bet Velnias made a mess in there." Heron smirked, then looked at Avril, who was still reeling from the loss. "He'll be okay, babe. He's resourceful. And we'll get him out of there before they take him away. We're going into stage two now, anyway." He then looked at Jax and me. "Right?"

"Yeah, as soon as the others—" Jax started, then paused as Caspian came to the garden, accompanied by Fiona, Zane, Pheng-Pheng, and Arrah. No Harper.

That dull pain I'd experienced earlier was back with a vengeance, tearing my stomach apart. I couldn't help but groan and take several deep breaths to keep myself on the level.

Dion checked the front of the mansion, then came back shaking his head. "They weren't followed, either," he said, touching his red lens to reposition it better.

"Did it work?" Jax asked.

Caspian was completely distraught. He barely even noticed Cadmus, until his lieutenant came up to him and gave him a friendly pat on the shoulder. They hugged like brothers, while I carefully checked the others' expressions. They were equally upset.

"It worked," Fiona murmured, crossing her arms. "They have Harper."

"They had traps waiting in the corridor outside Lumi's room," Zane explained. "You were right. They were ready for us, with or without a tip from us."

"I think they tranquilized her," Fiona added, her brow furrowed. "They injected her with something, and it knocked her out."

Caspian cursed under his breath. Cadmus stayed by his side. It was literally the only thing anyone could do at that point.

"I know it sounds awful, but that's very good," I muttered, crossing my arms. "It means—"

"It means that Harper is a prisoner!" Caspian shot back.

I had known this was coming. It had taken a lot of work to get him on board from the very beginning. He had every right to be angry. It was one thing to talk about planting your lover in the enemy's claws, and something else entirely to watch it happen.

"It means we have her on the inside now," I replied firmly. "You need your head on your shoulders for this one, Lord Kifo."

"We learned our lesson with Alles, where the enemy's resourcefulness is concerned," Jax interjected. "We made a tough call, but it had to be done. We need the Maras and the daemons to get comfortable and cocky. They have to think they've got the upper hand here. Whether they'll keep her as leverage to get the rest of us, or just consider this a first victory in picking us off, one by one, this is the first time we are truly one serious step ahead of them."

"It paves the way for stage two, as well," I added. "With Harper on the inside, we have a better shot at getting Lumi out. You said they had traps ready. Which means they suspected we'd come. They now think we played into their hands. And that, Lord Kifo, is very good."

The air got cold, all of a sudden. Nevis sure liked to make his presence known. He came onto the stone path, frost spreading beneath his bare feet. Colton and Neha were right behind him, clearly pissed off. I didn't see Caia and Blaze anywhere. Another groan escaped my throat, my stomach once again in tatters. I should've been content. The plan had worked flawlessly. But it still felt terrible.

My conscience be damned.

"Wait, where are Caia and Blaze?" Avril breathed, her eyes wide with horror.

"They're up on the seventh level, doing their part," Nevis replied.

"What the hell are you talking about?" Scarlett gasped, her gaze darting between him and me.

I pressed my fingers against my temples, fighting back an incoming migraine. "I'm sorry we didn't tell you," I said. "But only Nevis, Harper, Jax, and I knew about it. It was best if the rest of you didn't carry the burden, too."

"I presume you've been briefed on the way back," Jax muttered, raising his eyebrows at Colton and Neha, who replied with sullen grumbles and brief nods. Obviously, they weren't pleased either.

"We would've appreciated the heads up, though," Colton replied, scowling at Nevis.

The rest of our group was stunned, staring at us and probably unable to believe what was happening. Nevis, on the other hand, was as cool as a cucumber, offering a shrug in return.

"You all had deniability," he said. "The dragon and fae included. They certainly didn't see it coming."

"Did the Lords buy it, then?" Jax asked.

"They most certainly did. Lord Obara is expecting me tomorrow to sign truce papers," Nevis replied with a smirk.

Fiona scoffed, panting with rage. "What are you smiling about? Caia and Blaze are prisoners? You sold them out for... for what, for the mission? We need to get them back! We didn't agree to any of this!"

"You should've told us! This isn't right!" Avril snapped.

Just like Caspian, they had every right to be angry. But this was neither the time nor the place for us to nurture their broken hearts —even though it killed me on the inside.

"Everybody, calm down!" Jax hissed. "And keep your voices down, too. Control your emotions. You're GASP agents. We're at war here. Everything is part of the final plan. We didn't share it with everyone because we knew how you would react. And we understand your anger; we definitely do. But we need to get this done right."

"Velnias will be fine down there. Those COs are probably dead already. He's probably sabotaging the prison and the daemon tunnels as we speak," Zane chimed in. "I doubt he had any plans of coming back with the group tonight. In fact, I'm willing to bet we'll see him again, soon enough."

Avril sucked in a breath. "You think?"

"Absolutely," I cut in. "As for Caia and Blaze, we wouldn't have had them taken, had the Druids not come up with those anti-mind-bending lenses. They're safe down there. In fact, they're an added bonus right now, because the Maras think they've got our firepower all under their control."

"I'll tell you one thing," Nevis replied. "They're both quick and smart. They caught on fast and played their part. The dragon will still want to punch me, though, I'm pretty sure."

"I'd worry more about Caia, if I were you," Avril muttered. "That girl can pack a serious uppercut."

"Avril, I apologize for causing you and your friends grief. But it had to be done this way," Nevis replied. "I suggested it after everyone left because I knew it wouldn't sit well. But I have faith in your friends. They probably hate me right now, but they see the bigger picture, too."

"Right now, we have three agents on the inside," I reiterated. "The Maras think they've crippled us. They have no idea. Most importantly, they've also been made aware of Shaytan's failures, correct?" I added, looking at Nevis, who replied with a nod. "Which means they'll be summoning the daemon king to Azure Heights soon, since he refuses to let Darius go back. With the dragon in their possession, a creature that Shaytan covets, the Maras will get an upper hand on the daemons. Our aim was to sow discord and plant our agents inconspicuously. Mission accomplished."

A couple of moments passed. The noises in the city gradually died down.

"Now, we're all going back to Meredrin to set up stage two of our plan," Jax said, as Arrah opened the secret tunnel door.

"Our troops are in position throughout the gorge," Neha replied, putting an arm around Pheng-Pheng's shoulders and pulling her close. "Ready for our orders to attack."

"And we've planted charms and explosive charges in specific parts of the city," Patrik added.

"These are extreme measures we've taken, but they're taking us somewhere concrete," I replied.

Fiona cleared her throat. "Speaking of extreme measures, we discovered something in the Palisade, where they're keeping the witch," she said. "They had a spell going, through a hybrid contraption. A mixture of Druid and swamp witch magic. They used it to hijack Telluris and speak to GASP on our behalf, pretending to be us. Laughlan and Ryker might know something about the Druid part. Vincent said they tortured them for it."

My stomach dropped, finally defeated by everything to which it had been subjected. My knees got weak, and I took deep breaths in a bid to calm myself.

"Wait, what?" Jax replied, equally shocked.

"They've been talking to GASP," Fiona murmured. "Vincent destroyed the spell before we could get to him, though. He said his mother knows how to do it."

"So that's how they've been keeping GASP and Calliope at bay," I breathed.

"Well, the shield is doing its part, too," Zane replied, pursing his lips. "I knew they had tricks up their sleeves, but this was unexpected, even for me. The Exiled Maras are despicable, to say the least, but I've got to hand it to them. They're brilliant."

I scoffed. "Yeah, well, I look forward to watching their brilliant heads roll on the ground. Let's go," I said, then made my way into the tunnel. "We need to get ready for tomorrow. Shaytan will be coming to collect his prize, and we want to be there when that happens. Harper knows what she has to do."

One by one, we slipped through the tunnel—our nerves stretched beyond their means, our hearts riddled with a toxic mixture of hope, determination, and fear, and our minds focused on the single most important thing on our to-do list: survival.

39

HARPER

M y body felt heavy. My limbs made of lead. My mouth filled with cotton.

I licked my lips and lifted my head, instantly regretting the move. A sharp pain cut through my brain and settled somewhere behind my eyes, spreading into an uncomfortable heatwave.

My arms were stretched out. I tried to move them. Chains jingled.

Uh-oh.

I finally managed to open my eyes. I was in a dimly lit room, its walls covered in swamp witch symbols painted in—judging by the faint scent—blood. Upon a quick self-assessment, I found I was chained up to one of the walls.

My wrists and ankles had shackles with swamp witch symbols engraved on them.

All the weapons I'd been carrying on top of my leather suit, along with my backpack and shield, were gone. Nevertheless, I still had tricks up my sleeve.

I groaned from the pain, then stilled at the sight of my cellmate.

In the middle of the room, gagged and tied to a chair, was the swamp witch.

"Lumi," I breathed, suddenly over the moon, despite my circumstances.

Her head was down, and her eyes were closed.

They kept her clean and dressed in their Azure Heights style, with a simple but elegant black velvet gown, bodice, and white lace details included. Her hair was a peculiarly bright orange, pulled up into a waxed bun on the top of her head. There were black tattoos covering her temples, her cheeks, and her neck—a combination of swirls and squares, reminding me of Maori tattoos of New Zealand natives.

Her skin was pale. Her nostrils flared as she slowly opened her eyes.

They were so strange. The irises were streaks of white with a fine blue outer border. The pupils were tiny black dots. They looked as though they'd been carved out of marble and polished to perfection. They scanned the room, as she took deep breaths.

"Lumi?" I raised my voice.

Her head snapped up. Those tiny black pupils found me. Her eyes widened.

My heart broke to see her like this. Her aura flared red—so much pain. She'd been tied up and gagged like this for thousands of years. They probably kept her under a lot. I didn't even want to know how they fed her or how they gave her water. It sent chills down my spine to even think of millennia spent in a dark room, tied to a chair.

Every single one of these Maras deserved to die for what they had done to her.

"I'm Harper," I said softly. "I'm here to save you."

A minute went by in heavy silence. She then measured me from head to toe, her gaze lingering on my cuffs, and scoffed.

"Well, yeah, I know I don't look like I can do much right now, but trust me. I've got a plan," I added, then gave her a confident smirk. "We're getting you out of here, Lumi."

There was doubt in her almost-white eyes. Not that I could blame her.

I was chained to a freakin' wall.

But I was down there, with her, in the middle of enemy territory. It broke my heart to think of Caspian and what he was probably going through at this moment, but I drew strength from the hope that we'd be together again soon.

Stage one of our plan was a complete success, as far as I was concerned.

My next challenge was staying alive and whole and, most importantly, getting Lumi out of Azure Heights.

Almost there, Harper.

40

DEREK

Less than a day after we'd discovered the lies being fed to us through Telluris, I had the whole of GASP mobilized and taking action. Corrine and Ibrahim worked with Viola on developing a transporter for us—a ship, of sorts, that could be inserted into the interplanetary travel spell and transported across the galaxies to Neraka.

Draven continued his communications with the impostors on Neraka. It was imperative to keep the act going, to let them think they were still fooling us. That way, we had the element of surprise on our side. It made my blood boil each time he confirmed contact with them. We'd gone over possibilities of who the impostors were —at this point, however, the only likely culprits were the Exiled Maras.

We just couldn't understand why they were doing this. What was their end game?

And, most importantly, where was our team?

Sofia and I made our way up to the platform on top of Luceria. Corrine and Ibrahim had tweaked the final details on the ship. It was beautiful. It looked like a large capsule, capable of holding up to two hundred Shadians and Eritopians. The exterior was coated with a metal alloy designed to withstand any extreme temperature in the vacuum of space, from insane lows to scorching highs.

The Daughters of Eritopia had assisted Viola and Phoenix in preparing the interplanetary travel spell. Viola had even made tweaks to the spell, after having spent the entire night translating more of the swamp witches' book. She'd found a couple of useful modifications, which she'd applied to the final formula.

"This way, if we don't have access to Neraka, the spell will allow us to steer it to the nearest surface for landing," Viola explained as we went over the details.

Corrine, Ibrahim, and the other witches made the final preparations inside the capsule, setting up an atmosphere and gravity system, along with air filters and various other amenities, in case we had to spend more than twelve hours on that thing.

"Let me get this straight," Sofia said, crossing her arms as she looked at the capsule. "We have the destination, but we can't see it. We don't even know if it's still there. How will the interplanetary spell work?"

Viola sighed, flipping through her notes. She'd pulled her reddish pink hair into a loose bun, keeping a pencil behind her ear for quick modifications. I found her to be adorable, despite her goddess-like abilities. Fearsome, yet so kind and delicate. I could see why Phoenix was so smitten.

"If Neraka isn't there, for some insane reason, we have the red beads," she explained. "Which means the interplanetary spell will take us wherever Neraka is. If Neraka is still there, but hidden or shielded, making it impossible for us to land there, I've edited the spell in a way that allows me to manipulate its course and land the ship nearby—on a neighboring planet, or even one of Neraka's moons."

"And the ship is now ready," Corrine said as she emerged from the capsule, followed by Ibrahim, Shayla, and Arwyn. "There's an entire atmospheric system created inside the walls. You'll be able to use it for days on end, safely."

Sofia nodded slowly, then frowned. "What if we have no choice but to come back here?"

She was worried sick, and I couldn't blame her. Our children and friends were out there. We had no idea whether they were okay, or even still alive.

"I've got that covered," Viola replied with a confident smile. She held up a piece of obsidian glass. "This is from here. Phoenix has packed all the other ingredients we need for another inter-planetary spell to return, on top of other charms. You know. Just in case."

Phoenix came out from the other side of the platform, carrying the duffel bag he'd loaded with swamp witch spell ingre-dients. He was accompanied by the rest of the Daughters, all clad in colorful silks and wearing their golden masks. Viola was the only one who adhered to the Calliope dress style and didn't bother wearing a mask. She'd chosen to live among the people, anyway.

"Okay, we're ready to go," Phoenix announced.

He'd geared up, weapons and charms ready. I'd assembled a large team of GASP members and Eritopians to help us with this.

"The team is downstairs, waiting for your signal," I told Phoenix.

He nodded, then rushed downstairs and got the others. One by one, the veteran GASP members and allies joined us on the plat-form. They each gave me a brief salute as they went inside the capsule, guided by Corrine.

"I see you've put together quite the squadron of heavyweights," Ibrahim replied with a smirk.

"What choice did we have?" I muttered, as Sofia leaned against me.

Draven and Serena joined us, both geared up and ready to fly with us.

Lucas and Marion, Pippa and Jeramiah, Vivienne and Xavier, Benedict, Hazel and Tejus, Heath, and Grace and Lawrence were all making their way onto the ship. They were all fuming, eager to get their kids back. Field and the other Hawk brothers joined them, along with Anjani, Jovi, and Dmitri. We had a hefty alliance of werewolves and fire and ice dragons joining us from The Shade, along with several dozen vampires.

From the In-Between, Sherus had sent over two dozen fae fighters, and Draven had summoned Jax's wards along with the best warriors of White City. Several Druids had come to assist us as well, along with two dozen incubi and succubi.

"We'll join you, too," Safira, one of the Daughters, said, then nodded at Nova. "Our little sister can stay here and help Aida and the others look after Calliope while we are gone."

"I'm humbled and thankful," I replied, offering a curt bow.

"If the Exiled Maras did something terrible, it is our duty as Daughters to address that. Besides, we may not be as powerful outside of Eritopia, but we can still make any creature cower in fear before us," she said.

The Daughters joined the others, while Nova gave me a brief nod and rushed to the side of the platform. I had to admit, I was impressed.

We had a fearsome crew with us. And we were all extremely pissed off.

"Are you ready?" I asked Sofia.

Draven, Serena, Phoenix, Ibrahim, and the witches got into the capsule, and Viola began chanting the spell.

Sofia gave me a warm smile, squeezing my hand. "I've left our kids in charge in The Shade, and I'm about to go on a recovery mission with you, my love. Of course I'm ready."

"Good, then let's go get our people back and whip the living daylights out of whoever did this," I replied, then chuckled softly as she pulled my hand and took me inside.

I found myself breathless.

The interior of the capsule looked infinitely bigger than the exterior. It was made of a sturdy metallic framework, with a plethora of greenery in its enormous glass walls. The witches had put together an entire ecosystem inside the capsule, along with the basic facilities required for long hours of travel. The photosynthesis from the onboard plants delivered oxygen into the capsule's air ventilation system, aided by spells, and there were preservation charms in place on our food supplies.

Beams of white light crossed through the ceiling and the floor. The front of the capsule held a massive screen, doubling as a glass pane, through which we could see outside. Ibrahim and Corrine got to work on the keyboards mounted on both sides of the screen, just as Viola came inside.

"Okay, everybody stand still," Ibrahim said, pressing several buttons. "The airlock is on."

A hiss and a loud clang announced the hatch door had closed. Now sealed and prepared, our capsule was ready to go. Viola went to the front, positioning herself before the screen, then muttered the last lines of the spell.

Bright white light exploded outside. It engulfed the capsule.

The hum was familiar. I'd heard it before when the Neraka team's spell had taken off.

It was our turn to fly away. Only this time we weren't going to

Neraka to investigate or explore. The entire crew sat down on metal chairs attached to the glass walls, complete with seatbelts, and buckled up. Corrine had picked up a few tricks from the humans' space travel technologies.

"We have to be prepared for anything," she said, noticing my frown as I stared at my own belt. "I asked myself a lot of 'what if' questions when we put this ship together. What if the spell fails for some reason? What if we hit something that sends us tumbling away? And so on."

"No, no, I completely understand," I replied, squeezing Sofia's hand. "And I agree. Better to be prepared than get caught with our guard down."

The giant sphere of light swallowed the capsule whole.

"We have liftoff," Corrine announced.

For a second, we were all weightless, though strapped to our seats. The capsule left Luceria and shot through the sky.

Minutes later, it broke through the atmosphere and took us deep into the cold darkness of space.

Several hours later, Neraka's galaxy glimmered ahead.

Heath cursed under his breath, drawing our attention. Out of everyone with children potentially stuck on Neraka, Heath was, by far, the angriest.

"Heath, our kids are strong," Grace tried to comfort him. My heart broke a little more, because I could hear the tremor in her voice. She was as worried as the rest of us, no matter how hard she tried to hide it. "We'll get to the bottom of this."

Heath scoffed, shaking his head slowly. "You said Maras can be killed by fire, right?"

Jax's wards all stared at him, equal parts scared and impressed. The other Maras were on edge, as well, but none were as impressive as the wards. They'd seen Heath and Blaze in full dragon form, months ago. They'd seen what the father-son duo could do. They had every reason to be in awe of Heath, as well as the other dragons joining him. There were ten of them, in total.

"Yes," Draven replied, holding Serena's hand in his. He pressed it against his lips for a moment, as he looked out through the front glass screen. "Fire, sunlight, or decapitation."

"Good," Heath grumbled, crossing his arms.

Hazel let out an audible sigh. "What do you think they're doing now?" she murmured, staring at the plethora of stars whizzing past us.

Pippa chuckled nervously. "Knowing my Scarlett? Surviving, for sure."

"Fiona is quite good at breaking bones," Benedict replied, the shadow of a smile fluttering across his face.

"And Harper is pretty much the definition of a killing machine when she has to defend herself and the people she loves," Tejus chimed in, a proud smirk stretching his lips.

Despite the anger and the underlying despair, I could see the sliver of hope. We all beamed with the faith we had in our younglings. We'd raised and trained them to be fighters. To always question and debate. To hold their ground and tear into anyone or anything who threatened their livelihoods.

"Okay, now, everybody! Hold on," Corrine announced, as some of the temporarily loosened seatbelts clicked back into their slots. "We're about to attempt entry into Neraka's atmosphere."

"Wait, it's there?" I asked, then leaned forward to get a better look.

My breath hitched. A collective gasp emerged from the entire crew.

"It is. Sort of," Corrine muttered. "It's shielded. We couldn't see it through the telescope."

"Good grief," I murmured, my eyes widened with shock.

There was an empty slot between the third and fifth planets in the galaxy of three suns, just like we'd observed through the telescope. But it wasn't literally empty. The vacuum of space rippled around it, in the form of a giant sphere. Three moons orbited the seemingly empty space. There was an occasional glimmer across the invisible planet, the result of sun reflections.

"It's there," Sofia breathed.

"It's cloaked somehow," Draven said, staring at it.

"Hold on," Corrine said again, as the capsule hummed, then hurled toward the shielded planet. "We're going to try to pass through the shield now. Viola, get ready!"

Viola nodded, then unfastened her seatbelt and slid down on her knees, placing her palms on the metal floor.

The capsule headed straight for Neraka. We could hear the interplanetary spell whirr and whistle as it shot through space. A bright flash erupted before us. It blinded me, temporarily.

I heard Viola grunt, then mutter a swamp witch spell under her breath. She was affixed to the floor, connected to the capsule itself.

"Dammit, it won't go through!" Ibrahim snapped. "Corrine, help me keep it steady for Viola!"

I blinked several times until the image of those around me came back into focus. Viola's hands glowed a brilliant pink, fluorescent fuchsia veins stretching out from beneath and covering the entire floor.

The interplanetary spell crackled and shimmered, like a glitching TV screen, after having made contact with whatever shield was keeping Neraka hidden. Viola worked her combination of swamp witch magic and natural abilities as a Daughter of Eritopia, while her sisters murmured in the background.

Only then did I noticed the same fluorescent pink veins spreading out across the walls and ceiling, originating from beneath their naked feet. They were helping her, along with Ibrahim and Corrine, to override the original spell and steer the capsule onto one of Neraka's moons.

The white one was the closest. We shot toward it, the interplanetary spell groaning beyond the capsule walls, as if taking a life of its own and protesting the change in direction. The moon didn't have an atmosphere, so our landing was rather... weird.

The speed with which we came through was enough to hurl the capsule into the dusty white ground. We bounced around several times, turned upside down and back and forth. By the time the spell bubble stilled, we were all pretty pale and nauseated.

But at least we'd made it safely to one of the moons.

It took us a while to recover. Phoenix jumped out of his seat and rushed to take Viola in his arms. She was tired and covered in sweat, as she removed her hands from the floor. She'd put in one hell of an effort to get us to land on a moon.

"It's a cloaking spell of sorts," Viola murmured, rubbing her face as Phoenix held her close and dropped kisses on her forehead.

I unbuckled my seatbelt and stood.

We could see the seemingly empty space from where we'd landed. The sun's rays shimmered across the invisible surface.

"You mean swamp witch magic?" I asked, feeling my blood boil.

"I think so. On a literal global scale," she replied. "It's massive. Nothing else makes sense. Otherwise the interplanetary spell would have taken us through. Only swamp witch magic can resist or reject swamp witch magic."

I exhaled sharply, and Sofia got up and joined me in front of the screen. One by one, the rest of our crew stood and stretched their limbs.

"How do we get in?" Sofia asked Viola.

"I'm not sure yet," she replied, then looked at her sisters. "Any ideas?"

None of the Daughters had an answer—only shrugs.

"You should keep translating that book," Saphira suggested. "Perhaps there's something in there, somewhere in the last pages."

"This is serious swamp witch magic, though," Draven interjected with a frown. "Not the charms and mojos Rewa claimed the delegation swamp witch left them with. This is heavyweight stuff."

It hit me then, knocking the air out of my lungs.

"You mean to tell me this could've been set up by a swamp witch?" I muttered.

"Or maybe they got a lot more out of the delegation swamp witch to begin with," Draven replied, giving me a concerned look. "The delegation never came back in the first place. Now that we know we've been lied to, perhaps it's time to ask. What if the Druid delegation never got off Neraka?"

It was my turn to curse under my breath.

"This is getting even more complicated. All we're getting are more questions. Zero answers," I said, no longer able to hide my frustration.

"I'll dig through the tome, in the meantime," Viola offered, motioning for the duffel bag beneath Phoenix's chair. He fetched it for her. "Let me see if we can do something about that shield."

A thought crossed my mind, and I shifted my focus back to Draven.

"Can you try Telluris again?" I asked him.

He nodded, then closed his eyes.

"Telluris Hansa!" he called out. A minute later, he tried again. "Telluris Harper!"

Nothing. He shook his head.

"You can't feel them?" Serena replied.

"No answer. I haven't truly felt them since they first left Calliope," Draven reminded her.

"Then what do we do?" Sofia asked, resting her palms on my chest. "We're not leaving here until we get the kids back."

I thought about it for a few seconds, then looked at Viola.

"You're right, Viola. Keep searching through that book. There must be something there," I said. "In the meantime, the witches, the Druids, and the Daughters can work together on alternatives. We will stand by, ready to intervene and rip heads off the shoulders of Exiled Maras, if that's what it takes to get our people back!"

Everyone agreed. Heath, in particular, his brow permanently furrowed.

"It's fine, Derek. We're all here," he muttered. "No one takes our kids away from us and gets away with it."

One of Jax's wards came next to him, placing a friendly hand on his shoulder as he looked at me.

"Our Lord is down there," he said. "We're getting him back, one way or another."

"We're getting them all back," added Tejus, his arms wrapped around Hazel.

"This is war," I said.

Staring at the empty space where the hidden planet lay, I cemented my resolve with an extra layer of anger.

Heath was right. No one got away with causing any kind of pain to our people. To our friends and allies. To The Shade or Eritopia, for that matter.

There would be blood, soon enough.

READY FOR THE FINAL BOOK OF SEASON 7?

Dear Shaddict,

Thank you for reading *A Snare of Vengeance*.

The next book, *ASOV 59: A Battle of Souls*, is the thrilling FINAL book of Season 7!

A Battle of Souls releases **April 28th, 2018**.

Order your copy now: www.bellaforrest.net

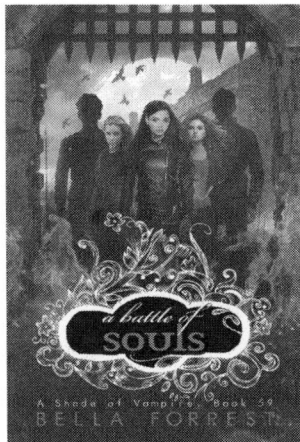

See you soon!

Love,

Bella x

P.S. Join my VIP email list and I'll send you a reminder as soon as I have a new book out. Visit here to sign up: **www.forrestbooks.com**

(Your email will be kept 100% private and you can unsubscribe at any time.)

P.P.S. Follow The Shade on Instagram and check out some of the beautiful graphics: @ashadeofvampire

You can also come say hi on Facebook: www.facebook.com/AShadeOfVampire

And Twitter: @ashadeofvampire

READ MORE BY BELLA FORREST

HOTBLOODS

(New supernatural romance series!)

Hotbloods (Book 1)

Coldbloods (Book 2)

Renegades (Book 3)

Venturers (Book 4)

Traitors (Book 5)

THE GIRL WHO DARED TO THINK

The Girl Who Dared to Think (Book 1)

The Girl Who Dared to Stand (Book 2)

The Girl Who Dared to Descend (Book 3)

The Girl Who Dared to Rise (Book 4)

The Girl Who Dared to Lead (Book 5)

The Girl Who Dared to Endure (Book 6)

The Girl Who Dared to Fight (Book 7)

THE GENDER GAME

(Completed series)

The Gender Game (Book 1)

The Gender Secret (Book 2)

The Gender Lie (Book 3)

The Gender War (Book 4)

The Gender Fall (Book 5)

The Gender Plan (Book 6)

The Gender End (Book 7)

A SHADE OF VAMPIRE SERIES

Series 1: Derek & Sofia's story

A Shade of Vampire (Book 1)

A Shade of Blood (Book 2)

A Castle of Sand (Book 3)

A Shadow of Light (Book 4)

A Blaze of Sun (Book 5)

A Gate of Night (Book 6)

A Break of Day (Book 7)

Series 2: Rose & Caleb's story

A Shade of Novak (Book 8)

A Bond of Blood (Book 9)

A Spell of Time (Book 10)

A Chase of Prey (Book 11)

A Shade of Doubt (Book 12)

A Turn of Tides (Book 13)

A Dawn of Strength (Book 14)

A Fall of Secrets (Book 15)

An End of Night (Book 16)

Series 3: The Shade continues with a new hero...

A Wind of Change (Book 17)

A Trail of Echoes (Book 18)

A Soldier of Shadows (Book 19)

A Hero of Realms (Book 20)

(Completed series)

The Secret of Spellshadow Manor (Book 1)

The Breaker (Book 2)

The Chain (Book 3)

The Keep (Book 4)

The Test (Book 5)

The Spell (Book 6)

BEAUTIFUL MONSTER DUOLOGY

Beautiful Monster 1

Beautiful Monster 2

DETECTIVE ERIN BOND (Adult thriller/mystery)

Lights, Camera, GONE

Write, Edit, KILL

For an updated list of Bella's books, please visit her website:
www.bellaforrest.net

Join Bella's VIP email list and she'll send you an email reminder as soon
as her next book is out: www.forrestbooks.com

Made in the USA
Lexington, KY
25 June 2018